FIGHTING BACK

By the same author

Novels

THE TRUTH WILL NOT HELP US
AFTER THE RAIN
THE CENTRE OF THE GREEN
STORYBOARD
THE BIRDCAGE
A WORLD ELSEWHERE
THE McGUFFIN
THE GIRLS

Biography

SQUEAK (*Faber*)

Plays

I LOVE YOU, MRS PATTERSON
AFTER THE RAIN (*Faber*)
THE FALL AND REDEMPTION OF MAN
LITTLE BOXES (*Samuel French*)
THE CORSICAN BROTHERS
THE WAITING ROOM (*Samuel French*)
THE DISORDERLY WOMEN (*Samuel French*)
MISS NIGHTINGALE (*Samuel French*)
HEIL, CAESAR (*Samuel French*)

Television Plays

THE ESSAY PRIZE
ROBIN REDBREAST

FIGHTING BACK

A NOVEL BY
JOHN BOWEN

HAMISH HAMILTON: LONDON

HAMISH HAMILTON LTD

Published by the Penguin Group
27 Wrights Lane, London W8 5TZ, England
Viking Penguin Inc, 40 West 23rd Street, New York, New York 10010, U.S.A.
Penguin Books Australia Ltd, Ringwood, Victoria, Australia
Penguin Books Canada Ltd, 2801 John Street, Markham, Ontario, Canada L3R 1B4
Penguin Books (N.Z.) Ltd, 182–190 Wairau Road, Auckland 10, New Zealand

Penguin Books Ltd, Registered Offices: Harmondsworth, Middlesex, England

First published in Great Britain 1989 by
Hamish Hamilton Ltd

British Library Cataloguing in Publication Data

Bowen, John, 1924–
Fighting back.
I. Title
823'.914 [F]

ISBN 0-241-12630-4

Printed and bound in Great Britain by
Richard Clay Ltd, Bungay, Suffolk

CONTENTS

Acknowledgements 9

(1) A Rabbit in the Garden 11

(2) Phonics 36

(3) Fathers and Sons 71

(4) A Christmas Outing 100

(5) Palace of Culture 123

(6) Cotswold Spring 137

(7) Wormald 167

(8) The Battle of Fawley Woods 193

FOR

ELAINE GREENE

As usual when writing a novel, I have relied heavily on others for information, advice and assistance. My thanks are due to Frank Kermode, Piers Mayfield, Ian Lapworth, Sally Thompson, Valerie and Charles Wood, Peter Brod, Tom Stoppard, Dan Jacobson, Sir Michael Howard, Roger Scruton, Dr Jeff Lewis of the Warwickshire Nature Conservancy Trust, Derek Altham of the Artificial Limb and Appliance Centre at Selly Oak, Penelope and Jack Lively and Colin Rogers. Two books I have found extremely useful have been A.J. Herman's *History of Czechoslovakia* (Viking) and *The Darkness is Light Enough, the Field Journal of a Night Naturalist*, by Chris Ferris (Sphere).

· 1 ·

A RABBIT
IN THE GARDEN

The top of the house was all shut up. They had intended to sell and move to a cottage when they grew old, but had become used to the house and fond of it, and had not in any case considered themselves to be old. Now Sophie was dead, and James was certainly old, but old age had made him obstinate, and he refused to move.

The house was not practical. There were three floors of it, all spacious. The top, as has been said, was shut up. It consisted of uncarpeted attics, the windows no longer cleaned, the contents only dust and old trunks filled with invoices, out-of-date tax-returns and notes of research long completed. There were also camp-beds intended for parties of young people, friends of the children, who might be stopping for the week-end, but no such week-end parties had ever been held, since the children seemed to make very few friends and none whom they were willing to invite home.

On the ground floor there was a large kitchen, with many wooden surfaces requiring to be scrubbed, and a Rayburn which ate scuttlesful of smokeless fuel. Between the kitchen and the front door (which was seldom used) a corridor of stone flags made a right angle – to one side the dining room and sitting room, both with large fireplaces for logs, to the other the library and a large cold room with a marble table; this room may once have been a conservatory, since the outside wall was of glass. All the rooms on the ground floor were difficult to heat in winter. Below them was a cellar, never heated, which contained bottles of Rioja

11

and the rotting tubers of dahlias. Between cellar and ground floor, made perilous by unexpected stone steps set at an angle, was the downstairs WC with a wash-basin.

The rooms of the first floor had lower ceilings, and were heated by portable electric fires. There was a double-bedroom, in which James now slept alone, the study, a guest-bedroom, a large and a dovecote which had been converted into a small self-contained flat, occupied by their daughter, Helen, until her mid-twenties, when she had suddenly married an antique-dealer and gone to live in Houston, Texas. The loo in the first-floor bathroom had a walnut seat and was enclosed in walnut casing. One mounted three steps to reach it, and might sit there, raised above the common level, reading or conversing with anyone who happened to be having a bath. All the loos in that house were approached by steps. It was no longer a practical house for an elderly gentleman living by himself.

The garden was even more impractical than the house. The lawn was large enough to require cutting by a petrol-driven lawn-mower on which one sat as if on a combine-harvester. It was shaded on one side by trees, and bordered by wide beds containing shrubs and perennial flowers, many of which now showed the signs of old age and creeping diseases. To one side of the lawn, and almost as large, was the vegetable garden, in which weeds grew thickly, and the crowns of asparagus rotted away. Some vegetables were still planted and still grew, far too many for an old man, and were taken away by the once-a-week gardener, and given to friends, or sold. Beyond the vegetable garden was a heated greenhouse, no longer heated, and, beyond that and the lawn, an orchard, already infested with briar and bramble, and enclosed in wire-netting to keep out the rabbits, which would otherwise invade the garden and destroy it, eating up the young lettuce and French beans and all the choicer flowers, and burrowing into the roots of shrubs to rear enormous families. Although the wire-netting had been dug into the ground, and was patched from time to time, in winter the tracks of rabbits could always be seen on the lawn in snow. Rabbits would make a mock of all one's efforts if they were allowed. It was a point of honour to keep them under control.

James was sixty-seven years old. His father was still alive at ninety-one, so James himself, he supposed, might reasonably expect at least another twenty years. What a gloomy prospect! His father lived, bright-eyed and talkative, in sheltered accommodation provided by a charity set up in the eighteenth century under the will of a particularly rapacious Governor of Madras to build almshouses for such of the East India Company's servants as might fall into want. Since very few of the Company's servants *had* fallen into want, very few almshouses had been built, and the legacy had grown and continued to grow long after the honourable East India Company's own power and administration had passed away. From the compost of its passing had emerged that noble flower, the Indian Civil Service, its most illustrious servants still drawn from the same families which once had served the Company. Some of these servants, however, since rapacity had gone out of fashion, did fall into want, and their widows even more so, and by the late nineteen-twenties, after a deal of correspondence and committee meetings, it was recognised that there was a need and the money to satisfy it. Almshouses no longer seemed appropriate. A settlement of small bungalows was built in the grounds of a bankrupt preparatory school near Maidstone, radiating in rows like spokes from the main building in which the administrative offices were housed (Matron's Office, the Sanatorium, the Staff Quarters) but which was largely given over to the uses of what was called "the Club" – its Dining Room, Bar, Billiards Room, Library, and separate rooms for Contract Bridge and Mah-jong.

The settlement was called Madras House. Its charges, being subsidised, were modest; a Collector's pension would easily cover them. Dignity, the frail important dignity of the old, was a primary consideration to Matron and her staff; the medical supervision was tactful, and such of the residents as became overtly incontinent or senile were unobtrusively transferred to the geriatric ward of the local hospital so as to avoid distressing the others. Madras House satisfied the desire in an elderly person of the professional classes for both privacy and company. The bungalows (some single, some double) were private, and one might keep in them such of one's own things – cherished mementoes, family heirlooms – as would fit into the space. By day one might look after oneself, brew cocoa or settle into a good read, and spend the evenings in the company of like-minded people at the Club, as in the old days, enjoying a couple of *chota pegs* in the Bar before dinner and a game of Bridge after.

James's mother had died, as Sophie had done, suddenly in her mid-sixties, and his father had been quite unable to cope. Close to despair, James had searched for somewhere to keep him, until a colleague, the Reader in Indian History, had told him of this admirable institution. He and Sophie had made a point of visiting at every Easter and Christmas, and the old man had taken pleasure in showing them off to the residents – "My son, the professor" – but had not seemed sorry to see them go. His life, interests, memories, opinions, friends – they were all contained by Madras House now. Of course its own time must also be coming to an end, since the Indianisation of the ICS had greatly diminished the number of those qualified for a place, but it would last the old man out.

Were there similar institutions for retired academics? Should James look about, reserve a place? Well, to be sure there were such, or had been; they were the Oxford and Cambridge colleges, but even were he permitted, as a Fellow Emeritus, to live out the rest of his life in college rooms, dining at High Table and slopping his port afterwards in the Combination Room, he would not do so. Auden had not been happy at Christ Church, nor Forster at King's. A college was a place of work, or should be. One's

14

own home was the place to die.

He remembered coming across Faraday, the retiring Regius Professor, alone in his rooms at college, sitting on the floor in front of the hearth in tears among books piled up all anyhow. James had knocked, of course, but had mistaken the blubbering for permission to enter, and had so found him, red-eyed and puffy-faced.

"It's the books. I've nowhere for them." Faraday and his crippled sister lived in a bungalow adapted to her needs. With so many ramps and hand-rails, there was little space for shelving. He had accumulated a library in the rooms he must now vacate.

"Sell them."

"There's three thousand. More. Most of them out of print."

"All the more valuable. You'll be a rich man."

"I like having them about me. I'm used to them."

"You don't read them. When did you last read this?" Cook's *Life of Florence Nightingale* in two volumes, long superseded by Cecil Woodham-Smith.

"I don't intend to vegetate, you know. I shall need to consult them." The man had brought in a tea-chest which had overflowed. Snivelling idiot! James himself had taken his library with him when he moved out of college. In a large house, there is always room for books. His father had taken no books at all to Maidstone. Even James's mother's collection of Dorothy L. Sayers had gone for jumble.

James had begun to think increasingly of his father, whom he had never liked and did not wish to resemble. Yet, whenever he looked into a mirror these days, he saw his father staring angrily back at him.

He took to wandering about the house with the cordless telephone in his hand, but nobody phoned. He did not have to manage alone; there was no question of his managing alone. Elsie continued to come in one day a week from Chipping Norton as she had done when Sophie was alive and there was the gardener on Wednesdays. Sophie had died, after so short an illness, in January. She had fallen

15

over in the snow, and it had been difficult to get her up and back to the house. Either she had thought little of it, or she had felt some premonition, for she had refused to be taken to hospital, and the doctor had supported her refusal. She had died at night in the double-bed, with James on a Put-U-Up beside her. He had woken in the morning, and found her dead. Now the month was June, and the garden a mess. "Oh God!" he said. "I'm so lonely."

There was a cupboard in the kitchen, still full of jams and jellies made by Sophie, many several years old, since there are so few opportunities to eat jam, even if one liked the stuff. He took out a bottle, and held it: Magnum Bonum Plum and Almond Conserve, 1985. She had made it angrily, her hands sticky with juice as she cut away the plum flesh from the stones and weighed the stoned fruit. The plums had been brought by old Mr Proctor, who was still working for them then, and would bring fruit and vegetables from his own garden to compound the glut they had already. The new man took from the garden; he did not bring. "Why don't you throw the bloody plums away?" James had said. "Put them in the garbage bag, and tie it up. He'll never know." But of course one could not do such a thing, when Mr Proctor had picked the plums from his own tree, and brought them in his own basket. Magnum Bonum plums, the greatest goodness. Each plum quartered, the flesh stripped from the stone, and the stones gathered into a muslin bag which would be boiled with the jam. And Sophie swearing.

He ought never to have slept, never to have allowed himself to sleep. What could he have been thinking, to have let her die at two, three, four in the morning, between dark and dawn with no one to comfort her? He might have held her hand at least, even in sleep he might have held her hand and felt her leave him, a final clasping of hands in goodbye before the journey. "So good to have seen you! Drive safely! Telephone –" he wept so easily these days, such easy old man's tears, leaning against the jamb of the door, and wiping his nose and eyes with the crook of his

16

arm – "Remember to phone as soon as you get there."
Why, if she had felt the moment close, had she not cried out
to wake him for farewell?

James had been born three weeks prematurely (his mother
had told him) during a tennis party. His mother had been
in pain with her stomach off and on since two in the
morning but, as the baby had not been due for three
weeks, the pain had been ascribed to nerves, or flatulence,
or most likely flatulence brought about by nerves. His
mother had been on station less than a year, and had
suffered greatly with her nerves, owing to her ignorance of
the social conventions prevailing amongst the professional,
military and commercial families of Rangpur, which had
been partly derived from Edwardian books of etiquette and
partly (as it seemed to her) invented by some spiteful
person. The older women of the community, particularly
the Barra Memsahib, wife to the Collector, had put themselves out to advise and explain, but James's mother had
suffered nevertheless.
   The tennis party had, of course, included Wormald.
James himself could not remember Wormald, though he
must have met the man, but any meeting would have been
before James was six, so the memory could not be expected
to stick. He remembered the name; it was so much part of
his parents' memories, the conversational small change of
their domestic life – Wormald's misadventures, his little
errors (which had to be tidied up), his women (who either
went sadly back to Shropshire or had to be persuaded to
marry someone else). Wormald must have followed
James's parents about the Indian sub-continent from posting to posting, which seemed odd when one considered
that, although he and James's father might reasonably have
been expected to have mounted the rungs of the Service at
the same rate, they would hardly have been posted to the
same districts. Yet there he was, a constant in every period
of reminiscence; he even seemed to have gone on holiday
with them. Was Wormald in the Service at all? James could

17

not remember that he had a rank, or even any particular job. He was not "Mr Wormald" or "Captain", "Doctor", "Padre", far less "Paul" or "Adrian" or "Bill", just "Wormald" *tout court*. He was everywhere at every time, yet did nothing in particular but play tennis and cards, come over for dinner or a drink, get cheated by his bearer, poisoned by his cook, bitten by a rabid dog and injected in the stomach with a hypodermic as big as a bicycle pump, find a cobra in the thunderbox and a krait under the verandah steps, try to cure his prickly heat by standing naked in the rain and his ringworm with gentian violet, which came off on the sofa. There he had been at the tennis party, standing up to the net for James's father (Wormald was a tiger at the net), and when the ayah had gathered courage to interrupt the play and to communicate her opinion that the memsahib was in labour, Wormald had laughed, and told James's father not to worry, since women were known to get these false preliminary pains, that he himself knew a chap whose wife had suffered in the same way, and it had cost this chap a packet at the Nursing Home, the whole damned shooting match having to be gone through again three weeks later at the proper time. So they had let matters take their natural course, and by 17:15 hours, when James's head had appeared, his mother could no longer be moved, and the ayah herself had bitten through the umbilical cord, and an army doctor, summoned by bicycle, had stitched James's mother up without anaesthetic and rather clumsily since this kind of thing was out of his usual line of work, and as a bachelor he was embarrassed by her nakedness.

"I thought you were the most wonderful thing that had ever happened," she had told James later. "You looked like a very old Chinaman, all scrawny and yellow." He had been taken to the hospital every day by boat, poled by a native boatman, his mother sitting on a wooden thwart with her feet in water holding the swaddled yellow baby. He had put on very little weight, and had developed boils. The doctors at the hospital had extracted pus from the boils and injected him with the pus, but it had done no good so they had given up on him, since babies did easily die in that climate at that time, and his mother was young enough to bear others. But James's father had gone secretly into debt against the rules of the Service, and had sent mother and child to Darjeeling in March to escape the hot weather, and there the boils had dried up, to return in James's thirties as no more than hay fever which itself grew less vexatious with the passing years. Of course the debt, which was to old Pandit the money-lender, must have been known and excused by the circumstances. Nothing the British did in India during the nineteen-twenties was secret, even to each other.

She had thought him the most wonderful thing in the world, and had sent him Home – meaning to England, which had not up to that time been his home – just before his sixth birthday, to be shuttled between grandparents and aunts until he was old enough for a prep school, which would leave only the holidays to worry about. She had travelled across India with him, two days and two nights in the train, and either did not tell him or he did not understand that she would not be going with him, and when they were on board in all the noise and bustle of Bombay Docks, she had said, "I have to go ashore now," and had held him close and kissed him, and left him still not understanding that she would not be coming back, and when the ship began to move he had not been at the rail to wave, but had wandered through staterooms and corridors looking for her until a steward had found him in the tiny ship's library searching in cupboards, and had returned him to the care of Mrs Golightly, who had promised his parents that she would look after him during the voyage. And his mother had travelled back across India alone, two days and two nights in the train.

That was in the days when calling cards were left with one corner turned down, at least in Bihar. He remembered now that Wormald had a ginger moustache, clipped as close as sandpaper, and that gravy would dry on it.

*

19

Was it there, was it all there in childhood, as has so often been suggested? A lonely child, he had taken to reading, three books a day sometimes from the public library. It had been compulsive, as children these days sniff glue, a craving for print – *All Quiet on the Western Front* at the age of twelve, *The Forsyte Saga*, humorous essays by Anthony Armstrong, and the plays of A.A. Milne. He had found a hoard of back numbers of *Punch* in the wash-house by the mangle, and gone through the lot, reading even the advertisements for Abdullah cigarettes on the back page. Sexton Blake, a different long story every week, and the boys' weeklies of that time, *Magnet*, *Gem*, *Triumph*, *Champion*, *Hotspur*, *Wizard*, they had all gone in between the eyes and left his appetite undiminished. His Aunt Enid had warned him that too much reading weakened the sight, but it was she who had suffered from nervous headaches and ended stone-blind in Porthcawl. Now there were no boys' weeklies, and even *Punch* had become a dull thing, fashion-hungry like a colour supplement without the colour. Since the end of the war, two generations had grown up without the habit of reading, and even he – J.M. Elphinstone, who had been whipped for stealing money from the Whitehaven aunt's purse to buy bound back numbers of *The Strand Magazine* for the E. Nesbit serial – even he opened a book reluctantly these days, expecting little from it.

There had been servants then – well, *a* servant, Belle, who had lived in with his grandparents. In India there had been many servants, even for those most junior in the Service – the bearer, cook, ayah, sweeper, night-watchman, and three gardeners – but that was in another country, and besides . . . Belle had bought him a stencil-set and paints for his eighth birthday with her own money, and he had loved her. While he was away at school, Belle had been taken to the cottage hospital, where a cyst as big as an orange had been removed from her stomach, but she had recovered, and often spoke of it. Dear Belle! He could not eat an orange these days without remembering her.

Dear Belle! Dearest Sophie! And his mother, of course. When he closed his eyes for sleep or for any other reason, the faces of the women he had loved would appear among the after-images, dissolving into each other as the other images did, falling to pieces, becoming leprous, radiant, ageing, changing sex. The other after-images were usually of strangers; only rarely might they resemble some casual acquaintance, a person brushed against in the street. He could not imagine why Belle and his mother should appear among their number.

And besides the girl was dead.

Like his father, James had been of an age to participate when war broke out, just coming up nineteen, a Scholar of Merton College, and about to begin his second year at Oxford. Bad luck! If he had completed his second, his call-up would have been deferred to allow him to graduate. As matters were, James had spent an undistinguished war, and put on his scholar's gown again seven years later in order to cram three years' work into two and achieve his First.

His father had been eighteen in 1914, but there was no conscription until two years later, and by that time James's father was already in residence at Trinity College, Dublin, where there was no conscription at all throughout the war. James had never understood it, not truly to the bottom, how it could have been done in that time of white feathers and left no stain. His father had been, as James himself later was, a member of Le Bas House at Haileybury; he had been Head of House (as James never was), trusted with responsibility, a moral influence; he had flogged other boys and kept good discipline. There had been a relationship of some sort with his housemaster, probably affectionate on both sides without being in any way sexual. James's father's own father had been abroad in the Service, and the housemaster was childless; he and James's father would have been surrogates for each other. They had been on a walking tour together in North Wales, hill-walking by day, reading

21

together in the evenings in preparation for James's father's entrance to university. August, 1914. The conversation had taken place in a stone cottage not far from Blaenau Ffestiniog. It had been put to James's father that there might be a higher duty for a lad of his background and experience, that any fool could rush to enlist, but the Empire would need a governing class long after the war with Germany had been forgotten. There would have been tears in the housemaster's eyes; he knew the sacrifice he was asking. James's father would have been genuinely torn; he would have had difficulty in speaking; like James, he was an only son, but with two fathers. The housemaster had connections with Trinity College, Dublin; Latin was better taught there than at any English university. After 1916, James's father had not returned to England during the vacations, having already made the acquaintance of the young lady who was to become James's mother. After 1918, with so many qualified men killed, the ICS had been glad to accept a recruit with James's father's training and family background, and in 1939 he was already in his forties, and with a job to do; there was no question then of his being conscripted. James's father had survived two wars by not taking part in either.

James looked back on his life, having so little else to do in that big house, and what he often saw was his father whom, during that life, he had seen so seldom. What guilt was he trying to transfer? There had been no ladies with white feathers in 1939. Like most of his generation, James would have dodged the call-up if he could, but had not been given the opportunity.

Ever since his first term at Merton, back in Michaelmas 1938 when scholarship was not fashionable among undergraduates, James had known that he wished to be a scholar resident at some university, preferably Oxford. He had no particular inclination to teach, but would do as much as might be required; what he wished was to live in college, and to read books and write about them. The war had been an interruption. Throughout its course, James held fast to

22

his ambition. Among his fellow-soldiers, at least among the more educated of them and those who believed that they had been denied the education they deserved, literature became a popular diversion; quite apart from the prevailing boredom, if one expected to be blown to pieces at any moment, it seemed somehow important to read a poem or write one before that happened. Books were passed from hand to hand, even inherited, or stolen from the dead like a watch or signet ring. Editions of *Penguin New Writing* were sold out almost as soon as published. Messrs Faber & Faber exploited an exploding demand for the poetry of T.S. Eliot, and Messrs Gollancz for the politics of John Strachey. With Hitler's invasion of the USSR, a sudden interest in Tchekov and Turgenev disseminated the prose style of Constance Garnett to every corner of the English-speaking world. But literature was not a mere diversion to James; it was food for the future. Scott, Thackeray, Fielding, Trollope, Jane Austen, George Eliot, Dickens, the Brontës, Richardson, even Sterne, he gobbled them up, as once he had gobbled Galsworthy and Somerset Maugham. His copies of the Pocket Oxford Classics were heavily annotated in the margins. These annotated volumes were never lent to his comrades, but deposited at his grandparents' house near Appledore whenever he went on leave, together with notebooks containing detailed analyses of structure, symbolism and social context. He discovered D.H. Lawrence, read Flaubert in French, and used the Italian Campaign to bone up on Manzoni.

Then he was back at Oxford at last, coming up twenty-seven, never having put his head above the Second World War's equivalent of a parapet, one of that generation of undergraduates with no time to waste, already as it seemed to them half-way to retirement age, who manipulated the Union Society and the political clubs, the OUDS, *Isis*, Film Society, every college and university institution of which they could get their hands on the levers, even the drinking clubs, to their own ambitious purposes. James already knew that he had chosen the wrong university for a degree

23

in English unless he proposed to be a medievalist or specialise in Anglo-Saxon, that Cambridge and even Manchester were the places to be, but he made the best of what there was, secured his First, and departed immediately for the USA (which was almost as good a place to be as Manchester) and two years at Columbia on a Fulbright Fellowship. James was twenty-eight, and Sophie, who had been reading History at Lady Margaret Hall, twenty-six; they were almost a middle-aged couple, but could not marry until James had a job, which was in the autumn of 1951 at Bristol, where they lived in a large room with kitchen alcove and a bathroom and toilet across the landing, shared with the staff and customers of the first Espresso Coffee Bar in what is now the County of Avon.

At Bristol his early work on Lawrence was published, which led naturally to Birmingham where Helen was born, and then a year at the University of Indiana in Bloomington, of which it has been said that one receives one's first intimations of immortality there, since every Sunday afternoon lasts three weeks. Then York in the sixties, a new foundation and James's first professorship. They had been happy at York. James closed his eyes and saw again the campus on a November afternoon, spattered with the fallen leaves of trees which had not yet grown shoulder-high, and the grey concrete of the buildings darkening with the rain. There had been a fountain, and Muscovy ducks and a lake, which had been constructed by enlarging the Heslington village pond. The Department of Biology had stocked the lake with coi and other exotic fish, both for decoration and for study, but none of the villagers had informed either builders or biologists that a pike lived in the pond. Thousands of pounds' worth of delicate Oriental fish, gold and silver, scarlet and blue, had been poured into the lake at public expense to feed the pike. Even the nestlings of the Muscovy ducks had been taken.

Yes, they had been happy at York. The children had been pre-pubescent and still likeable. The university was near enough to the city to make access easy, yet far enough for

24

country quiet, the undergraduates biddable and his colleagues malleable. James and Marie-Louise Huntingdon, a passionate philologist who had been hounded from the University of Penang and would refer to James and herself as "us Wogs", had created the Department in their own image, and although the task had taken longer than seven days they had looked at it and seen that it was good. Sophie had once said to him – it was long before the time at York; it was on their honeymoon, something to do with his not wanting to get up and dance and break plates in that taverna on the harbour – she had said, "The trouble with you, James Elphinstone, is that you won't enter any situation you can't control," and she had seen to the heart of him as she always did. At York he had been in control both of his own work (*Demolitions* and *The Pathology of Romanticism*, both still in print) and of his Department, as he had never been since.

How better to punish a man than to give him what he has always wanted? He had wished to pass his life as a scholar at some university, preferably Oxford, and when the opportunity came he had not been able to refuse it. *"My son, the professor! He's at Oxford, you know."* At Oxford, the professorships are attached to specific colleges; one becomes a fellow of the college by being appointed to the professorship. At Cambridge, a professor can at least negotiate his attachment; once again, Cambridge would have been the better place to be. James had found himself a fellow of a college of which some malicious person had once remarked that the dons seemed to spend their time trying to convince each other that they were not at a provincial university. The remark had been made during the fifties. Since then the college had deteriorated and, during James's own time there, enlarged its numbers, turned increasingly towards the applied sciences, elected an Olympic hurdler as Master, and appeared to be aspiring towards the condition of a polytechnic. That would not have mattered; none of that would have mattered. James had rooms in college, but was not required to live in them.

25

He dined in Hall no more than once a week during term time, was rarely seen in the Senior Common Room, and his attendances at College Meetings were desultory. He and Sophie had bought the Manor House in Little Easeley; that was where his life lay. There was always room to entertain friends, not that they made many in Oxford, but they did not need to look for friends; they were good company for each other. In York, of course, they had made no such distinction between public and private life.

What could not have been foreseen was that he would become bored with his work. There is a limited amount to be discovered between the lines of the novels of Henry James. A critical study of the later works of Joyce soon begins to resemble the task set by the Nazis for the inmates of concentration camps, to carry huge stones across a courtyard and back again. In his search for subjects of some kind of importance or interest, James had moved steadily backwards through time, beginning with D.H. Lawrence and ending with the Word of God, or at least with the more obscure rabbinical commentaries on it. He discovered that colleagues called him "the Exegete". In 1984, on the edge of retirement, when boredom had become, as it so often does, a form of flippancy, he turned back to some of the trash he had devoured during his early adolescence, and published his last critical work, *The Passionate Imagination*, a study of popular fiction between the wars, with essays on *The Green Hat*, *The Constant Nymph*, *Precious Bane*, *Of Human Bondage* and *Rogue Herries*, the structure dissected, the language analysed, the sub-text so teased out as to leave the novels themselves looking decidedly threadbare. This received the reviewers' approval which an earlier work on the Essene Gospels had been denied. "My whimper," said James to Sophie, "appears to have become something of a small bang."

He was in the state of those who see their world pass away as they move upwards through it, so that one looks down as from a roller-coaster, and sees only the drop. What good would those annotated texts and notebooks deposited at Appledore be to any scholar twenty years younger? The whole study of literature had taken a different path; *The Common Pursuit, The Romantic Agony*, those seminal works of his youth, were irrelevant now. Moral values? social context? symbolism? narrative? characterisation? all, all had gone, the old familiar notions, and even ambiguity held the field with less confidence. It had begun before the war, of course, with the separation of the poem from the poet, a useful device, and then along had come the French with semiology, and the points had clicked over; the scholars were on a new track, moving through cuttings towards a long tunnel. Semiology (which confusingly became semiotics in the USA) was defined in the Oxford English Dictionary as late as 1973 as "the pathology of symptoms", but the French did not feel themselves bound by the OED and appropriated the word for "communication studies" to mean "the science of signs".

So it had gone. Structuralism arose naturally from semiology. Language was no longer to be considered diachronically (i.e. in terms of its evolution – farewell philology!) but synchronically – the language as it is in use at the present time. The new linguists said, in effect, "We have abolished yesterday," which was hardly a statement likely to be found endearing by a man in his sixties. At the University of Konstanz, the bloody Krauts went further, with a new "Aesthetic of Reception", which was not concerned with the work, but with the reader's response to it.

James had not been required to engage in such studies, but he had been expected to have an opinion of them. *And he could not condemn them*, was expected to do so, but could not. It seemed to him that the whole bloody chase – the Krauts, Frogs and Yanks in the lead, with the Brits running a rather scrappy fourth, impeded as usual by their compulsion to keep licking the feet of the Yanks in front of them – the whole chase was an expression of and reaction to what he himself suffered, the boredom, the growing and overmastering boredom, not so much with literature itself as with the necessity of finding something to say about it.

27

Learned articles and books had to be published if hungry academics (as he had been) were to find jobs, lectures had to be given, but what on earth was there left to say that any reasonable person might wish to hear? He had not been sorry to give up his Chair, to move his books, to vacate his rooms in college, to settle into domestic life at the Manor with Sophie. They would not vegetate. There would continue to be colloquia, symposia, conferences all over the world, to which James could still secure an invitation, and which would pay their expenses and a little over. They would visit Helen in Houston. James would deliver a few old lectures, lightly refurbished, in Manitoba, Hawaii or New Zealand. Like Prospero he would break his staff, but he would keep the wizard's cloak for occasional wear. He and Sophie would stroll together at their own pace through rustic ways towards a distant death, which would come when it would come, but not yet and not separately.

Sophie! Sophie! an academic's daughter who had married an academic! She had produced three slim gracefully written scholarly volumes of Social History (*Aspects of Everyday Life in the Eighteenth Century, I – A Cotswold Village, II – A Market Town, III – A University City*) and then two children, and then no more books or children. Her hair always smelled of onions because, when cooking, as with any task which demanded concentration, she would run her right hand through it. Sophie!

Marie-Louise had been retired now from York with some unpleasantness, as he had heard, owing to her not wanting to go. James supposed that if language, of which the roots go back so far, were to be studied synchronically, then History itself might be hijacked into synchronism and reader-response, becoming no longer an investigation of what had happened but of what people at the present time chose to believe, which might do wonders for Mary Queen of Scots. It occurred to him that this was already being done in the Soviet Union with the continuous revision of the encyclopaedias. Ah, Sophie, Sophie!

*

Within three weeks of Sophie's death, logic had led him to the conclusion that no useful purpose would be served by his continuing to live. This was different from a mere wish not to be alive; he had wished to die more or less continuously from the moment he had found Sophie dead, but that was emotionalism, a self-indulgence which must not be allowed to influence decision. He had allowed emotionalism a free rein, at least in private, until after the funeral, then a further fortnight, and had then sat down to consider the matter logically.

He was of no further use to himself or to others. That would not matter if he were, on balance, enjoying life, since he had earned his retirement, but he was not enjoying life. Of course Helen had made the offer that he should go and live with them in Houston, Texas, but what would James do as a hanger-on in Houston, a grossly inflated housing-estate with skyscrapers? The logical course of action would be to use the shot-gun. If what he had read were true, the immediate shock of the explosion would act as an anaesthetic; he would be dead before he had time to feel pain; the thing was done by placing the muzzle in the mouth, pointing upwards. Even so, it would be rash to act immediately. A life, which in February was lonely and burdensome with no prospect of amelioration, might become less so, either by habit or happenchance, with the passage of time. He might even become useful again; the experience of adversity might awaken in him a critical interest in the Book of Job or an impulse to re-evaluate *Urn Burial*. The advent of summer might make a difference; it had been Sophie more than he who had responded to nature, but thinking of her so much, as he did, remembering her so much, missing her so much, he might begin after a while to see through her eyes. He would allow six months for reconsideration. By the end of four, it was already clear that there would be no reconsideration.

The single-barrelled shot-gun was kept in a cupboard in James's study, the door secured by padlock and chain in compliance with the police regulations. The intention had been that if any rabbit were to breach the orchard wire and make an appearance on the lawn, it might be shot from the study window. In fact, on those rare occasions when a rabbit had actually made such an appearance, it had always disappeared within the time taken to remove the padlock and chain, take the gun from the cupboard, and load it. The shot-gun had hardly been used, but it was in good condition; it would see James off. Lately he had taken to fingering it, cleaning it, talking to it sometimes. *"I do not set my life at a pin's fee."* This was clearly eccentric behaviour, indicating a deterioration in his mental condition. All the more reason to get the business over.

He would set a date and stick to it. July 25th, the first that came into his mind. His will was at the bank, and would require no adjustment; it already contained provision in case Sophie should die before him. He would have to write letters, one to Helen at least, and if he did not write to Richard as well, it would cause comment; he was not sure of Richard's address, but this was not a problem; that young man would come running to the scent of money. He would not post the letters, but leave them on the kitchen table to be discovered by Elsie. The discovery of himself would be bound to be unpleasant for her. The shot would blow out the back of his head; his brains would be scattered all over the study. Never mind; it could not be helped, and would give her importance in Chipping Norton. She would have her photograph in the local paper, and be interviewed by one of its three reporters. He decided nevertheless to leave her a hundred pounds in an envelope, in addition to the small bequest she would receive under his will. It occurred to him that, since Elsie always came to clean on a Thursday, it would be better to choose a Wednesday for the suicide, some time in the afternoon after the gardener had left; any longer and he might begin to stink; it would be inconsiderate to cause Elsie any more distress than was unavoidable. He consulted the diary. July 25th was a Saturday. Very well, July 29th, then.

Why had he chosen July 29th instead of the 22nd? Was it

30

possible that he still had qualms? He locked the house, and went for a long walk, through the orchard, across the water-meadow, up the further hill, through the copse, and back by the road. Nature did not speak to him as it would have spoken to Sophie. He had no qualms. The later date gave more time for preparation; that was all.

On July 29th he lay in bed late. He heard the gardener arrive, and clump about in the shed. This new man put more energy into clumping and clattering than into hoeing. Old Mr Proctor had worked quietly and methodically, digging and preparing great tracts of the vegetable garden until well into his eighties, when arthritis and a hernia had slowed him down; in his seventy-ninth year, Mr Proctor had lifted stones the weight of a ram and trimmed the hedge from a step-ladder. Punctually at eleven he would come in for his coffee, and sit with Sophie in the kitchen, telling old tales of when the village houses were all thatched and the roads unmade and how he would go out with his father to plough their only field by lamplight, the boy walking ahead with the lamp and the father himself pulling the plough. The new man wore a flat cap, skulked behind bean-rows, and when he conversed at all it was of what he had seen on television the night before.

James drank a mug of tea and ate an apple. Though there were two bridges and a gap he still had most of his own teeth, and he cleaned them as thoroughly as always, using floss and an interdental brush. He felt no fear at what was to be done that day. Consequently his bowels were not loose; he spent only the customary amount of time on his walnut throne reading an article on pheromones in an old copy of *The New York Review of Books*. Five minutes afterwards, he had no recollection of what he had read. He went downstairs, still in his dressing-gown, and washed every dirty dish and pan in the kitchen and scrubbed the table, then prepared a mug of instant coffee, and took it out as usual for the gardener with his weekly money in an envelope. The milk left blobs on top of the liquid, but did not taste odd, and the man did not complain.

31

He went back upstairs, made the bed with clean sheets and pillow-cases from the airing-cupboard, got out the hoover, and cleaned all the carpets upstairs and down. He decided not to dust, because his hands were sometimes a little shaky, and he did not wish to break anything. Besides, if one started dusting, it would never end; even Elsie never tackled the books more than once a year.

At one o'clock the gardener clattered off. James drank a glass of Rioja with wholemeal bread and cheese for lunch. After lunch he walked in the garden, crushed a leaf of bergamot between his fingers, and smelled a rose. He sat for a while on the wooden bench under the yew tree, but this "having a last look round" would not do; it was a pointless occupation; he was not storing up memories for any afterwards, because there would be no afterwards.

He bathed, and put on clean underwear and a clean shirt. He considered wearing a suit, but that would be almost Japanese; that would be making a gesture, not merely carrying out a decision based on rational grounds; his act was to be logical, not histrionic; old cords and a light pull-over would be appropriate. The letters for Helen and Richard and the envelope for Elsie had been prepared the evening before. He left them on the scrubbed kitchen table, went upstairs to his study, took the phone off the rest, unlocked the padlock, and removed the shot-gun from the cupboard.

He broke the gun open, and looked into the barrel. It was clean of course; he had spent days cleaning it with Three-in-One Oil and a cleaning-rod bought at an auction. There were two ducks etched into the metal of the stock; they were not in flight, but seemed to be ordinary farmyard ducks, walking, perhaps the only models the etcher had been able to find. He did not think the gun had ever been used for duck. He had bought it from the widow of a man in the village who had kept ferrets, and had clearly been a rabbiting man. The widow had offered to throw the ferrets in with the gun at a reduced rate, but James had declined.

The cartridges were Winchester GB Chasse, Number 6;

there were instructions for use and various warnings printed on the box in English and French. Print of any sort still held some compulsion for James; he read the instructions before inserting a cartridge in the chamber. He would sit at his desk; that would be appropriate for a scholar. The base of the shot-gun would have to rest on some solid surface to absorb the kick. Not the desk itself, which would be too high; obviously, the floor. He should have rehearsed all this; there must be no muddle, which might only cause mutilation and pain instead of death; it must all be efficiently done. Never mind; he would rehearse it now; there was plenty of time. He removed the cartridge from the chamber, and rested the gun with its base on the floor and the muzzle against the roof of his mouth. He would easily be able to pull the trigger, but the floor was of polished boards, and the base of the gun showed a tendency to slip. Very well, he would hold the base of the gun with his feet, the stock clamped between his knees. Probably the blast would send him backwards and topple the chair, so that he would be found sprawled on the floor among the mess instead of sitting at his desk like a scholar, but that could not be helped. It was just as well there was no carpet; the floor would be easier to clean, though perhaps the ceiling . . . but one really must not allow oneself to worry about such matters. He put the cartridge back in the chamber. Right! the thing must be done, and now was the time to do it. If he found himself shivering, that was natural; Sir Walter Raleigh had shivered on the scaffold, but had made a good end none the less, unlike the Duke of Monmouth whose execution had required several strokes of the axe. Shot-gun in position and firmly held, safety catch off, the direction of the barrel correct, insofar as James was able to judge, for blowing the back off the top of his head. He moved his right hand down towards the trigger-guard. Interesting! It was as if the air had thickened a little around the fingers; one had to make a definite push. Political prisoners, he had read, were blindfolded and tied to a post, or lined up facing a wall before being shot. *Close your eyes.*

33

This won't hurt a bit. It always did hurt, though. He would not close his eyes. He was James Elphinstone. He would look out once more at the world, and then leave it. He raised his chin, and looked out through the study window.

There was a rabbit in the garden.

It was at the far end of the lawn. It was nibbling at something, not grass, a tender plant, probably the meconopsis. James moved the gun very cautiously from between his knees. Luckily the window was already open on this summer afternoon. There ought to be a carpet; the noise of his chair moving back against the bare boards might startle the rabbit. Gun down gently across the desk, chair moved, lifting and lowering it so as not to scrape, gun picked up again, one step and then another to the window. The gun would be steadier resting against the sill than held to his shoulder. So be it; take the easy way; this was not sport. He had the rabbit in the sight, held steady. It was sitting up, listening, and would be off in a moment. He aimed for the base of the rabbit so as to allow for the kick, and squeezed the trigger carefully. The rabbit jumped as he shot it (or was lifted off its feet) and fell over. He must go down and finish it off at once if it were not already dead.

But the rabbit had died at once, or at least between being shot and the time taken for James to reach it. There was blood on its nose. It lay on the edge of the lawn, limp and warm like a child. James took it by the hind legs, carried it into the orchard, and threw it over the wire; the body would disappear during the night. Now he would clean the gun, and put it away.

And put it away. It came to him that his hand had actually been on the trigger when he had seen the rabbit. It came to him that he had shot the rabbit, not himself. It was like the case of Abraham and Isaac, when the Almighty had substituted a lamb for the little boy, with Abraham's knife already in the air. James did not believe in Jehovah or any other god, but there was no denying that it would not be James's corpse the foxes would be crunching that night. He realised . . . he saw that now . . . he felt a little faint, and

34

had to sit down on the bench. He realised that he had suffered a form of release, and could now do anything. He had been about to pull the trigger and blow his head off, would certainly have done it, and therefore could now do anything, need fear nothing except lingering pain from which he might always free himself simply by finishing the unfinished business. He was no longer bound to any way of life, to any place, any obligation, because he had already been at the very point of leaving behind all such obligations and considerations; practically speaking, he might act as if he were already dead. James had become a free man, and must decide how to use his freedom. "I shall do such things," he said, "what they are yet I know not, but they shall be the terrors of the earth."

· 2 ·
PHONICS

"I shall do such things. What they are yet I know not." That was the problem; what they should be, he knew not.

He had decided not to waste his death, but did not know to what purpose he should apply it. He had no great liking for humanity in general, nor for those human beings in particular with whom he was himself acquainted, yet clearly his death, if it were to have any meaning, ought to serve humanity in some way. He was not even sure whether he should be considering an act or course of action likely to lead to death, which should serve some cause, or whether he should regard the life he had now resumed as being owed to the service of a cause, which service should continue until ended by death in a way not of his own choosing. The dilemma was not entirely semantic.

Was there a way of serving humanity without actually having to mingle with it? Yes, there was the transcendental alternative. James thought of Thomas à Beckett, scabby and louse-ridden beneath his hair-shirt, but the mortification of the flesh did not go so far these days; a little fasting should suffice. If James were to enter a monastery, there to devote what remained of his life to the service and glory of a God in Whom he must make himself believe (but perhaps even belief was not necessary, only submission), he might, as he understood the matter, by prayer and by silence, by holy thoughts and a strict adherence to rule, atone in his own person for the sins of the silly fellows outside, or at least make it a little easier for them at the Final Judgement. James considered the transcendental alternative for about the length of time it took to formulate, and then rejected it.

What of its opposite, by which service to humanity may consist of the violent removal of those baser parts of it? Should James, like the elderly heroes of the American revenge movies, walk inner-city streets by night, executing in various unpleasant ways the muggers and rapists who loitered there? It seemed to him that there might be the danger of misunderstandings, so much more embarrassing than the mere sacrifice of one's life. One would feel remarkably foolish if a bolt from one's crossbow impaled a rapist who turned out only to be enjoying energetic coitus with a friend; in such a case, apologies would not be enough. If the removal of what was base were to be his choice, it might be better to stick to what he knew, shifting secretly from one university to another, eliminating structuralists. Such murders are always thought to be motiveless, since the police do not know where to look for a motive; he would get a fair run before they caught him. Perhaps he could combine the shooting of structuralists with sending poisoned chocolates to television newsreaders, who believe that "strata" and "media" are singular feminine nouns and speak of "decimation" when the slaughter is far greater than one in ten. And when at last he had been found out and the structuralists and the newsreaders hit back, battering him with their microphones, burying him under mounds of learned articles, he would be remembered by a simple plaque set into the spot, "James Mountstuart Elphinstone. For Services to the English Language." It would be enough. Better the English Language than humanity.

James played with such notions for a while, cherishing them, devising itineraries, compiling lists like Koko in *The Mikado*. He did not once think of Sophie at such times. It was exhilarating, invigorating, not at all boring; he was as engrossed as he had been when he shot the rabbit. But of course it would not do.

He turned his mind to more mundane matters. The

Citizens' Advice Bureau, he discovered, had very little use for a retired professor of English. "If you had only been a solicitor, age would not be a consideration," they told him. "We can never get enough of them." The Samaritans chose to regard him as a client, not a volunteer, and he left the interview tight-lipped. In the late fifties he had loosely supported the Campaign for Nuclear Disarmament, because it had seemed to him that the development of nuclear weapons was at an early stage, and might by agreement be prevented. He and Sophie had walked part of the way from Aldermaston, and pressed their protesting bodies against the linked arms of policemen in Trafalgar Square. But time had passed without agreement. Nuclear weapons and the nations possessing them had proliferated; there was no longer, as it seemed to James, any turning back. When it came to the nuclear issue, he had rather be a bee, and sting while dying, than a fly to be swatted for sport.

No CAB or CND, no Samaritans. There were societies for the amelioration of most human ills, and all had a great need of money, but little work for elderly academics. Oh, to be a *sanyasi*, and sit beside the road with a begging bowl of brass! Such behaviour would have been ill-regarded in North Oxfordshire; the police would have had him away in a van. And, in any case, he had already rejected one transcendental alternative.

Opium poppies bloomed in the garden, purple and pink. Convolvulus had invaded the far border, twining at first unnoticed among the stems of astilbe and agapanthus; there was mildew on the roses. James took glyphosate gel to the convolvulus and a fungicide spray to the roses, wearing rubber gloves for both operations and an old scarf of Sophie's over the lower part of his face for the second, such precautions being needful now that his own life had become valuable again. It had never occurred to him to dispose of Sophie's clothes, or any of her things, which occupied the same space in the house as before.

It came to him that in this matter of not wasting his death, three considerations were conjoined. First, what he did should be of service to some person or cause outside himself; second, the person or cause should deserve, at least in James's opinion, such a service; third, it must be a service which he himself was suited to perform – as solicitors, accountants and estate agents must be suited to the Citizens' Advice Bureau. Thinking himself to be someone desirable, one of the Great and the Good who sit on Royal Commissions and the Arts Council, he had ignored the third consideration, and must now give it proper importance. What were retired professors of English Literature particularly suited to? The answer seemed to be "retirement". He remembered having read somewhere of classes in literacy for adults, that after over fifty years of compulsory free education there were still grown-up people who could not read, and that classes were organised to teach them. James himself could not remember ever having learned to read; he had taken reading for granted like breathing. Even though there was so little worth reading these days, it must be humiliating not to have at least the option of rejecting the rubbish there was.

He made enquiries. As between Chipping Norton and Burford, the locality was well served with evening classes in flower arranging, furniture restoring, computer programming, brass rubbing, Indian cookery, Commercial French and how to run small businesses. There were no classes for teaching adults to read, but he supposed that in the small towns and villages of the area an adult unable to read would not care to have his illiteracy known, and would travel to Banbury or Oxford.

He had avoided Oxford since his retirement, and particularly since Sophie's death. He did not wish to bump into acquaintances who might feel obliged to make helpless small talk about his bereavement, and in any case Oxford had become so loathsome a place these days, with its concrete car parks higher than the spires, its pedestrian precincts and shopping centres, a city of neon tubes and polystyrene, where visitors paid to enter Christ Church as

39

if it were a branch of Disneyland. Nevertheless he went.

The office of the Adult Literacy and Basic Education Scheme was at Littlemore, on the outskirts of the city, and was only open in the mornings. "Most of us in Adult Literacy are part-timers, you see," the Tutor said. "It doesn't come high among the government's priorities, I'm afraid, probably because illiterates very rarely vote. I hope you wouldn't expect to be paid."

"I should not expect to be paid."

"When would you like to start? There's a training course, but it's not arduous – three two-hour sessions."

"Are you sure I should be suitable?"

"Oh, we take almost anyone who offers. It's a one-to-one business, you see, so we need as many volunteers as there are students. They drop out during training or soon afterwards if they find they can't cope. The students drop out too, but not so quickly, so there's always a waiting list. We daren't advertise. People just find out we're here."

"Why do the students drop out?"

"It's a very inefficient method of teaching."

"One-to-one? Surely the best?"

"Two hours once a week, usually on a Monday or Tuesday evening. They can't retain what they've learned. Half an hour a day would be infinitely more effective, even if one only kept to week-days, but the system's not geared to that. If the teachers aren't being paid, one can't expect them to come in five days a week. As things are, a student would take six years from not being able to read at all to mastering a morning paper, assuming he's not mentally handicapped to begin with, which of course some of them are. They get discouraged, and give up. It leaves a bad taste sometimes. If you get a real tryer, he'll blame the teacher not the system, and then she blames herself. I remember one old chap – not so old, really – fiftyish, a scrap-dealer; his mother looked after the accounts and what letters there were. Well, she was in her seventies, and growing forgetful, and her fingers swelled, so he put her into a Home, and enrolled with us. After three years, he could manage street

40

signs, but even single-entry book-keeping was beyond him, so he walked out, and tried to get his mother back from the Home; unfortunately she was quite gaga by then. The volunteer took it personally."

"I offered myself to the Samaritans. They seemed doubtful of my motives for making the offer."

"Surely that's your own business? I don't think many of our volunteers have a vocation to teach illiterates to read. Boredom . . . loneliness . . . the need for a surrogate child . . . the need to feel superior to some other human being . . . to make some kind of life outside a partner's shadow . . . just wanting a reason to get out of the house for a while; we don't ask. Most of them are women, many of them elderly, and it's the older women who tend to stay. Some are men; the ratio's about one to five. The men are usually younger, as a matter of fact – younger than yourself – business executives in early middle age who feel they'd like to do something worthwhile; they never last. No, motive's quite irrelevant; it's a question of whether one can do the work."

"Is the work difficult?"

"Not in the least; that's the trouble. The work is extremely easy, but repetitive. It requires reserves of patience, and the ability to rise above persistent disappointment."

"You believe I should be capable of it?"

"Frankly, no. It would be below your capabilities."

"Very well. I shall enroll for training, if I may."

"You wouldn't prefer to lecture? It's not my department, but the Centre here caters for adult education in many forms."

"Brass rubbing!"

"Oh, yes. And flower arranging . . . Macramé . . . all that sort of thing; it's called the Useful Arts Option. But there are classes in literature also; they're not always very well attended but, unlike our people, the lecturers do get paid."

"Payment is not my first consideration. When does your

41

training course begin?"

"*Obstinate!*" the Tutor thought as James left the office, "*That might get him through for a while. Horses for courses, though. We shan't give him anyone handicapped.*"

James himself, as he drove home, wondered what he could be thinking of. This wasn't really what he wanted to do at all. It came to him that teaching illiterates to read was not only not his sort of thing; it was Sophie's sort of thing, and she would have done it well. It came to him that he was behaving like some damned novelist who, in order to delay the process of writing, casts about in futile directions (transferred epithet), and calls what he is doing "research". Nevertheless he would give it a whirl. One couldn't allow oneself to be put down by someone whose corduroy trousers did not fasten at the top. The Tutor, he supposed, had given up smoking, and consequently run to fat, but that was an explanation for slovenliness, not an excuse. It came to him that what his situation really required was a whiff of danger. Well, that would come if he put himself in the way of it.

That evening he sat in the living room, and listened to a recording of the Symphonic Variations of César Franck, which had been one of Sophie's favourites but too romantic for his own taste, and for the first time since her death he felt her presence in the room, and found it comforting.

One pays for such comfort. He had felt her presence, and must again, alone in the double bed, endure her absence. Sleep eluded him. He had recourse to the bubble.

The bubble was a device of the mind – of fancy, if you like. James did not approve of sleeping pills or tranquillisers, though the doctor had prescribed both. In the last days of his retirement and after, when he had lain awake wondering how he had wasted his talent, Sophie had tried to teach him the use of a mantra, and he had lain obediently beside her in the dark, breathing from the diaphragm and attempting to strip the word "alluvial" of its meaning until it should become no more than a sleepy humming in his brain. It had not worked; Sophie had known it would not. James's immediate question had been "Why 'alluvial'?" One does not ask such questions, or any questions. The point of a mantra is that, although the word is personal to oneself, and must be kept secret, any word will do. "Alluvial" had never even begun to hum for James. Like the Hound of Heaven, he had chased it down the nights and down the days, across continents, through delta and polder, from the Ganges and the Brahmaputra to the malarial marshes of the Ivory Coast, then eastwards to Siberia by way of the Wash. After a week, Sophie had given him relief by taking it back again. While she was with him, he had not needed a mantra; sleep would come in the end from her. The touch of her behind against his beneath the sheets had been reassurance enough; to take her hand in the darkness and hold it against him had been enough.

What would be enough now that he was alone, pills being excluded? Soldiers and prisoners were said to use masturbation as a cure for insomnia, drifting for a while on waves of post-orgasmic languour far from the boredom and the fear to which they must nevertheless return. Old age, James thought, is a prison, in which the bars keep getting closer and closer as freedom of choice and even movement are more and more restricted by the inadequate flesh. To extend the metaphor, those unfortuate people who had the AIDS virus were like prisoners on Death Row; there was no question but that they would eventually be killed in some unpleasant way; the only question was for how long and by what tricks one would be able to stave off the killing. He wondered whether Richard might have contracted the virus, or even the disease; if either were the case, he himself would be unlikely to be told. Even Helen . . . the disease was rife in the USA, and really he knew very little about her husband except that the fellow had written a pamphlet on aspects of Hepplewhite. He turned his thoughts another way, but not to masturbation; his libido had not survived retirement. His toes were curled by tension; he would have cramps unless he could uncurl them. Deep-breathing

43

would not do. "Alluvial" would not do. Far from being stripped of meaning; it had acquired an accretion of memories. He would have to try the bubble.

Of course one had to be careful with the bubble, first not to overuse it, then to play fair within it.

He closed his eyes, and let it settle into place. The bubble resembled one of those snug semispheres of plexiglass which will one day provide an artificial atmosphere for colonies on the moon, except that it was permeable; people could move in and out of it without even knowing it was there. James did not bother himself with the mechanics of its construction; it simply *was*. It could be extended to a radius of about five miles so as to take in a section of the A34 should he require to influence passing motorists, but usually it fitted around the house and the village. Within the bubble, James ruled, but his power was limited by the rules which he himself had imposed. Theoretically, as the onlie begetter of the bubble, he could amend those rules or even rescind them, but if he were to do so he would risk destroying the reality of the bubble, which was sustained by rules, and which would then become ineffable and therefore inefficacious.

Of course some rules had been changed. Time had changed them. The bubble had been created so long ago; James could not remember exactly when; it had been after his coming to England, but probably before prep school. Some had been changed as circumstances had changed; some had simply been forgotten. What was important was that one could not change a rule merely because it had become inconvenient, and one could not impose a rule which would benefit only oneself. Thus James could and did forbid the smoking of tobacco, sniffing of cocaine and glue, the injection of heroin; he could abolish murder, theft, child-abuse, habitual drunkenness and the splitting of infinitives inside the bubble; he could compel rats, mice, cockroaches, aphids, all sucking and stinging insects and various fungi hostile to plants to remove themselves outside the bubble; he could cause bindweed, couch grass,

44

ground elder, nettle, thistle and dandelion to die back at the roots and their seeds to become infertile. Rabbits were excluded from the bubble – it was not permeable by them – but badgers and hedgehogs were cherished. There was much James could do to ameliorate the behaviour and circumstances of his people inside the bubble and motorists who went in and out of it by way of the A34, even to the gradual dissolving of cancerous cells and their replacement with healthy tissue. But he could not bring Sophie back from the dead, or Helen from Houston. He could do nothing directly to ameliorate his own circumstances; in that respect the rules of the bubble were those governing the receipt of gifts by officers of the Indian Civil Service.

Except that inside the bubble, unwilled, unnoticed, he did grow younger.

Of course the reason for the bubble, the reason why James had created it all those years ago, was that inside it he had control. Sophie had seen to the heart of that right from the beginning of their life together, even before the dreams began. *"The trouble with you, James Elphinstone, is that you won't enter any situation you can't control."* The dreams were about that, the bad dreams and the nightmares, both in their different ways about not having control, those dreams from which he would wake to reach out to her for comfort, which she would grumblingly give. *"Why do you have to have these dreams while I'm asleep?"* and then, if it were a nightmare and not just a bad dream, *"Jimmy! You're soaked with sweat. It's so inconsiderate."* Inconsiderate or no, she would hold him and kiss his eyelids, drifting back herself almost immediately into sleep, while he lay wakeful holding her in the crook of his arm.

The bad dreams and the nightmares, different in kind as well as in degree. The bad dreams were about losing control, the nightmares about not having it. The bad dreams – a class, seminar, lecture, in which his presence carried no authority, his information no interest except to himself to whom it was of high importance, the students talking and laughing amongst themselves, trying out

45

scraps of popular song, going in and out of the room at will, ignoring him. Or he would have caught a train to some destination it was important to reach, but would be unsure if he were on the right train or where he should change, and would be unable to make out from his compartment the names of the stations through which the train passed or where it briefly stopped . . . Santahar . . . Parbatipur . . . Asansol . . . Dhanbad; the station signs would be unclear or obscured, or the train would overshoot and come to a halt just beyond the platform. Even if he were able to recognise the station, and know he must alight there, he would be unable to get his luggage from the rack, and the train would move on, leaving Sophie on the platform, himself still in the corridor, and only half the luggage out. Sometimes it would be Sophie who would be carried away by the train, while James struggled on the platform with the management of coolies who ran in every direction with pieces of luggage, some of which did not seem to be his. He would end up alone without money or baggage in some bazaar or desert with the train, even that wrong train, long departed and no other expected, and the station staff unco-operative, refusing to work the telegraph. Often in the bad dreams he would lose clothing, particularly shoes; he would beggar himself buying new shoes in replacement, and lose them almost as he left the shop. Shoeless, sometimes trouserless also, luggageless, he would never-theless find Sophie at last, but she would be with someone else and in the wrong hotel. Sometimes she would pretend not to know him, sometimes had genuinely forgotten him. *"Bad dream! bad dream!" "Snuggle up close, Jimmy dear, and try not to fart."*

The nightmares were of a different order. No question of his ever having been in control, James would be an observer, his punishment to watch. The caravan of peace-ful travellers, the women decently veiled, trotting in the dust beside the mules on which the children sat clutching at the pommels of the saddle, resting their legs on bales of cloth, nets of melons and cooking pots and chickens still

46

alive, the old men leading the mules or gossiping together at the rear, the leader, bountifully turbanned, on his white horse, with his musket which would explode if it were fired, and his two teenage sons with their curved swords, never yet used. Then the camp in the evening among trees not far from the road, the brushwood fires, the cooking smells, the bedding rolls laid out, mothers with their children lying beside them, lying close beside them, twitching in sleep . . . (*"Bad dream!" "Snuggle up close, my dear."*), the teenage sons and the old men suddenly sleepy, the leader with his cheek resting on the stock of his musket, only the assassins wakeful, bustling amongst the sleepers with their silken cords, and James watching from the shelter of a tree, watching it all, each murder, unable to prevent it, unable to save even a child, even a young girl half-waking to fear as the cord was twisted, unable even to turn away and run further into the wood, James who had known who the men were and what they would do, but had given no warning. Or the walled town and the secret alley beneath and between the walls, to which only James held the key and he had given it up, and must now, under guard, watch the flames and smell the scorching flesh, hear the screaming, smell the blood which spurted from slashed throats, see the infants impaled like kebabs on sharpened stakes. Or he would look down on tended fields from a high place amongst mounted men in winged helmets, who would laugh, and ride onwards, leaving James to watch them hunt the villagers like rabbits through the corn. Always the observer, usually the betrayer, himself never harmed but powerless, unable even to warn, far less to prevent. *"Bad dream!" "You're soaked with sweat."* He reached out in the dark, and did not find her.

"I'm supposed to talk to you."

"Aren't we going to do reading?"

"In a little while. I have to talk to you first to find out what your interests are. Then I make up sentences out of what we've been talking about, and you read them to me."

47

"I've got a lot of interests."

The boy only had one hand. James had been warned of this. The boy had not lost the hand; he had never had it. His name was Pavel Borek. The father had been a Czech refugee from the Russian Intervention of 1968, a lawyer from Brno, who had been the guest for a while of some committee hastily formed to assist such people, who are asked to Christmas parties in Twickenham or Chelsea, kitted out with overcoats and introductions and then allowed to drift; if such people do not find work with the BBC World Service, they are often unable to find any work at all commensurate with their abilities. Those who have been able to bring out money, or have access to any, may open a small shop; the women go cleaning. Pavel's father had been an activist, his name marked from the beginning, and had escaped only two jumps ahead of the police, wearing his best suit and two gold watches and with a spare shirt and underwear in his briefcase. The watches had not lasted long. A thorough grounding in Roman Law did not qualify him even as a solicitor's clerk in Britain, and few British firms had commercial dealings at that time with Czechoslovakia, while those which did would have found his attachment to their staff embarrassing. Though he spoke German and a little Latin, his grasp of the English language was insecure. He had found employment at last as an agricultural labourer on a farm near Garsington, and married a local girl who, after Pavel's birth, developed post-natal depression, or at any rate discovered that she could neither stand nor understand her husband, and ran away to London, whence she had often returned, but never for long. During one such return, when Pavel was twelve, she had walked into the river, and drowned. The father had died eighteen months later of pleurisy during the bitter winter of 1983, and Pavel, too old at fourteen for fostering, had been found a place at a Children's Home.

It was amazing that the boy seemed so cheerful. One could see the fingers, tiny pink buds in the stump of his wrist. There was a diagram in the Adult Literacy Tutors'

48

Training Manual, "The Cycle of Deprivation Related to Reading": the Manual was full of such diagrams and lists – lists of common and less common and immediately useful words, lists of teaching methods and lists of the advantages and disadvantages of each method. The Cycle of Deprivation showed (in a box) illiterate parents who did not read themselves and therefore could not (second box) assist their children to do so; the children therefore (third box) fell behind at school, regarding reading as alien to them, becoming in their turn illiterate parents (fourth box) unable to assist and unwilling to encourage their children to read. One could apply this cycle to Pavel only up to a point. The father had been a highly literate person, but in the wrong language, had worked long hours, mostly solitary, at the farm, and been unable to improve his English. The mother had been absent more often than not. There had been no television, and the cheap radio had been tuned usually to music programmes. At the village school, there had been suspicion of the boy's foreignness, disapproval of his peripatetic mother and distrust of his disability. Pavel had set himself to win the respect of his fellows, and this was not done by reading, but by physical prowess, even though handicapped. He had earned that respect and, with even more difficulty and after the most bruising fights, the respect of his peers at the Children's Home.

There was a heavy file on Pavel, and James had been allowed to read part of it. Files came naturally to that family. The Czech police had kept a file on his father.

Tiny pink vestigial buds like the promise, the unfulfilled promise of fingers. How often he must have watered them in the hope that they might grow! Pavel said, "We can talk about my hand if you like. You've been looking at it long enough."

"I'm most sincerely sorry."

"You don't have to be. Everyone looks at it."

"Nevertheless I imagine that talking about it may embarrass you."

"Not really. I have to come to terms with it, you see. Well, I

49

have come to terms with it in myself. What I still have to do is help other people come to terms with it."

The pity of it! The boy was clearly intelligent. He should, in that case, be easy to teach. They would make a start, as the Course Supervisor had suggested, with the Language Experience Technique, and hope to proceed swiftly to Phonics.

"We'll talk about your hand, then, or rather the lack of it, and devise some sentences together. You won't mind if I consult the Manual from time to time? I've never taught anyone to read before."

"But you're a professor." They had told James much about Pavel, and must have told Pavel at least a little about James.

"Not at this. I was a Professor of Literature before my retirement. Was it thalidomide? – something like that?"

"Eh?"

"Anything your mother took during pregnancy?"

"She took pills, but that was after. She'd take anything, my mum, all sorts."

"What did she tell you . . . about . . . ?"

Pavel shook his head. "It was my dad explained it. There's little signals inside you, see, tell your body what it's going to be. It's in code, messages in code. I didn't have enough of them. Simple really."

"To what extent do you find it limits you?"

"Not a lot. Or in the reading, do you mean? And the writing?"

The boy was right to make the distinction. Reading and writing were different activities, in his own case particularly so.

"Yes," James said, "Writing would present a physical problem; I see that."

"Physical problems don't bother me. There's not much I can't do; I can master most tasks. I set myself that goal right from the beginning, as soon as I could understand, to do what everyone else can do. Some things I can't manage. Climbing ropes or hand-over-hand up the wall-bars in the

50

gym, I can't do that. But I can play football, cricket, pool, tennis. Squash, I can play; basket-ball even."

"Your school seems to have been very well equipped."

"I find places. Sports Centres. I seek out new sports. You get in free if you're disabled."

"And the practical side of life? Day-to-day?"

"I can drive a car. Did the training at the Centre. They train you for anything; you only have to ask. I do have difficulty peeling small potatoes, and there's some DIY still beyond me. I have to depend on my teeth a lot to hold things still."

"Forgive me if I misunderstand. 'The Centre'? You were in a Home, I think?"

"Right. There's two places – the Centre and the Home. Very different; you couldn't confuse them."

"The Home is the Children's Home?"

"John Radclyffe Home, yes. I've left now. They throw you out at eighteen. It's a jungle. Nice blokes; don't get me wrong; I still go back sometimes, to visit for the company. You get lonely living by yourself."

"Yes, one does."

"Just the same, it's everyone for himself there, has to be. With my disability, I'd have been down at the bottom with the epileptics; they'd have poured shit on me. I had to fight my way up."

James looked at the stump of the arm with its tiny pink buds of fingers. "It can't have been easy."

"Took me a time. Just as well my dad didn't die any sooner, or I'd never have managed it. But with the training at the Centre, and keeping myself fit, at my peak of physical fitness, and I was fourteen, see; I'd got me strength, so I won through; I won their respect. I mean, either you give up or you win; you got no other choice. They gave me a hook at the Centre for a bit, and I was tempted to ask for it back; it would have come in useful."

"And the Centre is . . . ?"

"Disability Centre. I been going there since I was six, off and on, for the training. They gave me that hook, but I never

51

took to it. Then they made me wear an artificial hand all through school – hand in a glove, bloody stupid that was; everybody knew; when I had the choice, I refused it; I hate deception; the only way to get through, you got to face up to things."

"You still go?"

"When I want to. They rely on you not to take advantage. I help them a bit sometimes. There was a boy had his arm ripped off by farm machinery. I helped to teach him."

"You seem to have made an excellent adjustment."

"Not really. It's always a fight. Like I'm still nervous to approach people socially. Like discos, going to discos, I'll make myself go, but my hand is in my pocket most of the time."

"And you dance like that, with one hand in your pocket?"

"Looks cool. I don't know how people like me managed in the old days."

"Waltzes? Foxtrots? Yes, I can see it would be difficult. Tangos."

"Right! Old Tyme Dancing. You couldn't do it."

James had waltzed. Rather well, as he now remembered. He and Sophie had waltzed together sometimes in the front room at York, to the record-player, with the children beating time. They had waltzed and foxtrotted too (and hadn't there been something called the quickstep?) on the planked floor of the marquee at the Magdalen Commem nearly forty years ago, he and Sophie, James in a borrowed dinner-jacket with a carnation, Sophie in a dress of blue and silver panels, long since cut up to cover cushions. They had consumed cold salmon, champagne and strawberries in somebody's rooms at two in the morning – whose rooms? – was it Charles Fawcett or that Gibraltan? They had strolled round Addison's Walk, hand in hand in the misty dawn, and had breakfasted together at Ma Brown's in the Market. Bliss was it in that dawn to be alive, but to be young . . .

"I'm sorry," he said. "I seem to have forgotten to make any notes."

52

"And at the swimming-pool," Pavel said. "I've never managed that. Stripping off."

"You feel vulnerable?"

"Right! I'll do it, though; I make myself."

"And the reading?"

"Sorry?"

"You said earlier, 'Either you give up, or you win.' You gave up on reading?"

"Different."

"How?"

"Nobody reckoned reading. They teach it at school, but they don't expect anything. It doesn't win you any respect."

"Didn't your father reckon it?"

"He reckoned it, but he couldn't do it, could he? Not in English."

"He never taught you Czech? Or German?"

The boy fell silent. Slowly his complexion grew redder, and one could see that the blush spread up from his face to his ears and the scalp beneath the short fair hair. It was as if he were fighting the blush as he fought all forms of personal weakness, but time passed, and the blush won. He said, "I can speak Czech. Some."

"But not read it?"

"There wasn't any books to read. At first my mum didn't want me . . . wouldn't let me, but she went away. Him and me, we'd speak together; I was the only person he could really talk to. Sometimes when people had come to the house, social workers and that, and people about mum, he'd ask me what they'd said. He knew; he just wanted to make sure he was right; he could always understand more English than he let on. He hated the English, but he didn't have any money to go anywhere else."

"He was an educated man. A lawyer."

"Wasn't no good to him. Nobody reckoned it."

"Perhaps I'd better try to make up a few sentences, based on what you've told me. I'll write them out carefully in pencil and read them to you while you look at the text. Then you

53

go over the pencil-writing with a felt-tipped pen – getting the feel of the words, as one might say, tracing out the shape for yourself. Then we read a sentence a few times together, and then you read it on your own. When you can read that sentence without any help, we go on to the next, and, if I've been clever enough, you'll probably find some words you recognise. We could begin with the Disability Centre if you like."

Had he been a Gibraltan or a Greek? Cypriot perhaps; he had been of that complexion. Kenneth Tynan had made an appearance at midnight in a dinner-suit of strawberry velvet, and was said to have climbed in. A.J.P. Taylor had locked his door against intruders, and Tynan had raced snails up it.

The boy was amazingly quick. He had already taught himself to recognise any sign which was likely to be important to him, "ENTRANCE", "EXIT", "OPEN", "CLOSED", "PRIVATE", "SQUASH COURTS", "GYMNASIUM", "CHANGING ROOM", "RECEPTION", "GENTLE-MEN", signs which may confuse adult illiterates, and lead them into embarrassment. A teacher's first priority may be to familiarise the student with the appearance of such signs, but it was clear that James would not be required to do so in Pavel's case. The Language Experience Technique was one to which Pavel had already, in practice, accustomed himself, and he made such swift progress that he had soon mastered the appearance of the seventy-six words, from "a" to "your" which make up on average (the Manual stated) a half of all reading. Both he and James wished to get on to Phonics. The Language Experience Technique was not natural to James, and seemed retrograde, as if he were teaching the boy ideograms; the alphabet had been invented to free the human mind from such slavery. As for Pavel, he well remembered Phonics from his days at the Garsington Church Primary School. It had not been called Phonics then; it had been called Reading, and he had failed at it – well, not failed; Pavel never failed; he had chosen to evade it. Pavel now proposed to confront Phonics head on.

So they proceeded to Phonics, to the alphabet, to that simple system by which sounds are represented by twenty-four basic symbols in combination, which has brought written communication all the way from the stick-creatures scratched on the walls of caves by paleolithic man to the metaphysics of Kant, the existentialism of Sartre, the economic determinism of Marx, to the poetry of Shelley and Matthew Arnold, to *Playboy* and *Suck* and the newspapers of Rupert Murdoch, to blue books and white papers and discussion documents, to school reports and police dossiers, and *The Guinness Book of Records*. And James was reminded of what literate people so easily forget: the illogicality, the downright inexplicability of a written language in which the bow made from the waist and the bow with which one ties one's shoelaces are identically spelled, have different meanings and are differently pronounced. "Bow" and "bow", "cough" and "ought", "ought" and "taught", "taught" and "taut", these and so many others he re-discovered, and to Pavel could only say, "I'm sorry. I don't know why."

Long ago he and Sophie had tried to learn Greek in preparation for a summer vacation with the children in a rented villa on Spetzai, and had employed a young woman from the Greek Consulate to come in twice a week to give them lessons. She had been a serious young woman, and took her duties seriously. She wished the professor and his lady to speak – and certainly to write – her language correctly and not to shame her, yet she also knew that what they would for the most part need would be *demotiki*, the demotic speech of shop-keepers, cleaners, waiters and the drivers of buses, of, in fact, almost everybody in conversation if not in writing. So, whenever James and Sophie had mastered a particularly elegant construction, and demonstrated their mastery to her approval, she would add, "But of course we never *say* that," and Sophie would observe James's knuckles tighten, and kick him under the table.

55

James had been vexed at the time, but came now to realise that the vexation he had endured under the tutelage of that serious young woman was little in comparison to what she herself must have suffered while she acquired the fluency in written English which would qualify her for employment in the Greek Consular Service. "Break" and "speak", "sew" and "few", "horse" and "worse" – James began to perceive advantages in the ideogrammatic approach.

He had been advised not to insist on the niceties of spelling; if being able to read is the primary object, simply to make out the meaning will do well enough. It was Pavel who insisted on having everything exactly right. *"You give up or you win"*: there was nothing in between for Pavel. It came to James that the boy seriously believed that he could, by diligence and application, in one year or maybe two acquire the qualifications for a white-collar job, that literacy, once mastered, was to be the key to unlock History, Geography, English and Commercial Studies.

Obligations, once undertaken, may not easily be laid down. James had drifted into teaching literacy to an adult illiterate on a one-to-one basis for two hours a week. *"I shall do such things. What they are yet I know not, but they shall be the terrors of the earth."* After so large a promise, what he had actually found to do smacked a little of anti-climax. Yet it satisfied most of the criteria he had set. James was being of service to another person outside himself, Pavel did deserve such a service, and although James felt that he himself was not very well qualified to perform it, he suspected that this must be the case with most teachers of literacy; they would have to pick up the skill as they went along, or else drop out. (It never occurred to him that he had been carefully matched to the only applicant of that year's intake whom he would be able to teach.) Certainly there was no whiff of danger; the feeling of anti-climax, he supposed, must be due to that. If some more demanding service, of which one of the elements should be just such a whiff, were to present itself, he would have to find some way of combining it with what he was already doing. Pavel could not be abandoned. His expectations were too high.

Once Littlemore was a pretty working village outside Oxford, the parish a university living, held for a while by John Henry Newman before he defected to Rome and became a cardinal. Now cottages and church, as with so many of the small towns and villages of Oxfordshire, are embedded like a nut in a pulp of cheap housing units with attendant laundromat and minimarkets, separated from the industrial sprawl of Cowley only by the Oxford Ring Road. Littlemore has become overspill; a hospital and two schools have been fitted in with the housing. From almost any point in the village, and certainly from the Portakabins of the Further Education Centre, one can hear the passage of sixteen-axle lorries on their way from the M40 to Newbury, Swindon, Cheltenham, Birmingham, Banbury or Northampton. The beds in the hospital (some empty because of cuts in the National Health Service) rattle gently to their passing, and small flakes of rust drop off the scaffolding which seems to be a permanent part of the ravaged school-buildings, their doors padlocked and chained every evening against vandalism.

A Tuesday evening in October, the fogs not yet come, and the leaves still green on the trees. James had asked whether the lessons might be twice a week instead of once, since he had the time and Pavel the enthusiasm, but the Portakabin would not be free. He had wondered whether to invite the boy to the house, but this practice was not encouraged by the permanent staff since it might lead to entanglement, and in any case James's house was too far away; the country buses did not run so late, and Pavel, although he had learned at the Disability Centre to drive a car, and had actually passed his test and been awarded a licence, had no car of his own, or access to one. James had considered, and was still considering, suggesting that they should meet once a week in a café, some place of tea and buns if such places still existed, but could one teach in such a place? It would be bound to attract attention.

If one still existed! Of course they existed; they must exist; it is a kind of snobbery to pretend that the places of common resort of one's youth no longer exist. But it is true that Fuller's Walnut Cake no longer exists. James had invited Sophie to tea in his rooms, and they had consumed Fuller's Walnut Cake and toast made at the electric fire. He had sat on the floor to make the toast, and stared up at her legs. Then, when after so many years of married life, they had returned to Oxford, Fuller's Walnut Cake was no longer to be found.

There was a man fiddling with the windscreen-wipers of the car parked next to James's Volvo. He looked round as James approached.

"Professor Elphinstone? Good evening!"

"Yes?"

"Stephen Baker. I've a research fellowship at Nuffield and do a little teaching here, for my sins. Basic Economic Theory, an hour a week."

"Ah! Yes. Good evening." Even before his retirement James had rarely spoken to economists, and knew nobody at Nuffield. However, Adult Education makes strange bedfellows. The man would be, in some sense, a colleague; the small change of politeness was required. He hesitated, searching for some neutral observation, which would not provoke much in the way of further chat. Just so do lonely people quietly strive to antagonise those who might otherwise offer a little social solace.

It was odd that the fellow should know him, both by sight and by name. An hour a week hardly seemed enough for Basic Economic Theory, just as two hours were nothing like enough for Adult Literacy. They were not liberal with their time at the Further Education Centre. The tutor had said that these semi-academic courses were paid. A research fellowship would not bring in much. The man looked to be in his thirties, and would need the extra money. He had an educated voice, and seemed likely to be what he claimed to be, but it was odd, nevertheless, to be greeted by name in the car park by a total stranger.

"I trust your course is well attended." Idiotic observation, since it was bound to provoke a reply!

"You fear it may not be, but it is; my course is invariably oversubscribed." James took his car-key from the pocket of his overcoat with one gloved hand, and held it across the fingers of the other in the attitude of one politely prepared to listen but clearly with a journey to complete. "So many people continue, in spite of the politicians' promises, to be made redundant, and take the opportunity offered by the redundancy money to start a little business – antiques often, home-made chocolates, a tea-shop or delicatessen, wrought iron, monumental masonry to individual commissions, photocopying. Husbands and wives do it together. Previously the husband's employment kept them separate; now redundancy will bring new life to their marriage, a real companionship. They imagine that my course will teach them the essentials of business practice, and by the time they discover that Economic Theory has almost nothing to do with making a living, it's too late to cancel. Since they've paid for the whole course in advance, it usually takes them some time to drop out, but by halfway through I'm left with six or seven serious students, which is how I like it. How are you yourself getting on with young Borek?"

James dropped the car-key, and both men stooped to recover it, almost banging their heads together. The stranger found it amongst gravel, and handed it to him. "I'm so sorry. I'm delaying you."

"You are acquainted with my pupil, Borek?"

"Not to speak to. He's a countryman of mine, in a sense. I take a mild interest."

The situation continued to be odd, irritatingly so. The man spoke with a standard English accent, and had introduced himself as Stephen Baker.

"I have dual nationality, I should explain, or I suppose I have, if I ever wanted to avail myself of it. I was born in Ealing, and went to school in Nova Scotia, but both my parents were Czech – are, indeed; they live just outside

Chippenham, where my father has a small factory, making shoes."

"You take an interest, you said?"

"A mild interest. One wouldn't want to get involved."

If the man did not wish to get involved, why had he mentioned Pavel at all? There were deep waters here. James said carefully, "I very much doubt whether young Borek would consider himself to be Czech."

"He keeps the name."

"It was his father's name. He had no choice but to keep it. You don't suggest that an adolescent, hardly educated and with no resources, would change his name by deed-poll?"

"Keeps the 'Pavel'. Doesn't call himself 'Paul'. Odd that, when one considers the pressures to conform."

" 'Pavel' may have been his father's name also."

"No, it's his uncle's name."

"He has an uncle in this country? I had no idea."

"In Brno. His uncle is a cleaner in a hospital. I could lend you one of his books."

The man was being wilfully confusing. He must have an object. Why should he wish James to be confused? The fiddling with his windscreen-wiper had been diversionary, designed to conceal the fact that he was waiting for James to appear. Since his own class lasted only an hour against James's two, he would have arrived later, and deliberately parked next to the Volvo. No! He would have arrived earlier, watched where James parked, then moved his own car.

"It's a Mental Hospital. Pavel Borek's uncle – also Pavel Borek – cleans the floors of the wards, the corridors and the lavatories, and is sometimes allowed to assist in restraining some of the less co-operative patients."

"And you admire his books?"

"Highly. He was a professor of Philosophy, but fell out of favour for obvious reasons. Anyway the Czech universities don't have faculties of Philosophy as such, not any more; there's no call for that kind of thing."

"What are you trying to say?"

"Not a great deal at this stage, but I hope we may chance

60

to meet and talk again. My own course goes on until Christmas, and I shall hope to be asked to give another. You'll find the travelling a little difficult later on, I'm afraid. It gets very foggy here, more so than out your own way. The pollution from the factories at Cowley combines with the mists from the river." The door of the man's car was already open. "Goodnight, Professor Elphinstone."

"Goodnight." James looked at the key of his own car as if he did not quite know what to do with it, as if the turning of any key at this time was an action he was not eager to initiate. It was a bit of a rum do, no doubt of that. The man Baker's car reversed out of the parking space. It would be easy enough to confirm that he was, in fact, a Research Fellow of Nuffield, although he would hardly have said so if it were not true. James watched the rear lights and flashing indicator as the car turned right at the exit from the car park. A rum do! He drove home thoughtfully. The father an agricultural labourer, the uncle a hospital cleaner; such ends did Philosophy and the Law attain. It was surprising that Pavel himself had developed such an appetite for education.

Tuesday morning. Two slices of wholemeal toast and a lightly boiled egg. A wind had sprung up overnight, and was working on the trees, but it was too early; the leaves still had sap in them, and clung on. "Pathetic fallacy!" James said to the wind. "I shall be sere soon enough, but not yet." James did not often talk to himself, was careful not to do so, but sometimes he would talk to Sophie, and often to inanimate objects which he met about the house, to plants in the garden, and to such natural forces as the wind and rain. Never to animals, because he saw so few. When the children were young, there had been a dog called Mr Fingers to whom the whole family spoke freely, but he had died long ago of some malfunction of the liver and had never been replaced. The woman at the Samaritans had suggested James should buy a dog, rear one from a pup; it would provide an interest, and sleep by his bed at night.

61

Where did the Samaritans find such people? What should James do, at his age, with a dog? He had gone to them in good faith, offering to work for them in any capacity, and they had suggested he should buy a dog.

He telephoned Nuffield College, and discovered, as he had expected, that Stephen Baker held a research fellowship there. It would be more difficult to confirm the existence of a Czech philosopher named Pavel Borek unless James were to accept Baker's offer to lend him a book, which he did not yet wish to do. If Borek's books had been translated into English and published, there would be copies at the British Library, which received a copy of every book published in Britain, and even if they had not, the BL might have bought one in, though its funds were limited and it was unlikely that Czech philosophers rated highly on its list of priorities. Sophie had met the Head of the British Library's Eastern European Section at a party, he remembered, and had reported that he was awfully nice, but Sophie brought out the best in everyone, except perhaps her own son.

Take the train to London, then, and spend the afternoon at the BL? Or Bodley; there might be something in Bodley, no need to go even as far as London. He walked in the orchard, where windfalls lay thick, and wasps gorged on them. Really he would prefer another opinion. Since moving out of his college rooms two years previously, James had not revisited the Senior Common Room, but he continued to receive – unsolicited – the *College Record* and numerous appeals for donations which would allow the acquisition of premises (a brewery off Walton Street, an abandoned cinema in Headington) to be converted into residential accommodation; in this way the college hoped to build up a strong undergraduate presence in Mechanical Engineering. He must still have dining rights, might dine in college, he supposed, seven nights a week during term if he wished to do so and were prepared to pay. There had been a philosopher among the fellows of the college, a Moral Philosopher or Political (the two were the same, practically

62

speaking), certainly not one of the Linguistic lot; he had tutored undergraduates on the Social Contract theories of Hobbes, Locke and Rousseau, and had lectured on Proudhon. The philosopher, Borek, would have been of his kind, not Linguistic, James was sure of it, before his demotion to cleaning a Mental Hospital; one did not get into such trouble for splitting hairs. What was the man's name – Ellis – blue chin and a corduroy jacket – would Ellis know Borek, or at least know of him, have an opinion of his work? If Ellis were married, or had become so during the last two years, he would not often dine in college, perhaps only on Guest Nights, Wednesdays, that was to say, tomorrow. James would telephone the Manciple, and give notice that he himself would dine tomorrow. He would get into conversation with Ellis (or was it Barrow?); he would get some sort of line on Borek, which would either confirm or modify what he had been told.

In the event it was simple enough. James put on a suit, and took his gown, unworn for two years, from the hook on the back of the door of his study. Barrow was wearing a cravat of some pastel shade, probably apricot, over a shirt of chocolate brown; the whirligig of time had brought back to those of an aesthetic turn the undergraduate fashions of the late forties, which had themselves looked back to the eighteen-nineties. James remembered now; Barrow was of homosexual inclinations, and unlikely to marry. He was editing a quarterly these days, was a member of the Editorial Board at any rate: *Reflections*, the Journal of the New Philosophical Society; he occasionally printed contributions from Polish scholars, but nothing came out of Czechoslovakia. He himself knew nothing of Borek but, as is the way in Oxford, knew who would know, the Reader in European Studies, who was attached to St Anthony's, and said to be extremely accessible.

What was said to be so proved to be so. The Reader in European Studies confirmed that the philosopher, Borek, had been a member of the Chartist Group, fell consequently into disfavour but had since been permitted by the authorities to undertake employment of a menial nature. Not a very original thinker; there had been two books of essays stodgily translated by someone at Brandeis College in up-state New York, a compatriot teaching there. Neither volume had achieved any wide circulation. Compared with Havel, Borek was rather small beer. The sympathies of Western intellectuals can only comprehend a limited number of dissidents.

The man Baker's story held up at all points where it could be checked. One couldn't, of course, be sure that the philosopher was young Borek's uncle; Pavel Borek might be a common combination of names in Czechoslovakia. But there seemed to be no good reason why Baker should have invented the connection, just as there seemed to be no good reason why Baker should have communicated any of this information to himself, James Elphinstone. Why wait, fiddling with a windscreen-wiper, for James, when he could easily have accosted the boy directly? *"I take a mild interest. One wouldn't want to get involved."* The whole affair remained a puzzle.

The dons of the SCR had been extraordinarily solicitous; not just Barrow, they had all gone out of their way to be attentive, had urged dry sherry on him before the meal, madeira and whisky after. Whisky and madeira in any quantity would lead to sleepless nights, already common enough, but they could not know that; their intention had been hospitable. They had expressed themselves as pleased to see him in the Common Room again after so long, and hoped that he would dine in college often; it was so easy to fall out of touch. They had never, to his recollection, expressed any such sentiments while James was still professor. James supposed that they had believed he had come to college because he was lonely and in need of company. They were foolish fellows; he was not lonely, or if he was, it was not a condition any of them was able to remedy. He missed, he greatly missed, the company of his wife, which could not ever be replaced by theirs.

However, they had meant well, though they would not

be greatly disappointed that he did not come among them again. He must remember to write Barrow a note of thanks.

"B."

"Buh."

"B A."

"Ba."

"Now we add a T."

"Ba-tuh. Bat." Pavel grinned. This was all going over old ground. He didn't need the "tuh", could easily have gone straight to "bat", but put the "tuh" in to oblige.

"Now an E."

"B A T E" was new to Pavel, and he studied the combination curiously. "Bat-uh. Batter?"

"No. Remember." James put a finger over the B to erase it momentarily. "A T E."

"Ate." James removed the finger. "Bate? Like fishing?"

"No, I'm afraid that's another spelling – B A I T – pronounced the same way. This is a word you're not actually likely to come across." How many times during these few weeks had James said that? *"Rather old-fashioned", "Not likely to come across."* Yet Pavel's cheerfulness continued unabated. He was prepared to acquire any word on the off-chance that it might come in useful. "I've used it partly as a step to a longer word, and partly to illustrate the principle that a vowel after a consonant lengthens the vowel before. B A T – 'bat' – short 'a'. Add an 'e' and it becomes 'bate' like 'ate'. Perhaps I might have chosen a better example." James wrote "M A T".

"Mat."

"Add an E?" Adding it.

"Mate."

"P A T."

"Pat."

"Add an E."

"Pate?"

Another archaic word. Were all the words James knew archaic? "An old-fashioned word for 'head'." At least he

65

was remembering to avoid "cat" and "cate". "F A T?"

"Fat."

"Add an E."

"Fate. Why do they spell the fishing bait a different way?" With Pavel it was always "they"; he never blamed his teacher.

James said, "I'm not sure. It must be an exception again. I don't think there are any other "ai" words like it. Wait a minute! – there is; 'gait'."

"Like in a garden?"

"No, that's G A T E. 'Gait' is an –"

"– old-fashioned word?"

"For how one walks. Pavel, I don't know how anyone manages to learn to read."

"Don't worry. Keep at it. You're doing all right."

"I've been thinking that once a week isn't enough."

"I've been thinking that. I could come in more often."

"I've been wondering if we should meet in a tea-shop."

"Snack Bar? There'd be people listening."

"And watching – yes! And tea spilled on the tables."

"You wouldn't like it. Me neither." Pavel took a deep breath. "There's my place, if you like. It's just a room. One-room flat, it's called, with use of facilities. Sink and a cooker, bed and a table, gas fire and two chairs; it's all together, very convenient. Toilet on the first floor, bath upstairs; you put money in it. The Social Worker found it. She asked if I'd rather a hostel, but I told her I wanted to be independent. It's not as big as this; we'd be a bit crowded. Be warmer in the winter."

"What would your landlady think?"

"It's a Pakistani, doesn't live there himself; he's standing for the Council. There's a lot of us in the house, mostly unemployed. Social Security pays the rent; we don't see it; goes straight to him. There's a caretaker lives in the base-ment – Irish; he doesn't do much. You're not supposed to take women back, but nobody bothers."

"Do you take women back?" Pavel shook his head. "But you'd take me back?"

66

"You're my teacher. It's like the Social Worker, isn't it? She comes round sometimes."

"Not exactly like. I'm not sure it would do." James was ashamed. He might have offered his own home, distant as it was. They were not tied to the evenings; the buses ran by day, and Pavel's days were free. Perhaps in time he might make the suggestion, defying the disapproval of the permanent staff, and risking entanglement. It would be all round the village that a young cripple was visiting him on a regular basis, but that was of no great concern. "My own home's rather a long way away," he said, "and the buses are infrequent." *"I shall do such things . . ."* Yes, his reluctance was shameful.

"Don't worry. We'll work something out."

During these few weeks of lessons, two hours a week together in a Portakabin, a change had taken place in their relationship. James was the teacher, but Pavel was by way of becoming the leader. James said, "You seem to be of a very managing temperament."

"Managing?"

"Capable. You manage. Cope."

"Had to since my mum died. That's another reason why I didn't . . . at school, I couldn't . . . My dad worked long hours, see, and it was a dirty job. He wasn't any good with his hands; it was hard enough, the farming."

"You had to look after the house?"

"I didn't mind."

"Cook and clean?"

"He couldn't do it himself. Not used to it. He'd break things. He did what he could. There was someone came in for a bit, but she left. I never minded. They'd've took me away if the place got too bad. He wouldn't've liked that; he needed me. Then when he died, and I went to the Home, it came in useful. One of the girls – staff, she was, worked in the kitchen for a bit – she said they took advantage of me. I was always cleaning up after the others. Habit. I look after my own place now, keep it nice; I clean my shoes twice a day sometimes for something to do. I love a high shine."

67

He would use his one hand to apply the polish and to brush. How did he grasp the shoe? – in the crook of an arm? between his knees? with a foot? his teeth? James said, "Don't you have any kin, Pavel? Uncles and aunts? On your mother's side perhaps? Grandparents?"

Passage of a cloud over the sun. "Don't want to know, do they?"

"I think I should want to know if I were your grandparent."

"Not them." Pavel looked sideways at his stump. "Said I was good for nothing, like my dad. But I'm as good as them."

"If that's what they said, I'm sure you're better."

"Said it was my dad's fault I was born like this. Said he was a foreigner. Bad blood. Didn't mix right. Said she'd've never married him if she hadn't been in the Club with me. Kids at school told me that, had it off their mums. She could've got rid of me, had me cut out, took pills to bring it on early, only she wouldn't. She wanted to marry him. He was an educated man; she was nothing, like my gran."

It was not clear who had told him what, but clear enough that he had been mocked at school, his father denigrated by the villagers of Garsington, the mother's parents prominent amongst them. "Did your mother talk to you about it at all? About the circumstances?"

"Never talked much. Kept going away. Kids at school said she had anybody in London, anyone who wanted, do it for a cigarette up against a wall, anywhere. Told me that when I didn't know where to put it meself, didn't know what they were talking about half the time, just knew it was dirty. You get some funny ideas. Then she drowned."

Momentarily James wished that he himself were in a position to drown the man Baker, pushing his head with both hands beneath the surface of some polluted canal. He had intended his enquiries about the mother's family to lead naturally to the father's, and had stumbled instead into a waste of pain and remembered humiliation. He had better move quickly onto safer ground. "Do you ever hear

68

from anyone in your father's family?"

Pavel stared at him. "How could I?"

"I wondered if they'd made any kind of contact."

"How?"

"Letters?"

"I can't read."

"No." Bugger Baker! "I suppose I thought . . . It's not easy to get out of Czechoslovakia, but people do go and come back."

"How would they know who I was?"

"If any message had reached your father?"

"He's dead. And I don't live there no more. We'd better get on with our reading. We haven't got much time."

"I'm sorry. It was just that I was wondering . . . You've kept the name 'Pavel' when you could so easily have changed it to 'Paul'. Since so much of your effort has been directed to fitting in." This was a mistake; it continued to be a mistake. "I wondered if you had any reason for your attachment to the name."

"There was kids in the Home tried to call me 'Paulie'. I made them stop."

"Ah!"

"My dad gave me my name. He wanted me to have it. I'm English, just like anyone else but I haven't got an English name, all right? It was important to my dad; it was what he called me. Nobody else reckoned him, and he didn't reckon himself much, but I loved him; I looked after him, and when he got sick, it wasn't my fault; it was the cold. The doctor told me, 'You mustn't blame yourself. You did everything.' " There were bright tears in both eyes, ready to fall. "I think we should do reading now, sir, if you don't mind." Pavel's head went down into the crook of his bad arm. The back of his neck was as red as his face. The tears had begun to fall, and were flowing freely.

"Oh, shit!" James put a hand out to the boy's shoulder. It was not a professorial gesture, not teacher-like, but instinctive, to share distress. "Shit! shit! shit! I'm sorry. You must think me very unfeeling. I really didn't mean to upset you.

69

'Pavel Borek' is your uncle's name. I wondered if you knew."

The sobbing ceased. Slowly the boy's face was lifted from the crook of his handless arm. "What uncle?"

A thought came to James, amazed, appalled. *"I am your father now."*

But it would not do. James had a son already, unsatisfactory, untrustworthy, unlikeable, but of his own getting. It would not do at all to undertake another.

· 3 ·
FATHERS AND SONS

One looks back, "Where did we go wrong?", a pointless exercise. Facts are facts; all else is speculation. Even the facts, as they move from the present into the past, become distorted in memory. Blame and extenuation become equally irrelevant, the merest mental small-talk, occupying the mind to the exclusion of more important matters.

What more important matters? James had very few important matters these days to occupy his mind.

One might blame oneself; one might blame the school; one might blame oneself for choosing that school. James had broken with family tradition; he had not sent his son to Haileybury. Academic snobbery! he had hoped for a high-flyer, and there had seemed to be some justification for his hope since, at thirteen, when they had made the move from York to Oxford, Richard had already been more fluent in Latin than his father. Haileybury had been, in James's own experience of it, a school more concerned to form character than to nurture scholarship. His thoughts had turned towards Winchester and St Paul's.

Sophie had not wanted a boarding-school at all for either of her children. At York, as day-scholars, both Richard and Helen had been assiduous in their studies, engaged vigorously in various competitive outdoor sports, played respectively the recorder and the cello in the school orchestra, a sheep and an angel in the Passion Play; they had shared the life of both school and home and been the better for both. Sophie saw no reason to send her children away to school and turn them into strangers. Helen had been sixteen at the time of the move, and presented no problem; there was the Quaker School at Sibford Gower, into which she settled quickly, and soon became an opinion-leader. Sibford Gower would not do for Richard (or at least it would not do for James), but there were two boys' public schools in Oxford itself, both academically respected, both accepting day-boys. Sophie's reasons and James's reasons came together to the same conclusion. Richard went off dutifully to day-school in Oxford, at first driven by his father until he himself insisted on the bus. There his academic talents were recognised and encouraged. Nevertheless he became a stranger to his parents. For Sophie this stranger, whom she saw every day and who slept in her house, was harder to bear than a school-holiday stranger would have been.

The estrangement had begun when Richard took to wearing a cap. It was an eccentric decision. The cap was of thick tweed, not at all, one would have thought, suitable as a symbol of adolescent rebellion, but of the sort worn by old-fashioned country gentlemen when at the races or rough-shooting in the rain. It had been left at the house by one of James's pupils, able enough in his way, but one who aspired to the condition of a Young Fogey. He had not reclaimed his headgear, and James had forgotten to tell him that it had been found, and then term had ended, the Long Vacation had begun, the Young Fogey had left for a walking-tour of Spain in the footprints of Hilaire Belloc, and the cap had been appropriated by Richard, who wore it indoors and out, so that it rapidly shed all its connotations of Young Fogeydom.

This was also the period when Richard made new friends and began smoking dope. They had said at the school that this was of no great consequence, that marijuana had ceased to be a problem amongst adolescents in the nineteen-seventies, was hardly ever smoked, far less eaten, by their boys, was seldom discovered in lockers or pockets, had gone altogether out of fashion, and that alcoholism these days was the real problem. If smoking dope had gone out of fashion, nobody had bothered to tell Richard and his new friends, many of whom were undesirables who had dropped out of education altogether and taken various menial jobs. He stayed out late at night, hitch-hiking home in the early hours or sometimes not coming home at all. He became streetwise, and developed ways of teasing the police, inducing them sometimes to stop and search him when he was clean, but acquiring total inconspicuousness when carrying. When he was at home, he played punk rock on his music centre, which could be heard all over the house. He rarely bathed, slept late whenever he could, and his sheets were filthy. He continued to wear the cap. James and Sophie, who never quarrelled, now quarrelled over their son, neither having any clear notion of how to restore him to what they believed to be normality (or at least to socially acceptable behaviour), but each certain that the other's way was wrong. One night, with the Provost of Worcester among the guests at a rare dinner party, and Richard then seventeen, sitting at table with dirty fingernails and still wearing the cap, Sophie broke down, and screamed at him, "Take off that bloody cap!" Richard did not take it off, nor did he leave the table, and after a silence the dinner-table conversation was resumed.

It was not at all what either James or Sophie had expected. Both remembered their later adolescence as a time of cultural Renaissance. Sophie had read the poems of Christopher Cauldwell in an apple orchard, and burst into tears; James had discovered Telemann. Neither was prepared to allow that Richard also had experienced a cultural rebirth, and that reciting Alan Ginsberg's flowing lines in a haze of dope and the discovery of punk rock might be his equivalent to their own experience.

But he did work. Richard continued to work. He was bright. He knew well enough that, if the school were to throw him out, he would end up at Sibford Gower among the Quakers. Also he enjoyed the Classics; his view of Aristophanes was that he was a precursor of punk. Therefore, at odd times of his own choosing, he continued to

73

work, and had no difficulty in passing, when the time came, the University Entrance examination.

James believed that he had chosen the wrong university for himself, and as a consequence of that belief chose the wrong university for his son. Oxford was wrong for English, but would have been right for Classics. James had read English at Oxford, and sent Richard to read Classics at Cambridge, where the English Faculty is a jewel in the crown of Academe but many of those studying for the Classical Tripos switch subjects after the second year. In any case it would not have done for Richard to have been an undergraduate of a university where his father was a professor; even though he would have been a member of a different college, and studying a different discipline, it would have been bound to cause embarrassment to them both. As for Sophie, she desperately wanted Richard out of the house, at least for the twenty-four weeks of the academic year; she needed to rest from controlling, day after day, her dislike of her own son and her guilt at what he had become.

Richard was interviewed by a college renowned for English, and accepted for his father's sake, although the tutor in Classics found his opinions on Aristophanes heretical. In the pub afterwards, he said to Sophie, "This is a horrible place. I don't want to go," and dribbled moodily into his Coca Cola; it was one of Richard's many irritating characteristics that he did not drink alcohol. During the summer before taking up residence, when most boys of his age, class and education were travelling to South America or Kathmandu, doing voluntary work, often among lepers, or at least island-hopping in the Aegean, Richard worked locally as a hospital porter, not out of any identification with the sick and suffering, but because (he said) he needed the money. He continued to engage in heavy dope-smoking and the occasional dropping of acid with his new friends, who had by now become old friends. James and Sophie found his behaviour irresponsible. They did not sufficiently appreciate that the smoking of dope is a serious

74

business, since one must not only give proper consideration to the actual smoking of the stuff in congenial surroundings, but even the acquisition of it is a continual preoccupation; one must not only find the money to buy it, but keep oneself continually cognisant of who, in that shifting world, has it to sell and where they may be found.

It was hard for parents in the seventies to understand, far less sympathise with, the paranoia of adolescent dope-smokers, which was expressed in the sentiment, "The people with whom I smoke are my friends, the people I can trust. The rest are the enemy." This paranoia was not entirely paranoid, since it was caused partly by the parents' own persistent disapproval and partly by the children's knowledge that what they were doing was illegal. Meanwhile the parents worried that the children's paranoia and peculiarities of behaviour (late rising, loud music, dirt, apparent inability to remember even the mildest admonitions or prohibitions) might be symptoms of schizophrenia, and worried almost as much that they themselves were in danger of imprisonment as a consequence of cannabis being discovered in the house. So one thing led to the other, and the snake bit its own tail. The seventies were a hard time for parents. One cannot be sure that the eighties have been very different.

In October 1977, Richard went up to Cambridge, and was sent down just over a year later. It was not dope that did for him; the college was rather tolerant in a high-minded way about that sort of thing provided that the police did not become involved. It was not even sloth, although sloth was suggested, for Richard continued to work in his own fashion, even though much of his work was received with disapproval or disdain. No, Richard Elphinstone was sent down for slugabed behaviour; he habitually stayed in bed until three in the afternoon. His tutor attempted to convince him that, by cutting himself off from much of the communal life of the college, Richard was depriving himself of the spiritual enrichment and intellectual stimulation which collegiate life in our older universities is intended to

75

provide, but since the main reason why Richard found it difficult to get out of bed was his strong dislike of the communal life of the college, the attempt failed. His tutor thereafter scheduled all Richard's tutorials at nine a.m., and, when Richard consistently failed to attend, he was sent down.

So onwards and downwards. Richard found an unpaid job writing continuity of increasing opacity for a pirate radio station in Oxford, which was followed by another unpaid job as a disc jockey in a cellar-club. Then he moved to London to work for one of his friends who had started a video-magazine. This was during video's boom-time, when anything seemed possible provided that it was presented in images and lasted for under ten minutes. The magazine consisted partly of trailers for films available for hire as video-cassettes (this material being free), partly of interviews with in-people at in-places usually at night (the facilities of the in-places being free), partly of "video-features" (Freudian psycho-analytic theory condensed to six minutes with a heavy beat), and partly of pure images which dissolved into each other and were expensive to put together. The public was said to be hungry for video in any form, but its hunger did not extend to the magazine, which turned out not to be what Richard's friend called "a saleable option"; the public preferred *The Sound of Music* and various forms of sadistic pornography. Within three years most of the creative talent of the video-boom had been diverted to the making of pop-promos, and Richard had found a job as a barman, dispensing to an increasingly younger clientele the cocktails of the nineteen-twenties, which had come back into fashion. He no longer read Aristophanes in Greek for pleasure.

"All this," James said to himself, "is from my own point of view; I remember only from my own point of view. The tone is ironic. Even when I make excuses for him, even when I note my own failures and Sophie's failures in understanding and in sympathy, the irony persists. I am incapable of thought without irony these days, except

76

when I think of Sophie and of our life together; I exclude even the children from that privacy. I do not understand Richard, because I do not see him clearly as himself, but always as our son, and perhaps I have never truly wanted to see him in any other way. And Sophie did want to do so, but could not. He has defeated us both by detaching himself from us. Perhaps he is not dislikeable in himself, not untrustworthy, but only our view of him is that." It did not occur to James that the other person about whom he sometimes thought without irony was his pupil, Borek.

Pavel's room was even smaller than his description had suggested, and would not contain two people comfortably, not at least if they wished to move about. Every surface which could be wiped had been wiped, those to which polish could be applied had been polished, a clean coverlet had been placed over the bed, the glittering linoleum reflected the flames of the gas fire, and the single armchair was still damp with fabric shampoo. Above the mantel, a large poster of a badger had been taped to the wall.

"You're a naturalist? I thought we'd already discussed all your interests."

"Not allowed to talk about it."

"Why not?"

"Oath of silence."

"I hope you didn't do all this cleaning just for me."

"I've got plenty of time. Do you want some coffee?"

The boy had bought biscuits, chocolate digestive, taken them from the packet, and arranged them on a plastic plate. There was a jar of freeze-dried instant coffee granules, when almost certainly Pavel could only afford powdered instant coffee, and milk had been poured into a jug.

James said, "You keep up more style than I do. Most people who live alone just use the carton."

"Borrowed it. I like to do things right."

From whom could Pavel borrow a milk-jug? Not from the other unemployed people lodging in the house, not from the Disability Centre or the John Radclyffe Home, surely not from his Social Worker. The jug had been bought specially, as the jar of Connoisseurs' Blend Instant Coffee Granules had been bought. "Connoisseur" was still some way beyond Pavel as a word to read off a label; he would have bought the most expensive. Well, it could not be helped, but must not be allowed to develop into a routine. James said, "This is extremely thoughtful. You've been to a great deal of trouble, I'm afraid." Oh God! there were lumps of sugar in a bowl. How much of Pavel's weekly dole from the Department of Health and Social Security had been spent in order to entertain Professor Elphinstone in the style considered appropriate to his status? Too much, almost certainly much too much. Next week James would bring a picnic-basket, and when summer came they would lunch *al fresco* in the Botanical Gardens.

"I've been wondering if we ought to start on a Reader."

"I'm the reader. Aren't I? You said I was quick."

"You are. I'm most pleased and astonished. No sugar, thanks. I meant a book. One of those books –" he bit back the words "small children use" – "beginners use. Short words; simple sentences; stories rather easy to follow." James had been told during the course that he must cultivate a non-élitist and sharing attitude, and, although that did not come easily, it was coming. "I went through my own book-shelves before I came out, but I couldn't find anything suitable." Sophie and he had never bought such books for Helen and Richard, who had found their own way to literacy. Most of Helen's books were still in the converted dovecote; she had taken nothing of her growing-up with her to Houston. He had run his fingers along the tops of her collection of E. Nesbit . . . *The Wouldbegoods* . . . *The Enchanted Garden* . . . *The Railway Children* . . . *Five Children and It*. They would none of them do. Even if the words had been comprehensible to Pavel, the world was not. "I suppose we could borrow something from the class-room. Nobody would mind; there's a cupboard full. Delicious biscuits!"

Pavel went to the bed, and pulled a suitcase from underneath it. James sipped coffee, and looked into the fire; if that was where the boy kept his secrets, James must not appear curious. He heard the clasps of the case open, something taken from it, and the case was closed again. Then the suitcase was replaced under the bed, and Pavel brought a book to the table, a thin book of thick pages with a cover of laminated card on which there was a picture of a large badger with a protective expression standing in front of a bank of wild flowers at the foot of which two lovable cubs were sporting. The title of the book was *Brock*. Pavel said, "I've got this."

"You have books?"

"Just this. I got it from a shop."

Would he have gone to one of the bookshops in Broad Street, Blackwell's or Parker's, and stood there among undergraduates present and past, visiting Americans, tourists, dons, eccentrics of various sorts, librarians, shop-lifters, the intellectually upwardly mobile and the depressed wives of academics trying to slow their down-ward drift into domesticity? – all the book-people, some bustling, some browsing, some actually trying to make a purchase while the shop-assistants played their game of "Now you see me, now you don't"? Would he have wandered bemused among shelf upon shelf of books, room after room of pretty boxes of information or diversion which he did not yet know how to open, in search of a book about badgers, and found at last by the picture on the cover a Reader for seven-year-olds in the Children's Department? Any of his contemporaries at the Children's Home would have stolen the book, except that none of them would have entered a bookshop anyway, but Pavel had bought it, just as he had bought the chocolate digestive biscuits, the milk-jug and the bowl. James was himself indifferent honest, yet he had hungered sometimes in adolescence for books he could not afford, and had stolen a few, albeit fearfully.

"A badger again!" Pavel would tell him in time why badgers were an important interest, or he wouldn't; James was content to wait. "Have you tried to read it?" Pavel

79

shook his head. "Shall we make a start?"

The book was by some woman with three names, the pictures boldly drawn and coloured, the narrative uncompelling and unambiguous. James had noticed that the Readers in the Portakabin were of much the same standard; if one is reading a word at a time, one cannot hold in memory a story of any complication or moral ambiguity. *"Old Brock lived with his wife and three chil-dren deep in a grassy bank in the woods. He and Mrs Brock had built their own home to-gether, and they had fur-nished it with leaves to keep the fam-ily warm."* Pavel made a flying start with "old" and managed "Brock" by phonics. "Lived" gave little trouble, and "with" and "his" were already familiar.

"Brock? That's his name?"

"Yes."

Pavel grunted. "Badgers don't have names."

"Shall we go on?"

"Wuh . . . I F – 'if'. Wiff?"

"No, vowel after the consonant makes it long." James wrote, "WINE, WISE, WIPE, LIFE."

"Wife?"

"Good. Old Brock lived with his wife."

"He's a badger."

"Yes. 'Brock's' an old-fashioned word for badger." It had pleased James that, no more than he, had the woman with three names been able to avoid the use of old-fashioned words, even in a Reader. "Next?"

" 'And'. Badgers don't have wives either."

" 'Mate', I suppose, would be the better word."

"They're not people."

"I agree. The book says he lived with his wife and three children, but I agree. I don't think one can altogether avoid anthropomorphism in this sort of story, though, do you?"

"A male badger's a boar. A female's a sow. They don't have children; they have cubs. They're not like people; they go their own ways."

"Boar? They're a kind of pig, then?" Mr Proctor had told Sophie long ago that country people used to smoke badger

80

hams, and that they were reckoned to taste better than those of the domestic pig.

"No, I don't know why they call them that. It's stoats and weasels, the family; I don't know the name. Ferrets – except badgers aren't vicious. They're very peaceable; they'd never attack you."

"You seem to know a lot about them."

Pavel said, "It's no good, is it, this book?"

"Not as a book about badgers."

James watched this go in. He had learned to read the boy's expressions. Money ill-afforded had been wasted, said Pavel's face; it could not be helped, but would not be repeated. Pavel would strive and apply himself; he would extend his abilities; he would not give up. James said, "Would you like me to try to find you something better?"

"About badgers?"

"We could find a better book, and read it together."

Pavel said, "I don't mind you knowing, but I swore an oath."

"Keep it. I don't need to know."

"There's a group of us. Protecting them. Badger Protection Commando."

"Sounds admirable."

"I can't explain it. I don't mind you knowing, but it has to be secret. We have to do things . . . You don't get anywhere by just talking; there's a lot of danger in it; you have to be prepared for that. Some things . . . you can only go so far, then you have to carry the war to the enemy. There's a lot of danger, so it has to be secret."

James said, "Do you think we should go on with the book, since we've made a start?"

James went to Blackwell's himself, and found a better book, Dr Ernest Neal's *The Badger* in Messrs Collins' series of New Naturalist Monographs. This book also had a picture of a badger on the cover, which might do something to diminish Pavel's sense of shame at having bought the other, but inside there were photographs, plans, anatom-

81

ical drawings and sketches to show how one could distinguish between the tracks of badgers and of foxes in snow, and the chapters had headings like "The Musk Glands and Their Uses"; it seemed altogether more likely to be Pavel's kind of thing. Of course it was far too advanced for him, containing words such as "embryology" and "subspeciation", but they would manage together, and if they discovered some words of which James himself did not know the meaning, that would be a blow against élitism.

Pavel was right to reject the Reader. All the Portakabin's Readers were similar. They lacked nourishment. If the ambition of an adult illiterate extends no higher than to be able to read Mr Rupert Murdoch's *Sun* or Mr Robert Maxwell's *Daily Mirror*, then clearly *Brock* and his fam-ily or *Tommy and His Chums* are steps on the way; they may go beyond the way. But Pavel's ambition did extend higher; he wished to open boxes, all the boxes.

They sat side by side at the table in the Portakabin. James wore an overcoat against the November cold, Pavel a donkey-jacket. Pavel had no difficulty with the title of the first chapter, "The Badger at Home", which was anyway in capitals, but ran into trouble with the second word of the first sentence, "naturalist". James said, "I think what we'd better do is that I'll read it aloud fairly slowly, with you following the text. We'll do that for pleasure and to get the meaning. Then we'll go over it again in detail, concentrating on some difficult words but not bothering with those which are too specialised." He was using a method of teaching which was not recommended, not even mentioned in the Training Manual since it was clearly so unsuitable. If the Tutor were to make one of his casual visits, not to check up, of course, far less to supervise, but just to see how they were getting on, there would be trouble, just as there would be trouble if it were discovered that Pavel was receiving extra tuition in his own bed-sitter. But what could the Tutor do? Once he had made the connection between Pavel and James, he could not disconnect them; he could do no more than to disapprove and perhaps to deny them the use of the Portakabin. James decided that he did not give a fig for the Tutor's disapproval. Disapproval, even to persecution and being crucified upside down, had not deterred the early Christians, and would not deter him.

They completed the first chapter and the second. "Yes," Pavel said. "It's like that. You get upwind of them, and keep still. They'll come close." They overstayed their allotted time in the Portakabin, which grew cold. In the car park the engines of Renault and Metro were switched on, and the beams of their headlights were diffused in fog. An old man came to the window, pressed his nose against the glass, rattled something metallic, and went away again. James skipped the third chapter, which was about population-levels in Britain, county by county, not very interesting in itself and seeming to be out of date, and went on to Chapter Four, "Getting to Know the Animals". At the end of this chapter was a description by Brian Vesey-Fitzgerald of a sow burying her dead mate.

"She came to the entrance to the sett, and let out a weird unearthly cry. Then she departed for a rabbit warren not far distant, where she excavated a large hole in preparation for the body of her mate . . . After some hours a second badger appeared, a male. The sow stood still with nose lowered to the ground and back ruffling agitatedly, and the male slowly approached with nose also lowered . . . The ritual over, they both retired down the sett. After some time they reappeared, the male dragging the dead badger by a hind leg, the sow helping from behind. They reached the warren, interred the body, and covered it with earth."

As he read, James found his throat tightening. He swallowed, and coughed to clear it. Pavel had ceased following the text, and was watching him closely. James continued, feeling his voice to be unsteady. Tears were forming behind his eyes. This was ridiculous. He would have stopped the reading, except that to do so would be to make his weakness manifest. It would not do. For Pavel to weep when reminded of the circumstances of his father's death and of his own guilt at not having prevented an occurrence which it was not in a fourteen-year-old boy's power to prevent, that was perfectly proper, that could be understood and condoned, but for James, a grown man, his teacher, a respected academic . . . Grief was private. Since February James had kept his grief private, hidden and cherished; he had repelled sympathy; his grief was his own. What had Sophie's death to do with a badger sow burying her dead mate? James turned away, trying to hide his face in the crook of his arm, just as the boy had done on that earlier occasion. His tears fell profusely, and his voice was choked. "I'm sorry," he said, "it's idiotic, I know, to be so affected."

Pavel said, "I'll tell you what we do at the Commando. You can come with me some time if you like."

"Why Baker? Simple. The family name is Brod; we claim Max Brod, Kafka's friend, as a distant cousin. So do most of the Brods of Czechoslovakia, of whom there are a great many, column after column of them in the Prague Telephone Directory, if one could ever get hold of such a thing. Change one letter, and 'Brod' becomes 'brot', the German word for 'bread'. 'Brod' equals 'brot' equals 'bread' equals 'Baker'. My father simply exchanged one common name for another."

This time there had been no waiting about in the darkness of the car park. Baker had telephoned to invite James to dinner at Nuffield, and since there seemed no strong reason to refuse, James had accepted. *I take a mild interest.* Let the man come out into the open, and declare his interest.

Nuffield College was built of Cotswold stone in the late nineteen-thirties just opposite Oxford Prison; it is without architectural interest, but warm in winter. The man Baker had rooms in college, dourly but comfortably furnished, which indicated that he was a person of some standing, not one of your bed-sitter research fellows. James had been delayed by weather, and arrived late; there was only time to gulp a glass of sherry and exchange apologies for greetings before they had to go in for dinner. If what Baker had to say required privacy, as it almost certainly did, he and James must endure a deal of academic small-talk before it could be said. Car park conversations had their advantages after all.

There were perhaps twenty dons at the High Table, perhaps forty graduate-students down below. The graduate-students, James noticed, were already eating before the dons entered Hall. There was a muttered grace, of which the graduate-students took no notice, and dinner at Nuffield began.

James was between Baker and a short don with broad shoulders to whom he had been introduced immediately before sitting down, and whose name he had already forgotten. Soup was served. Baker had turned to his other neighbour. James searched for something to say to the broad-shouldered don. Once upon a time this sort of thing had been so easy, one could do it on auto-pilot, but these days James, although he read *The Independent* over breakfast and watched the television news at night, seemed unable to retain much information about either child-abuse or the price of oil or any other topic of current concern. Could anything usefully be said about Northern Ireland, which had not been said a thousand times already? Or conifers, either the planting of them for purposes of tax-avoidance in Sites of Special Scientific Interest, or their imminent death by reason of acid rain? The broad-shouldered don lowered his head almost to the level of his plate, and began to attack the soup, in which the chef had been perhaps over-generous with vermicelli. James was irresistibly reminded of Dr Neal's description of a badger gulping worms. The broad-shouldered don was purring, which is the noise badgers make when they are pleased, and slurping, which is the way badgers deal with worms found lying on damp grass. "You don't know much about badgers, I suppose?" James said, and the don replied, "Sorry. Can't do conversation. You'd better try Stephen Baker on your other side. Makes a speciality of it."

James chose a moment when Baker's attention was

85

temporarily distracted by a *bon mot* from the don sitting opposite. "You don't know much about badgers, I suppose?"

"Ah, yes," Baker said, "your pupil's become involved with some rather funny people, as I hear. We'll talk about that later. How are you getting on with Pithers? He's a great trencherman," and turned away again to discuss the prospects of Oxford United Football Team with his other neighbour.

"I'm your guest," James thought. "You should be paying attention to me. Are you softening me up for something?" It was possible that softening up, as well as conversation, was one of the man Baker's specialities.

The food at Nuffield was like the rest of the college, unexciting but respectable. James remembered a Guest Night at New College during one of its egalitarian phases, when the Butler, as wide as he was high and all affronted professionalism, had offered a lightly steaming decanter, "Will you have cider or *Spanish* burgundy, sir?" There was none of that nonsense at Nuffield. Whiting in a pink sauce was followed by pork in a brown sauce. The broad-shouldered don unrolled his whiting like old Brock uncurling a hedgehog preliminary to disembowelling it. A dish of shape, in variously coloured stripes like an old-fashioned bathing-costume, appeared. James refused the shape. Another muttered grace. Many of the graduate-students seemed already to have left Hall. Then the dons processed to the Senior Common Room, where several months passed in the consumption of port and dessert.

James said, "Do you mind if we skip coffee? I'm worried about getting home in this weather."

"We'll have a night-cap in my rooms. 'A sealer', as the Irish say." A man with less gall than Baker would have couched the invitation as a question, not a statement, but James did not imagine that he had been invited to dinner merely to eat.

Even now, this late at night, with the strong probability of fog beyond Woodstock, the habit of conversation held

86

Baker. Perhaps it was not a matter of softening one up at all; the man Baker was simply unable to come to the point.

"The Czechs are a strange people, James." That they were on first-name terms had not been James's choice. " 'Pragmatic' is the word we use, but it covers a deep national neurosis. We never fight, you see. Our neighbours do, always at it, the Poles particularly. Think of the Polish cavalry in 1939, charging the Nazi tanks. No Czech general would order it; no Czech soldier would do it. When it comes to fighting, particularly some nation bigger than ourselves – and it always is some nation bigger than ourselves – we consider the situation carefully, conclude that we're bound to be defeated anyway, and give in. The Czech Army was mobilised in 1938 before the German invasion, and again in 1968 before the Soviet invasion, and demobilised both times almost immediately without firing a shot – rather like the Noble Duke of York and his ten thousand men. Of course when you're defeated, it all ends up much the same; Stalin's people murder the Polish officers in Katyn Wood, and the Nazis shoot all the male inhabitants of Lidice down to teenagers and destroy their village. But somehow if you've fought, it's a consolation. You don't feel you've deserved what they do."

"What exactly do you want me to do?"

"I'm coming to it." Outside all the clocks in Oxford were chiming midnight at five-second intervals. James's Volvo would have turned to mice. "I want you to understand my people."

"Young Borek knows nothing about his uncle."

"Only what you've told him, presumably."

"Which is no more than you yourself have told me. Which is very little."

"But you've been making enquiries, I hear."

"To little purpose. My enquiries confirmed what you had told me, but added little of significance to it. The uncle – if he truly is Borek's uncle –"

"He truly is."

"– is a disgraced political philosopher, not particularly

87

highly regarded in the West."

"The Czechs are never very happy with philosophy, political or any other kind. Jan Masaryk, you know, our dearly loved, deeply respected president for most of the twenty years of Czech independence (we never reached the jubilee), he actually taught philosophy for a while; he was an academic philosopher as well as a politician; we moonlight a lot, we Czechs. Where was I?"

James looked at his watch. "Masaryk and philosophy."

"Masaryk was a philosopher who distrusted philosophy. He'd look at the most elegant philosophical theories, and ask if they worked in practice. Pavel Borek, the uncle, is a philosopher in the Masaryk tradition, which may be why he is not respected by some Western philosophers. I'll come to the point. It's not easy to respect my people, though some of them, as you have already discovered, are remarkably easy to like."

"Pavel doesn't think of himself as Czech."

"You consider him, then, as his mother's son?"

Yes, there was rain driven in gusts against the window. It would be a beastly drive. "No."

"And he himself?"

"Loved his father. Scarcely knew his mother. I think you know the answers to these questions."

"I think you may need to be reminded of them."

Good God! the man was angry. James watched him trying to control his anger. Baker picked up the heavy decanter. James wondered if he intended to smash it against the fireplace or over James's own head. Baker said, "Whisky?"

"Thank you, no."

"Quite right. I shouldn't ask, when you're driving. Please try to understand. Many of my people, particularly the intellectuals, suffer deep feelings of inferiority. This is partly because they sometimes wonder if they are cowards, since pragmatism and cowardice may so easily be confused, and partly because they believe that the régime under which they now live is determined to *make* them

88

inferior by cutting them off from the culture of Western Europe of which Czech intellectuals have always felt themselves to be a part."

"Marx was European."

"Marxism has developed rather oddly in the Soviet Empire, don't you think, rather like Roman Catholicism in Ireland? It's moved a long way from Lenin, even further from Marx and Engels. Any philosophical and historical systems previous to it are only valued insofar as they may have led up to it. Any developments since, not just in philosophy or history, but in sociology, psychology, anthropology, even genetics, are regarded as bourgeois falsehoods, intended to divert attention from Marxist truth. Many of my own people are hungry for intellectual nourishment." (Pavel was hungry for nourishment.) "They reject – not publicly, of course – the pap they are given." (*"It's no good, is it, this book?"*) "Those who make a fuss are punished. Not any longer in the old Stalinist way. Back in the fifties, even the old Communists were given long prison sentences or shot, usually for nationalist deviation, but that kind of thing has quite gone out of fashion. The new deviationists – academics, writers, editors, musicians, lawyers, doctors – lose their privileges, then their jobs, their apartments. Some are sent to prison, but rarely for long; some are merely held in detention for a while. Most, like Pavel's uncle, after a period of probation are allowed to take menial jobs." (*"We must avoid élitism. Learning is sharing."*) "Even Dubcek was allowed to earn an honest living in the Slovakian outback. Hungry," Baker said, "hungry for nourishment. Hungry for self-esteem. I'm asking you to do something very much in your own line. Give a couple of letures. Conduct a seminar."

"I don't understand you."

"The people with whom my friends and I are concerned –"

"What friends?"

"Does it matter? Friends, colleagues, very few of them Czechs, all eminently respectable. The people whom we are concerned to help are people of our own kind, unfortunately placed – readers who are denied books, writers who are denied publication, thinkers who are forbidden to share their thoughts, educated people whose education goes to waste, cultured people cut off from a living culture, bright flames, some of them, which without oxygen will flicker and go out."

James shifted uneasily in his chair. "I'm afraid I find it hard to believe that anything I myself could say to such people . . . My own books . . ."

"They're not allowed to read your books."

"That doesn't seem to me a deprivation. My books are mostly out of fashion."

"They don't know the fashion. They still take literature seriously."

"But you'd like them to know the fashion, as I understand you."

"I'd like them to know what they choose to know, to have the opportunity of knowing, at least. At present they don't have a choice. Please take my request seriously. I shall understand, of course, if you refuse."

"Where would such a seminar take place? Hardly at a university under the circumstances you describe."

"In a room in somebody's apartment."

"Isn't it dangerous?" (*I shall do such things.*)

"Not in the least." (*What they are yet I know not.*) "A couple of window-cleaners, a hospital orderly and a road-sweeper discussing the novels of Thomas Hardy! – where's the harm in that? It's not political." (*They shall be the terrors of the earth.*)

"I'll think about it."

"No hurry. Good gracious, is that the time? And it's raining. How inconsiderate of me to keep you talking when you have so far to go!" Somehow they were both standing, and the man Baker was helping James into his raincoat. "I have an umbrella. I'll see you to your car."

It was a solidly built umbrella, like those used to stab Bulgarian defectors. James said, "You mentioned at the dinner-table that my pupil, Borek, has been involved with

90

some funny people."

"Odd lot. Animal Liberationists of some sort."

"You don't suggest anything criminal?" Militant animal-lovers, James had heard, set fire to fur-shops, and broke into laboratories to let loose upon the community monkeys infected with Lassa Fever. They had torn down the wire-mesh fences of a mink farm, and the rapidly multiplying naturalised mink had killed most of the smaller mammals of Leicestershire. Elitist or not, he had better try to explain to Pavel about the principle of ecological balance.

"Lord, no! More dotty than dangerous, I gather. Tunnels for toads and that sort of thing." *"We have to do things . . . there's a lot of danger in it."* Baker was lying for some reason, James supposed, or ill-informed on this matter, which was not like him. Pavel did not lie. There was more in it than tunnels for toads.

They were out of the college, and splashing down the pavement of New Road. The bottoms of James's trousers were soaking wet, and would steam in the car. *I grow old . . . I grow old. I shall wear the bottoms of my trousers rolled.* James said, "Your intention in inviting me here tonight was only to broach the matter of the seminar?"

"Quite so."

"It had nothing to do with Borek or his uncle?"

"The uncle would, I imagine, organise that aspect of your visit."

They had reached the car. "Ah!" James said. "I think the sirens will not sing to me. Thank you for your hospitality. Good night to you. I'll let you know."

The telephone rang at three in the afternoon. The staff of Madras House were not encouraged to make long-distance telephone calls at peak-time.

James had been lying down, partly to rest from the late dinner and drive the night before, partly to think in earnest about the matters which had been raised. "Tunnels for toads" – that was nonsense, part of the man Baker's show-and-run-away teasing. Pavel's interest as a naturalist

91

seemed to be almost exclusively in badgers. He and his friends of the Commando, those dismissively categorised by Baker as "dotty people", had set themselves to record the whereabouts and characteristics of the badgers of Oxfordshire, and to protect them against harassment. *"I'll tell you what we do."* In fact Pavel had not gone into detail because James himself had wished to bring his own grief under control and to conclude the lesson in the normal way, which, since they were already late, had to be done quickly. One must not forget that the prime reason for the conjunction of James Elphinstone and Pavel Borek was that Pavel should be taught to read and write; it had not been intended that they should share their lives. Nevertheless it was clear that Pavel would tell James in detail about the Commando – and probably at their next meeting – either because he was proud of his participation or because he had some doubts, and needed a confidant.

That being so, why consider the matter now? Why not wait for further information? But the man Baker had, in a sense, opened the thing from another angle, and it demanded consideration. James wished to have his mind clear before he met Pavel again.

"There's a lot of danger in it." Pavel had not referred directly to badger-baiting, but James knew that, even in the nineteen-eighties, though illegal it still went on, together with cock-fighting, dog-fighting, and some of the other common pursuits of the eighteenth and nineteenth centuries in which an enjoyment of cruelty is combined with gambling. There was money in it and, where money and illegality are combined, there is bound to be danger. So what did the Badger Commando actually do? Think it through. The punters would not come in their hundreds to the dark woods to lay bets on how long it would take four or five terriers to tear a normally unaggressive animal to pieces. The badger must first be trapped, loaded into a lorry or the boot of a car, and kept in a garden shed until a meet could be organised in some pit or barn, where the torture could take place with little risk of discovery. James had heard or

read somewhere – the information had been buried in memory, and now suddenly surfaced – that sometimes the badger's jaw was broken before the fight. The men with pitchforks and the dogs! James closed his eyes. To watch, and be unable to prevent – this was beginning to be too much like the nightmares. Forget the picture; follow the thought. The badger-baiters would be, then, of two sorts, the greater criminals who trapped the victim and organised the sport, and the lesser who watched and gambled. The Badger Commando would be in operation against the first. *"You can come with me if you like."* But Pavel would not take his teacher into any situation of peril. Would the mere presence of naturalists, "dotty people", inoffensive badger-watchers with a retired Regius Professor among their number, be enough to deter the trappers and send them off somewhere else. *"You can only go so far, and then you have to carry the war to the enemy."* How did the man Baker come to know about these people? The telephone rang.

"We've been a little worried about your father?"

"For what reason?"

"We've been wondering if you might have time to come and see us. And to see him, of course."

"He's not ill?"

"He's over ninety, Professor Elphinstone. Nobody of that age is entirely well. It's some time since we've seen you."

"My wife died."

"I'm sorry. We didn't know."

"I wrote to my father."

"He didn't mention it."

"No. Well, one wouldn't." There was no reason why James's father should have told Matron or anyone else that his daughter-in-law had died. What did he say to people down there? "Three No Trumps. Cold out. Shoulder's a bit dodgy. Been watching the cricket?" They talked about old times and warmer weather, of *badmashi* and *shikar*. The old man had liked Sophie in his own uncommitted way, and

93

had had the decency not to turn her death into a piece of conversational small-change. "When do you want me to come? I have a class tomorrow." Pavel's lessons were on Mondays in the Portakabin, Thursdays in his room. A letter, if James were to construct it of simple words and to type it, could be read, but would not arrive in time, and there was no telephone at the lodging-house, since the unemployed are given to vandalism when drunk or in despair.

"It's not urgent. Friday will do very well. We can find you a bed if you'd like to stop overnight."

If it was not urgent, then next week might as well have done. Nevertheless James rose early on Friday, and drove to Maidstone, and was received in Matron's office.

"Does he expect me?"

"I'm not sure. I told him you were coming, but he's grown a little forgetful. You mustn't be surprised if he keeps asking you what day it is."

"Why should he do that?"

Matron was embarrassed. "One of the standard medical tests for confusion among older people is to ask them what day of the week it is. Our older residents seem to have discovered this; I don't know how. Since the tests never vary, I suppose they become general knowledge among old people."

"Confusion? Do you mean dementia?"

"We never use the word. Since our older residents know about the test, they always want to know what the day of the week is, in case they should unexpectedly be asked. Then they forget the answer, and have to ask again. They don't ask the staff, of course, only visitors. One of the window-cleaners complained."

"Why should it matter what day it is? One day here must be very like another."

"Exactly. It's easy to lose track. Your father's a wonderful old gentleman for his age. Extremely independent." James felt the words "almost to a fault" were hovering on Matron's lips, but she refused to let them fall. "He does all

94

his own washing-up, and wiping of surfaces, and makes his own bed. Our policy here is to give our old people as much responsibility as they can take." She consulted a piece of paper on her desk. "Until February, 1986, he used to cut his own toe-nails and give himself a bath."

"Who cuts them now?"

"The chiropodist comes in once a month for all the older residents, and Mrs Griggs does the baths in the Warren Hastings Annexe."

"I thought there was a bath in his bungalow."

"That's one of the matters I wanted to talk to you about. If he were content to let Mrs Griggs bathe him, there'd be no problem, but sometimes he forgets, and he can't always get out, particularly late at night." James realised that his father must have been found in the morning, lying helpless in bath-water grown stone cold. "We think it's time for him to give up the bungalow, and move into Government House."

"Are you telling me my father has become confused?"

"Perhaps a little. It depends on the amount of his medication." James had not realised that his father would be on medication, but it was unlikely at his father's age that he would not be. "Digoxin's a difficult drug to handle; the effect seems to vary from old person to old person. Frankly, Professor Elphinstone, it's a matter of steering a middle course between kidney damage and an embolism." Medication at his father's age would be a matter of choosing how one killed people. James thought that the way which caused least pain to the person concerned and least inconvenience to others might be best, but that, he supposed, would lead to euthanasia.

"Very well. If he agrees, why not make the move? There'll be an extra charge, I imagine. If he can't meet it himself, I'll be happy to do so."

"That's the other matter." The other matter would be the important matter. "Our old people here have very little use for money as a general rule. A few rubbers of bridge at a penny a hundred, but when the same people always play together the reckoning runs on, and usually evens out. Everything else – the shop, the bar bill – it's all done by *chitti*; they sign for it, and it becomes an item in the monthly account. Although they don't go into town very much, your father not at all, it's a mistake for old people to carry money. We try to do without it almost entirely."

"It's not a problem, then?"

"It is a problem if he doesn't pay his bill."

"Refuses?"

"Forgets. Thinks he's paid it. Loses his cheque-book. We remind him, but one can't press old people too far; they start to believe they're being manipulated. He's three months behind."

"The problem must have come up before with other residents."

"Residents of your father's age don't usually manage their own affairs."

"You're suggesting?"

"A power of attorney."

"To Madras House?"

"That would be improper. To yourself. We send you the monthly account, fully itemised and with all supporting *chittis*. I have the papers ready. If you'll explain matters to him first, he can sign in my presence. My door is always open, except of course at lunch which will be at twelve-thirty. Perhaps you'd like to discuss the matter of the move at the same time."

"Very well. I'll talk to him." James stood up, and so did Matron. The woman had a smile like a steel trap. What a business! Would the old man agree? Presumably he had no option. They would throw him out otherwise, and James could not, would not take him in. But, if he were indeed confused, would he understand that, and if not, could the thing be managed without his participation? James said, "Is he to have no money of his own?"

"Pocket money at your discretion. It's usually distributed on Sunday afternoons. But really, you know, they don't need money. They can buy anything they want, within reason, at the shop.''

There was no answer to James's knock, so he entered uninvited, and found his father sitting in front of the television with the remote control unit, switching from channel to channel. The bed was unmade and in the kitchen alcove of the bungalow the sink was full of unwashed crockery and the surfaces looked singularly unwiped.

"May I come in?"

"You'll have to speak up." As James came further into the room, the old man turned his head without switching off the television. For a moment James had the impression that his father did not know who he was. Then the old man said, "My son, the professor."

"Yes, Father."

"Christmas early this year?"

"I came down to see you specially."

"Why?"

From the television screen a lovable bear was explaining to any children who might be watching that they must never play with sharp objects, such as scissors and knives.

"They want you to give me a power of attorney."

"All right."

"And they'd like you to move out of here into the main building."

Lips tightened. Nose twitched. His father's eyes, behind the heavy spectacles, had irises of milky blue over which a shadow now seemed to pass. The bear on the television screen had been joined by three young men in brightly coloured rompers, one of whom played comb-and-toilet-paper while another twanged a pair of kitchen gloves and the third beat upon a bread-board with a wooden spoon. The young men and the bear were singing a song about all the fun that could be found around the house. "I don't want that," the old man said.

James glanced sideways at the unwashed crocks and

unwiped surfaces. "They seemed to think it would be easier to look after you."

"Right. Don't want that. First step to the Funny Farm."

"Do you know that as a fact, father, or is it merely something generally believed among the residents?" This was too complicated a question, and only provoked a shaking of the head. The old man pressed a button of the remote control unit and the bear and his rompered friends gave way to a wise old owl in a supermarket. "Could we have that off?"

"Company."

"You'd get more company in the main building, surely? You'd be close to the Club."

"Don't want that."

"I don't see that we really have much choice."

The old man switched off the television. "What's we got to do with it?"

"You and I. We have to discuss the matter reasonably, and come to a decision."

"There isn't any we. You don't live here. I don't want you here. You're nothing to do with it. You've got fuck-all to do with it. They do what they want in Government House. In and out anytime. Look in your cupboard for whisky. Sniff around the sink to see if you've been pissing in it. First step to the Funny Farm. Gerry-bloody-atrics! They think we don't know the word. You won't stop them, will you?" James knew that he would not, and could not answer. "I'm the one who lives here. They make the decisions."

"But you like it here, father. Your friends are here. You talk about the old times. That wouldn't change if you moved to the main building. Your friends would be closer. There's no question of a geriatric ward or anything like that. It's just a matter of . . . of not having to do your own washing-up . . . of having people within call if you fell over or . . . felt unwell in any way."

"This is my place." He turned the television on again, and the wise old owl reappeared. "Choose my own company."

98

"Would you like to come with me to Matron? There are papers we have to sign."

"All right." The old man lifted himself out of his armchair. James took the remote control unit from him, and switched off the television. The old man was wearing slippers, and James looked about for shoes and something warmer than a cardigan against the weather. "What day is it?" the old man said.

· 4 ·

A CHRISTMAS OUTING

Helen and her husband invited him to Houston for Christmas, and James discovered that he did not want to go.

Last year, he and Sophie had spent Christmas together; it was less than eleven months ago, and seemed to be part of a different lifetime. They had gone down to Maidstone on the Sunday before, and taken the old man his present, a warm dressing-gown in navy with frogged braid at the wrists and collar. The old man's Christmas present was always a warm something – dressing-gown, Viyella shirt, pyjamas, sweater or scarf; it would have done no good to take a book. They had received in return – what? – James could not remember. There must be a trunkful of the old man's presents to them somewhere; for six Christmases in a row he had given them a decanter, until Sophie spoke to him. James would go down earlier this year to see how the old man had settled in to his new quarters. He would not need anything warm to wear; the main building was usually rather over-heated. Perhaps a book after all? – but even if the old man, having these days so little else to do, were to take up reading, how could one choose for him? Something to eat or drink would be best, liqueurs, a set of six half-bottles of cherry brandy and that kind of thing, Cointreau, Curaçao, Drambuie, that kind of thing; the old were said to develop a sweet tooth, though James had not found it in himself.

Sophie had made up the Christmas card list, as she always did, remembering who had died, and who had moved

100

house, and who had not sent a card in return for so many years that they might safely be struck off. There had been a woman in Andover, whom neither James nor Sophie had ever met, and who had been sending cards for over twenty years with friendly messages and news of her family written on the inside flaps. The woman had, as far as could be guessed, acquired their names in error, but every year Sophie had sent a card back, and over the twenty-odd years both women had moved house, and each had let the other know. The woman would send this year, would send early as she always did. Would James also send a card in return with a message on the inside flap, "I am sorry to have to tell you that my wife is dead"?

He would send no cards this year, and perhaps after a while others would cease to send cards to him. Except to Pavel; he would have to send a card to Pavel. He wondered whether the man Baker would have the impertinence to send a card.

No, he did not wish to spend Christmas at Houston, and must find a kind way of saying so. He loved his daughter – perhaps a little less since her marriage but that was natural – was at least fond of her, certainly did not wish to hurt her, but it would not do. He would be out of place in Houston, particularly at Christmas, which was a time, if one could manage it, for being *in* place. Christmas itself, James thought, would be out of place in Houston. Let Helen and her husband come to him if they wanted a family reunion. There was plenty of room in the house.

Sophie had pot-roasted a pheasant with carrots, celery and shallots harvested from the garden and stored in a crock. Calvados and cream had been stirred into the dish, and it had been served up with plain mashed potatoes and a bottle of claret. No holly, paper decorations or Christmas crackers, which would not be appropriate for an elderly couple keeping Christmas on their own; even the tree had been given up once the children were grown. Old Mr Proctor had always brought a wreath of holly and bay for the front door, but the new man did nothing he was not paid for. After dinner, James and Sophie had shared the sofa before the fire, he with his back against one corner and his feet stretched out towards the blazing logs, she lying with her head on his chest and her legs over the other corner of the sofa, and they had listened to music, Corelli and an early Beethoven piano trio for James, Rachmaninov for Sophie.

Sophie, he supposed, would have wanted him to send Christmas cards, which are said to be a solace to lonely people, though it is not clear whether the reception or the sending of the cards is the solace. He had ordered none from her own suppliers, UNICEF and the World Wildlife Fund, but there would still be some in the drawer of her desk, left over from last year. Perhaps he would send a few cards.

"Will you be spending Christmas here, or is there some sort of party at the Home?"

"They don't have a party; they have Christmas Dinner. I could go, I suppose. I'd have to ask first."

"And will you?"

"It's not the same when you don't live there no more."

"You anticipate resentment from those who do?"

"Right. You can't blame them. It's taking advantage. I mean, I can go back any time . . . see some of the lads . . . staff; they like to hear how you're getting on. But Christmas is special . . . Christmas Dinner; it's a special occasion. You get turkey and ice-cream; the shops give them from what they haven't sold; there's always turkeys over. And there's presents from the tree. People go out collecting, the Friends of the John Radclyffe Home; it's good quality, export rejects, all sorts of gear. I've got no part in that, not any more; I'm on my own now; I've got no rights there."

"So you won't ask?"

"Don't worry about me. I manage. I've got friends."

Clearly Pavel must have some friends, if only his fellow-members of the Badger Protection Commando. That James had never met any of them was natural enough if the

102

Commando's activities were really as secret and dangerous as had been suggested, and presumably for the same reason none of them had ever formed the basis, or even made an appearance in any of the exercises of the Language Experience Technique. It was true that Pavel had offered to take James with him on one of the Commando's expeditions, but that had been (and both knew it, since neither spoke of it) no more than a gesture of comfort, an emotional response to a display of emotional weakness; the boy had offered to share what was most precious to him, but had not really expected the offer to be accepted. In any case, James's own relationship with Pavel, though it had become close, was compartmentalised; even coming to the boy's room once a week for the lessons, he would be unlikely to meet any other of Pavel's acquaintances. Because one usually sees someone alone cannot be taken to imply that the someone continues to be alone when one is no longer in his company. There was no reason why Pavel should not enjoy, allowing for his disability, an active and varied social life. James said, "I myself have very few friends, as it happens. I shall certainly be eating my Christmas Dinner alone unless you'd like to eat it with me."

Pavel blushed. The boy did blush easily. Was it, as no doubt the man Baker would suggest, a characteristic of the Czechs to blush? It was hard to remember that Baker was an economist, his anthropology was so pat. It was more likely that Pavel, like James himself, found it extremely difficult to accept a kindness. Or – damnation! the thought came in too late – had James placed the boy under an obligation to accept the invitation by admitting that he himself would be alone? Perhaps the Commando gave a Christmas party in the house of one of its members. There would be dancing to recorded music, home-brewed beer and country wines on tap in the kitchen; hedgehog-flavoured crisps would be crushed into the carpet. Pavel would dance with one arm kept in his pocket, blushing freely from the good fellowship and the heat. There would be sleeping-bags in the attic for those who wished to stop overnight, and perhaps a girl

103

with whom to share a sleeping-bag. What a fool, what a patronising fool! Now Pavel would either have to give up the party for a boring dinner with an elderly gentleman in a large house, or else endure throughout it the thought of his teacher sitting down alone to frozen turkey. "Of course, it's still three weeks off," James said. "You might get a more congenial invitation. I shan't be at all put out if you do."

Pavel said, "Thank you. I'd like to see where you live. Little Easely. There's woods around there, isn't there? It's out of our area, but I'd like to take a look around."

James said, "Yes, there are woods. I wonder whether it's time we did an exercise on some of the less secret aspects of badger protection."

To save Pavel embarrassment and expense, James suggested that they should make a pact not to give each other Christmas presents. Pavel replied, "You'll promise, and then give me something anyway." This was true in substance. James's intention had been to buy some small thing, hardly to be considered as a present, which should combine elements of both necessity and luxury, something which the boy needed, but would not buy for himself, to wrap it as well as he could, and to leave it on the dinner-table by the boy's plate as a kind of Christmas cracker without the bang. Wrapping it as well as he could would not be to wrap it well; James was temperamentally unsuited to the manipulation of Sellotape, which had a way of sticking to present, wrapping paper and any manuscripts or correspondence which happened to be on his desk; he had once wrapped an angora shawl in two sheets of silver tissue and the proofs of an article for *The Modern Language Quarterly*. Sophie had always wrapped all presents but her own.

"What's your counter-suggestion?"

"You give me something which isn't expensive, so that I don't feel bad."

"What if I myself were to feel bad at giving something cheap? Or would that be part of the present?"

Such moral speculations were outside Pavel's consideration. "If it was difficult to get, you'd feel that was a real
present, wouldn't you, having to take the trouble?"

"You have an article in mind?"

"A cigarette-lighter."

"You don't smoke."

"One of that old-fashioned sort with a wick. You fill it
with fluid; I'd need it filled. It stays alight until you put it
out; there's a cap fits on top. It's called Zipper, I think."

"Zippo."

"Something like that. Doesn't have to be a Zip-thing.
Any of the old-fashioned ones will do, provided it's
cheap."

"And if I get you that –"

"– and no surprise extras."

"And no surprise extras," Pavel, although invariably
polite, could be bossy; James had noticed it before. Given
time and opportunity, he would become a natural leader. It
is the task of a teacher to develop such capabilities. "Do you
promise not to buy me a present in return?"

"I promise not to buy anything. I might write you a
Christmas card. Write the message, write the address on
the envelope, and post it. Posting it's the easy part."

"Would it be a long message?"

It was possible that the words, "Don't push your luck,"
hovered on the edge of Pavel's lips, but all he said was, "As
long as I can. Depends what I can think of. I'll use my
dictionary." James had thought it better, instead of provid-
ing the boy with a dictionary, that they should compile
their own of all the words he had learned to read as he
learned them. It was carefully written in a loose-leaf folder,
and grew larger with every lesson.

They would have smoked salmon, the preparation of
which is simply a matter of buying it already sliced and
laying it out on plates, and then pheasant again; cooked
Sophie's way, it would not spoil. James had wondered
whether, as an animal-lover, Pavel might be vegetarian,
but badgers are omnivorous, consuming over-ripe pears,

the bulbs of daffodils, worms, grubs, moles and baby rabbits with equal relish. Badgers would particularly enjoy a meal of pheasant, which is a rare treat to them, since it is only a sick or singularly unwary pheasant which will allow a badger to catch it. As for claret, it was hard for James to believe that anyone not afflicted by gout would dislike it, but he would provide Coca Cola and Perrier as alternatives.

He found a lighter easily enough in a Chipping Norton junk shop. He had anticipated more difficulty with the fluid, but discovered that it is still sold by small country tobacconists. Really this present was hardly a present at all, but he had made a promise, and must keep it. There was wrapping paper left over from last year, and the dreaded Sellotape. James extended himself almost beyond his abilities, and contrived a neat parcel.

Helen phoned on Christmas Eve. To be exact, she phoned at half-past one on Christmas morning. James was lying awake, the door of the bedroom open, and the telephone bell was like an alarm in the house; he was afraid it would wake the village. *"Silence that dreadful bell! It frights the isle from her propriety."* He made his way fuzzily downstairs, and her voice was so clear that he found the situation more confusing than distance and atmospherics would have made it. "Who? . . . What? . . . Are you in Oxford? Do you want me to collect you?" She had miscalculated the time-difference; it was six-thirty in Houston, the cocktail hour. She had lined up her husband and both infants to speak to their grandfather; the younger was barely able to speak at all. They thanked him for presents he had not sent and which – surely? – at six-thirty on Christmas Eve they could not yet have received. The conversation, some twenty minutes at God knew what expense, was barely coherent and rarely more than polite. Next year, Helen's husband said, James really must come to them; they would take no denial; Texas was beautiful at this time of year. James struggled to remember the man's first name, and heard himself saying that next year he hoped to be dead. He retired grumpily to bed. At least one could count on

Richard not to phone at such an hour, or any hour.

He made up a bed in Helen's flat. The guest-bedroom was only across the way from James's own room, and if he were to snore, as Sophie had often told him he did when lying on his back, the sound might carry. He had arranged to meet Pavel on Christmas morning at his lodgings off the Iffley Road, and drive him to the house. They would have soup for lunch, then a walk since Pavel had expressed a wish to see the locality, tea by the fire, a bath or a book or the television or all three until dinner, watch more television afterwards (the boy could not be expected to listen to music), and Pavel would stay the night and be taken back to Oxford whenever he wanted to go on Boxing Day. Rain would have confused this arrangement, but the day was fine, and more fine weather promised, with ground frost in the evening, but not heavy.

Pavel met him at the door. His face shone. James did not allow himself to presume that this shining morning face was in any way an expression of pleasure or the anticipation of it. No, the shine would have come from Pavel's face having been thoroughly scrubbed with some rough substance. The boy was wearing a sports jacket with a white shirt and a tie, garments James had never seen on him before, instead of jeans there were dark trousers of some artificial fibre, perhaps Dacron. The trousers also shone in places, although whether this was because of the nature of the fibre or from prolonged use was hard to tell. Shiniest of all, polished and burnished with brush and soft cloth, were the shoes which replaced the usual boots or trainers. Against that high shine, face and trousers faded; Pavel's shoes lit up the hallway.

"Hullo!" James said. "Happy Christmas! I'm glad to see you," and in fact he did feel pleasure, so perhaps part of Pavel's shining was pleasure also. The boy had brought a rucksack with him, in which the boots, jeans and roll-neck sweater to which James was accustomed had been packed against the afternoon's outing, and this was loaded into the back of the car. In all the windows of the lodging-house except Pavel's own, James noticed, the curtains were still drawn. The unemployed lodgers would not be about yet; Pavel would have had the bathroom to himself. What could the lodgers do in such places at Christmas, but try to sleep through the day? He drove the short way back via Longwall and the Parks and Woodstock Road, since there was so little traffic about, and reached the village in half an hour, to find the man Baker waiting in his BMW outside the house.

"I've driven all the way from Chippenham to wish you the compliments of the season. Don't thank me; it was the only way I could get out of going to church with my parents. I've brought you the book I promised." He presented a small parcel, wrapped as a present.

"I don't think you've met my pupil, Pavel Borek."

"I've been reserving that pleasure." Baker spoke fluently to Pavel in an incomprehensible language, presumably Czech, and held out a gloved hand to be shaken. His driving-gloves were of pigskin, and appeared to be new, perhaps a present, and he wore a cashmere scarf of powder-blue under a jacket of soft black leather. Pavel blushed, took the hand, shook it cautiously, let it go again, and said, "Thank you. Same to you." This reply reassured James, since it suggested that Baker had not mentioned the uncle, which might, on past experience, have upset the boy. James would have to remember not to unwrap the book until he was alone.

"Will you have a glass of sherry? I'm afraid I can't ask you to stay to lunch. There's no provision."

Baker looked at his wristwatch. "No, really, I shall have to get back. We're to have our lunch at two. It will be a traditional meal, I'm afraid. Traditionally English, that is. Turkey, mince-pies, Christmas crackers, brandy butter. My brother and his family are coming." Somebody was watching from the front window of the Tullivers' cottage, and there would be other watchers at other windows. A stranger in a BMW, exotically clad, who did not enter the house, and the professor bringing home a lad with only one hand. It could not be helped; one's *raison d'être*, in a country

108

village, is to provide gossip for one's neighbours. Meanwhile Baker, although he had refused the offer of hospitality, gave no sign of going.

"You drove all this way on Christmas morning to give me a book I could have collected from your rooms when I dined with you?" Age, treacherous age! He had had a thought, and spoken it in spite of his intention to keep the uncle out of their conversation.

"Athlone Press, distributing for the University of Milwaukee. It hadn't arrived. They're in short supply."

Again, it could be checked; the name of the Press would be on the book. The Reader in European Studies had said that the philosopher Borek's translator was at Brandeis College, but he could have moved to Milwaukee, or perhaps had some contact there; Brandeis College itself was unlikely to run to a university press. Everything the man Baker said was in some way unsatisfactory, and everything could be checked. He had not mentioned a brother before, but that was no reason why he should not have one. James said, "But you yourself are unmarried?"

"Interesting, isn't it? Czechs are naturally uxorious, so if I'm unmarried there has to be a reason."

True to form, Baker was not giving a direct answer to a direct question. James said, "You're always speaking of yourself as a Czech. When we first met, you told me you were British."

"I'm a Czech in Britain; it makes me special. If I were in Prague, or even Brno, I should be terribly British. However, I don't propose to go – except at this moment, if you'll forgive me, back to my family and the Christmas crackers. Have you given thought at all to the other matter we were discussing?"

"I've given it some thought. It may require more."

"Do please take all the time you need. I'll be back at Nuffield at the beginning of term, and the Extra-Mural people are renewing my Economics course at Littlemore, so we may meet in the car park. I imagine that your own work there is likely to persist for some time." He was in the car,

109

fastening the seat-belt. "Happy Christmas again, Pavel. I'm so glad to have met you," and then to James, "He's a younger brother, by the way."

The BMW had passed the pub on the corner and was two-thirds of the way round the village green before Pavel had taken his rucksack from the back seat of the Volvo. "What's 'uxorious'?"

"Another old-fashioned word, I'm afraid, meaning 'to be excessively fond of one's wife'. It's not a quality confined to Czechs."

Shown to Helen's flat, Pavel stood by the bookcase, fingering the spines of the books, just as James himself had stood some weeks earlier, wondering whether to take an E. Nesbit to the Portakabin. James suggested that the boy should change into his other clothes in preparation for their outing after lunch, and Pavel replied, "Right! I'll bring my map." Once again, the two of them being alone together, leadership had passed. James went downstairs to heat up the soup.

The map was, in fact, two maps, the first the printed Ordnance Survey map of the area, one inch to the mile, the second a section of the first, covering Fawley Woods, the scale considerably magnified, and with four crosses and a number of dotted lines neatly plotted on it in red ink. The dotted lines represented tracks not marked on the Ordnance Survey; the crosses marked the positions of badger setts.

"You made this?"

Pavel shook his head. "Friend. I have to give them back."

"You want us to go and look at the setts? Inspect them?" James had thought they might take Sophie's favourite walk together, and be back easily in time for tea. "I don't imagine that there will be any badgers actually on display."

"Please, if you don't mind. We'd have to go some of the way in your car if we want to see all the setts before it gets dark. If we can't see the spoil, we don't know if they're occupied." Pavel did not add that the time spent with the man Baker had put them behind the clock, but the thought was there.

"Of course. We'll start now. Will you guide me?" Interesting that Pavel should have no difficulty in reading a map, but one must remember that there were very few words on it.

"You'll need wellies."

"I'll get wellies." James greatly disliked driving in rubber boots, which would get muddy and therefore slippery if he were to go scrambling about in woodland. Luckily the Volvo had an automatic gear-shift; he could not have managed a clutch. "And gloves," Pavel said. "Wrap up warm, and wear leather gloves."

Fawley Woods were just over six miles away. The whole countryside around James was well-wooded, as the hedgerow trees – ash, sycamore, hawthorn, hedge-maple and even oak – had grown too large to be easily cut back, so that, even after the hedgerows themselves had been grubbed up, the trees remained, but the Woods proper covered the slopes of a valley owned by the estate of Fawley House. Once they had been part of a much larger forest in which stag and wild boar had been hunted by persons of noble birth and their verderers, and poachers had been impaled on stakes or hanged from the branches of deciduous trees, but that was long ago; the last man-trap had been removed from Fawley Woods in 1923, and the old forest trees had been replaced by conifers.

James drove over minor roads and then, under Pavel's direction, turned off the metalled carriageway through an open gate and onto a track, rutted but still maintained, since there were residues of asphalt and some of the potholes had been filled with hard-core. This track was marked on the Ordnance Survey map; James hoped they would not be moving onto one of the dotted lines. Pavel said, "We'll go as close as we can by car. There'll be a lot of walking to do when we get there."

Ahead, the road dipped and the woods began. They

111

were driving in sunlight, and the previous night's frost had melted. Once they were in the shade of the trees, would the ground be harder or muddy? James began to wish that he had studied natural phenomena more, and literature less. "Will there be room to turn the car, do you think? I'm not particularly good at reversing."

"There's a place halfway down the track, just after the bridle-path, where it gets wider. We can park there if there isn't a car already."

"That's on the map?"

"I was told about it."

"And if there is a car already?"

"We go down to the bottom, turn, and come back. Then we'd just be people out for a drive, who'd lost our way. But there won't be anyone. Too fine. Christmas afternoon. Bound to be people around – walkers, week-end drivers, all sorts."

James found it hard to follow the logic which suggested that because there were bound to be people around, enjoying the fine Christmas weather, therefore there would be nobody parked on the track. Nor had they seen any people at all since leaving the metalled road, but presumably Pavel knew what he was talking about. The track did widen just after being crossed by a bridle-path, and the space thus created was vacant. James parked the Volvo, and they left it locked, and set off up the bridle-path to the left in search of the first red cross. Since it was marked at some distance below the path, James supposed that they would have to scramble through undergrowth. However, the trees here were mainly larches. Their height and close planting discouraged undergrowth, of which there seemed to be more on the path than among the trees, where there was mainly leaf-mould. Old Mr Proctor would have been in his element here; he had had a considerable regard for leaf-mould, and often said that he could never get enough of it.

The first sett was unoccupied, as even James could tell. The heaps of spoil had been made months ago, and were covered with a light growth of moss or lichen, and the

112

entrances were filled with old twigs and leaves, obviously undisturbed. Two of the five entrances appeared to have been closed with rusty oil-drums. "Hunt does that," Pavel said. "Stopping earths. Bloody barbarians, the Hunt. Trap foxes, put 'em in a bag, cut their paws, then let them run, to be torn to pieces. But you can't do everything. Let's go on."

Picking his way from tree to tree down a slope that became increasingly steep, James began to feel that if Pavel were ever to decide that he *could* do everything, he himself would not care to be a member of the Hunt. The boy seemed tireless and extraordinarily nimble for someone with only one hand. When they left the car, he had produced a pair of leather gloves of his own, of which the left hand had no fingers, but a padded lump to fit over Pavel's stump; the contraption looked as if it had been home-made. With it he held back what brambles and blackthorn could not be circumvented, so that James should not snag his raglan overcoat on the thorns, and once, when James lost balance, and would have run down the hillside out of control bouncing off trees, Pavel's arm, with the speed of a bayonet-thrust, became a strong bar to catch him and hold him back.

Near the second sett a tree had fallen and, though it was held up by its fellows, its falling had let light into the wood, so that the scrub grew thicker. The tree was an oak, part of the old forest, immense, much of its bole rotten, the roots exposed and pulled some way out of the ground, bringing earth up with them so that a kind of cave had been formed, where already ferns and mosses grew. One of the entrances to the sett was in this cave; it was clearly occupied, the freshly dug earth easy to see, and some of the fern had been dragged in for bedding. "Stupid!" Pavel said. "Never clear up after themselves. Might as well hang out a signal."

The winter sunlight here shone through the trees, and suddenly, as James and Pavel drew closer, a patch of the dappled sunlight moved and became a woman, not a young woman, in fact a woman of pensionable age, dressed entirely in Army camouflage clothing, even to the

113

boots and a red beret. "Is there anything I can do for you, gentlemen?" the woman said.

"I'm sorry. Are we disturbing you?"

Pavel said, "That's all right. Just looking around."

"Show me your hand, then." Pavel held up his gloved stump. "Great!"

"How many are there denning?"

"Five. Two old 'uns and three cubs, 1M, 2F."

"Still with them?"

"Don't know why. Lazy buggers. Don't like digging, maybe. Mum'll have 'em out soon enough. She's impregnated again, due in February. Watched her and the old man at it last July. Thirty-five minutes by the clock! Makes you envious; my poor old feller never managed to last as long, rest his soul. Bloody important," the woman said to James. "Keep this little lot safe; got to. Five together, and one in pod. Bloody tragedy if they go."

Pavel said, "Seen anyone about?"

"God, yes! Bugger took a shot at me."

James said, "Surely you must be mistaken?"

"Didn't aim to hit. Wall-eyed bugger, done it before, doesn't like me, said so. He'll fire over your head, at your feet, break a branch by your side sometimes, just for the sport. If he hits one of those bloody oil-drums, the danger's in the ricochet. Does it partly to frighten me off, partly to warn his mates. They went off in a van."

It did not appear that the old woman had, in fact, been frightened off; on the contrary, she appeared elated. James thought, "It would frighten *me* off," and then, "I shall do such things . . . Shit!" On July 29th, in his own garden, long before he had met Pavel, he had committed himself to not being frightened off whatever he might find to do, and must abide by the commitment. The woman said, "Are you staying?"

There was Christmas cake for tea, and a pheasant to be cooked. Nevertheless James attempted to induce the word "Yes" to undertake the passage from his brain to his diaphragm up through his throat and on to his lips, but before he could complete the process Pavel said, "They won't be back till after midnight."

"Right! Boxing Day's traditional. Very early hours."

"Did you get the number of the van?"

"Not with these elderly peepers, baby," the old woman said. "It was blue. I don't know about make; could be Japanese, anything. Dirty old blue van; that's all I know."

Pavel said to James, "I would like to come back after midnight, sir. I can walk it easy." He had not called James "sir" since the very earliest lessons. After that it had been "Professor", then "Mr Elphinstone" and for some time nothing at all, since none of those forms of address felt right any longer, yet neither he nor his teacher would have been comfortable with "James".

Meanwhile James heard himself saying, "Of course. I'll come with you."

"Good show!" the camouflaged lady said.

Pavel said, "Have you got a camera with a flash?"

"I'm not sure. Such things get put away and forgotten. I could look."

The camouflaged lady said, "Don't bother. Never does any bloody good. They'll be wearing balaclavas for one thing, and for another they jump on you as soon as they see the flash go off, knock you down, and break the camera. Believe me; I've had some. Infra-red's the only thing, but it's bloody expensive. My poor old fellow left me badly provided for, rest his soul, or I'd get one." She laughed, one of those braying senior-memsahib laughs that came out of the very early past James was only now beginning to remember. "Got no other vices," she said.

This time they parked the car at some distance with others on the metalled road outside a row of cottages; it would not be noticed there. They had over a mile to walk to the place where the track widened, but Pavel said this would assist their night-vision. As Pavel explained it, night-vision was a shy fugitive quality, manifesting itself only slowly, particularly to those unaccustomed to using it, and retreating at

115

once from any form of light. The moon was still new, not yet in its first quarter, but there were stars. James was forbidden to gaze directly at either stars or moon, and soon found that he was able to distinguish hedges, and then the grass verge of the road, then gates and other irregularities in the hedges, the pot-holes of the track when they had turned onto it, the wire and posts of the fence that bounded it, and then they had reached the shadows of the wood, and he fell over a cattle-grid. "Takes time," Pavel said, helping him up.

The promised ground frost had not yet formed, and there had been only light frosts so far all through December. This was unfortunate; the ground would be easy to dig. Pavel had brought his rucksack, which now contained a length of cheap plastic hose he had found rolled up in James's tool-shed, a large ball of thick string from the depths of the kitchen cupboard, and a coil of thin wire which he had brought with him from Oxford. No doubt the purpose of these objects would be explained. James had offered to look about for a camera with a flash; there must certainly be a camera of some sort about somewhere. But, having regard to the old woman's warning, Pavel had refused it.

They reached the place where the track widened. No vehicle was parked there.

"Good!"

"You think they won't come?"

"Dunno. I think they will. It's the kind of night they like, and being a holiday makes it easier. They could do what we've done – park the van where it won't be noticed, and walk."

"They'll come this way, then?"

"Might go straight through the woods at the top. I better get to the sett. You stay here and watch."

"Here? What shall I do if the van comes?" What on earth was he intended to do, show himself and be shot at? Well, if that was the intention, he would do it. *"They shall be the terrors of the earth."* They were more likely to be the terrors of James Elphinstone. One could not be sure that the men would fire to miss, but they would carry lights, James supposed; they would see that his overcoat was a good one, and might be wary of winging a member of the professional class.

"We'll find you a place." A place of concealment was found further down the track, but up on the bank among trees. "Don't look at the headlights," Pavel said. "Turn your head away if you see the lights coming, then turn back when the van stops and they switch the headlights off. Try to remember everything you can about them – how many – they'll have a dog, maybe two – what they're wearing – anything."

"And if they don't come this way?"

"That's why I'm going to the sett. Fix trip-wires. They'll create so much noise, we're bound to hear." He put down his rucksack at James's feet, took the coil of wire from it, and slung it on his shoulders. He slapped the pocket of his anorak. "I borrowed your wire-cutters. I hope you don't mind." The wire was coated with dark green plastic, and would be hard to see even by torchlight. "If they do come this way, I need to know. I'll probably hear the van anyway, but . . ." The ball of string was taken from the rucksack. "Tie this to my left arm. It's bound to get snagged in bushes and stuff, so don't take no notice of any jerks you get from me." James had hoped that, in the course of conversation with his teacher twice a week, Pavel would lose the habit of the double negative, and he did seem to be using it less frequently, but at moments of stress it came back. "But if you see the van, or just the men walking – they'd have spades and a shot-gun probably –" How comforting to be reminded of the shot-gun! "– then you give three long pulls on the string, wait, and then another three. I'll come back to you. Right?"

"You may be at some hazardous place. I may pull you over."

"You won't pull me over. If you do, I'll pick meself up."

"And the hose-pipe?"

"Stays here in the rucksack. You look after it. Right?"

117

The boy was gone. Even encumbered by a coil of plastic wire, and with string tied to one arm just above the elbow, he moved amazingly silently. To James's improved night-vision the white string showed up clearly in the dark wood, but he supposed that the men in balaclavas would be unlikely to notice it because they would not be expecting any such thing. They would have a dog, maybe two. James was concealed, not only by the trees, but by the old nettles and brushwood that covered the bank beside the track, but to dogs these would be an irrelevance; the dogs would scent his fear. They would be terriers, Jack Russells or Staffordshire bull terrirers, bred and trained to savagery. Courage, Elphinstone! He was at some distance from where the van would be parked, and further down the track; the men would walk away from him to get to the bridle-path, and if their dogs wandered, they would be recalled. He hoped Pavel would come back soon.

Time passed. The string in James's gloved hand was for the most while slack, sometimes tightened, twitched and struggled a little, and then grew quiet again. Theseus in the labyrinth, Pavel Borek in the dark but penetrable wood, while night's black agents to their prey did rouse. *"My poor old fellow left me badly provided for, rest his soul."* Our partners, when they die, are bound to leave us ill-provided, since they themselves have been our provision. Was that why the old woman endured being knocked about and shot at by trappers, for occupation, for a sop to loneliness, or was it for love of the badgers themselves; had *they* become her provision? The photographs of badgers in Dr Neal's book had something of the appearance of the kind of poor old fellow who might have partnered the camouflaged woman; Badger in *The Wind in the Willows* is very much the kindly *barra sahib* of the Woodland Station. There was a glow in the sky at the top of the hill, and the sound of a van approaching. As the beams of the headlights cut into the dark, James turned his head away, and gave three long tugs at the string.

He had turned his head away as instructed, but could still

118

see the lower part of the track illuminated by the van's headlights on full beam. Although their activities were illegal, these people seemed to take no precautions against discovery. He closed his eyes. He heard the van stop, the engine switched off, doors opening. He opened his eyes, and turned his head back to observe. Two men (he supposed they were men) had vacated the front seats of the van, and were opening the doors at the back. Dogs spilled out as soon as the doors were opened, two of them, a Jack Russell and a lurcher, yapping and whining with excitement, and were followed out of the back of the van more stiffly and laboriously by a third person with spades. Was there a gun also? Yes, one of the men returned to the front of the van, brought out a shot-gun from between the seats, and tucked it under his arm. "I am an old man," James thought, "yet I have excellent night-vision, even though unpractised. I can distinguish a shot-gun from a rifle at sixty paces in the dark." Both dogs had cocked their legs, and the lurcher was now wandering down the track in his direction. Where was Pavel? James had been told to give the string three tugs twice, and had forgotten the second time. He tugged again, and the string was slack, and came in towards him; there was nothing for him to tug against. The lurcher had disappeared in shadow, and might be anywhere.

The men were moving away towards the bridle-path. One of them called the lurcher, who had only moved from the track to defecate, and now came to him running. Two of the men carried torches, which threw beams almost as powerful as the headlights of the van. Luckily the beams were turned away from James, so that he was neither discovered nor dazzled, but, put to it, he knew that he would not be able to describe the men to Pavel or anyone else, certainly not to identify them by daylight. There were three, probably all male, probably neither black nor Asian. They wore balaclavas, as he had been told they would (had he therefore seen what he expected to see?), with donkey-jackets, dark trousers and black rubber boots. He had heard

119

them speaking, and calling the dog, but could not remember what had been said, nor whether their accents had been local. What had they called the dog? That was hard evidence, the name of the dog, what was it? He could not remember what they had called the dog. None of it would stand up in a Magistrates' Court. *"A foolish, fond old man."* He felt a tear trickle down one cheek, but that was the cold. The men had gone now along the bridle-path. *"Five together, and one in pod! Bloody tragedy!"* What could a boy with one hand do against three men, armed, and two dogs? He had better try to find Pavel by following the string.

Pavel was by his side, had taken the end of the string from his hand, and wound it on to the ball, which he now dropped into the rucksack. He picked out the length of plastic hosepipe. "Come on!" he said. "We'd better take a look at the van."

It was a British Leyland Sherpa, by no means new. The men had left the back unlocked, careless in that as in all else. Pavel opened the right-hand door. He had brought with him the cigarette-lighter, his Christmas present from James unwrapped at dinner, and behind the shelter of the door he lit it, and held it up. The space behind the front seats of the van had been converted to a bank of cages, two on two. The man with the spades who had travelled in the back must have been uncomfortably crowded; perhaps he had put the dogs in the cages, which would account for their joy at being let out. "Buggers!" Pavel said. "Oh, the buggers, the cruel buggers!" Usually when Pavel was in the grip of strong emotion he blushed, but James could see that now his face, illuminated by the flickering flame of the cigarette-lighter, had gone a blueish white.

"Right!" Pavel said. "Better get on." Were they to follow the men, and deter them, by their presence as witnesses, from digging? So far the purposes of the wire and ball of string had been made clear, but not the garden-hose. Pavel was unscrewing the cap of the van's petrol tank, and put one end of the hose into it. That was it, then? He would siphon off the petrol, and, from the nearest unvandalised phone-box, they would telephone the police, who would catch the men *in flagrante* with badgers in cages. It would be hard on the badgers, some of whom, particularly the older male, might sustain injury or even death in the digging-out, but probably it was the best way. Pavel said, "Come on!" and began to unwind the hose down the track, James following.

The hosepipe was of some length. Surely the siphoning operation required very little, as long as one end was lower than the other? "Keep well back. Stand over there." James moved where he was told. Pavel put his mouth to the end of the hose, and sucked. It would take a little while for the petrol to emerge, but once a vacuum had been created, it would surely do so. Pavel spat, and put down his end of the hose. James had never had occasion to siphon petrol or anything else, and only knew the theory of it. Would there be a trickle, or would the petrol flow out strongly, and kill the surrounding vegetation? James moved closer, and Pavel waved him back. They would have to take the hosepipe away with them when the process was complete; one would not wish to be traced by one's garden hose. There was a strong smell of petrol. Pavel moved three paces backwards, took out the lighter again, lit it, and threw it forwards. It was like starting a bonfire with paraffin, when one throws the twist of lighted newspaper towards the pyre of garden rubbish. The petrol blazed up, melting the end of the plastic hosepipe from which more petrol was emerging, and so on and up the track, the plastic hose melting, the petrol vapour igniting, like some gigantic firework until the snake of flame had reached the van, which exploded and itself caught fire.

"Get back into the trees," Pavel said. The paint was aflame, the tyres were melting. From within the wood could be heard the shouting of men, the agitated barking of dogs. The men would have heard the explosion, might even be able to see the flames, which burned so high; they would know something had happened, and come running. It seemed possible from the confusion of noise that they had run into the trip-wires. One of the dogs had begun to scream. Pavel said, "I put down a couple of snares. I had time for that." The trees beside the van would be singed, perhaps killed, but were unlikely to ignite; it had been a rainy autumn. Pavel said, "Usually we put sugar in the petrol tank, and phone the police, but you wouldn't get anyone out on Christmas night. Anyway I know those men."

5

PALACE OF CULTURE

When the men had gone, Pavel returned to the interior of the wood, and removed the trip-wires and snares so that no other people or animals, particularly the badgers themselves, would be caught in them. There had been no digging at the sett, so the badgers would be unharmed, but after all the hullabaloo they would probably decide to move out for a while, and denn elsewhere. It was clear from the disturbance of bracken and bramble around the tree-trunk that some, perhaps all, of the men had fallen, and one of the snares had been pulled out of the earth, and the wire was sticky with blood. It would have been the Jack Russell's blood. One of the men, as they came blundering through the trees towards the burning van, had been carrying the dog inside his donkey-jacket. A scarf had been wrapped round the man's hand; the dog would have bitten him as he tried to release it. Perhaps their blood had mingled on the wire.

James was able to give little help in the removal of wires, and was asked for none. He seemed to be moving on auto-pilot, but not with any facility, and his night-vision had suffered a reverse, so that he could no longer be trusted not to walk into trees. Matters were made more difficult by Pavel's decision that, although the men had been gone a good half-hour, they might be waiting at the top of the track or at the road, so that he and James had better leave the woods by crossing the bridle-path and going out through the top, returning to the road further on by way of a ploughed field. For most of the journey, James held on to Pavel's handless arm; the cripple was leading the blind. "I'm afraid I'm not much good to you in this situation," he said, and Pavel replied that James had already been a lot of good to him, and that, without James, he would have been unable to manage. This was untrue, of course, but comforting.

The Volvo was where they had left it, outside the cottages, in one of the windows of which there was a tiny Christmas tree decorated with tinsel and coloured lights, and with a child's drawing of sheep and angels propped against the base. The tree had been there when they arrived, but James had thought that by now the lights would have been switched off; it seemed wasteful to keep the thing lit all night, when there was nobody to see it. God would see it, he supposed, if there was a God, and might be pleased at the profligacy, which He would construe as an act of devotion, like a toccata by J.S. Bach. James and Pavel had, after all, listened to music by the fire before leaving the house. It had passed the time, and Pavel had no objection to classical music, which he associated with his own childhood; the boy's father, being uninterested in the domestic affairs of the English, and not understanding the language, had kept his cheap radio almost permanently tuned to Radio Three. *"I am your father now."* Pavel seemed to be waiting for him to unlock the car. And get into the driving-seat. And switch on the ignition. "Seat-belt!" Pavel said.

Further down the road they passed the three men on foot with their two dogs, the Jack Russell still being carried inside a donkey-jacket. The men tried to hitch a lift, but no one, even in the country, would stop at four in the morning for three men in balaclavas with a shot-gun. James wondered if they would notice, and remember, the number of the car.

He decided that he would go to Czechoslovakia, but not on the man Baker's terms. He had nothing to say about literature which a person of ordinary intelligence could not work out for himself, certainly nothing that would justify

124

any dissident's placing himself in peril of the police to hear; James's common sense would not accept the prospect of a group of unfrocked academics gathered clandestinely to listen to a lecture on the moral ambiguities in the novels of Charles Dickens. Was there not, in any case, something called *glasnost* these days? The moral ambiguities of Dickens might be discussed safely on any street corner. He should have reminded Baker of *glasnost*; Baker might be out of date. James would get a sense of the situation on his own without commitment to Baker or anyone else, see what he might see, hear what he might hear, and then decide whether there were any service he could usefully perform for such culturally deprived persons as Pavel's uncle. *"I shall do such things"* – well, he had done such things; it was not every retired Regius Professor who spent the hours from midnight to dawn setting fire to the vans of badger-baiters. And he would do such other things, in or out of Czechoslovakia, as reason and decency might suggest. "Turn right here," Pavel said. "We'll be back at your house soon. I expect you could do with a lie-in."

In Prague it seemed rarely possible to pass a Milk Bar. "My God! I am a gannet," Jana cried. "Maybe it is because I am vegetarian, I am eating all the time." Jana's voice was piercing, and cut easily through the whispered cajolements of black marketeers attempting to persuade James to change money. Sometimes she would succeed for a while in breaking her addiction to milk shakes, and she would take James to shop in a supermarket, buying yoghurt and bread rolls to eat on the move between appointments.

James had replaced at short notice, as a British Council Cultural Exchange Visitor, the Curator of a Museum of Metropolitan Transport. It had been this man's habit to photograph vintage trams wherever he found them, and he had lost a toe in Milan, where it is considered unsafe to set up complicated photographic equipment in the middle of the road, and had been unable to complete his journey to Prague. The Czechs are not entirely inflexible. The pro-

125

gramme had been adjusted, literary persons being substituted as far as possible for civil engineers. The guided tour of the Metro and trip by funicular to Prague Castle had been retained, since they might be regarded as of touristic and cultural interest.

James lectured on *King Lear* to an extremely thin audience at Charles University; the university authorities, given only an hour's notice of the change of speaker, had managed to get rid of a full auditorium of Engineering students, but not to replace them. The Lecturer in English was Scottish, and had done his best in the time. "Made a mistake there," he said. "Went out looking for Literature students when I should have stuck to the Translation Section. Wonderful people, translators, salt of the earth. This country would come to a grinding halt without them; I can tell you that." He and Jana smiled at each other; she had been a favourite student of his predecessor. "Work their socks off, translators, come to any lecture, sit there taking notes, ask questions if prompted. You could do a linguistic analysis of the telephone directory, and they wouldn't care, just as long as your syntax was spot on. Translators hate sloppy syntax; it confuses them." James forbore to point out that several distinguished French scholars had already made linguistic analyses of telephone directories, that of the directory of Nantes being particularly admired. "And it always is *Lear*, you see," the Lecturer said. "I don't know why. Christopher Ricks did *Lear* here, and hardly anyone turned up. When he went to Bratislava he switched to Bob Dylan, and had them dancing in the aisles."

"I'm afraid I had very little time to prepare." James had not expected, when he had suggested himself to the British Council, that his tour would be arranged so soon, but the Czech Embassy had rushed the visa through, being at first under the impression that the replacement for Dr Jovis would also be an expert on metropolitan transport. "The lecture on *Lear* was to hand; it always has gone down very well abroad. I offered *The Pauline Epistles Reconsidered*, but it was rejected."

126

"Nothing religious. There's said to be a religious revival. Them Up Top don't like it."

The Pauline Epistles had been so thoroughly reconsidered that there was very little religion left in them, but Them Up Top, James supposed, would not know that. He had been in Prague six days, four of which had been working days during which he had made formal and polite conversation, all of it translated both ways by Jana, with a succession of administrators and academics, none of whom had been quite sure who he was or why he had come to see them and, since James had not been quite sure either, the conversations had taken on a repetitious quality, as if he had become trapped in a time-loop. On the remaining two days Jana had shown him the tourist-attractions of the city very thoroughly, as she had shown them with equal thoroughness to her many charges before him – biochemists, computer-engineers, laser-surgeons and her particular favourite, a woman to whom she alluded often, Miss Hoost, who had made a definitive study of the bacteria to be found in the udders of native cattle.

James's responses to the art and architecture of Prague had been measured against those of Miss Hoost, and had usually fallen below them. He had stood before a succession of dimly lit baroque masterpieces, and had not known what to say. Often his attention had wandered. In St Nicholas Church the young guide to a party of German tourists had put them into four pews, and was waving his umbrella over them as if scattering holy water as he talked; it would be part of the religious revival of which Them Up Top disapproved. "Are you looking? Please look! Look here!" Jana had redirected his attention from the party of tourists to the marble statue of St Nicholas before which she had placed him; Jana was never stern, but she was firm. Miss Hoost had been reminded by the statue of English pictures of Santa Claus, which was appropriate; when James himself had later observed that the portrait of Ludwig Rittersburg by Antonin Machek in the Monastery of St Agnes reminded him of his son Richard, that was merely

127

anecdotal. How could Professor Elphinstone explain to Jana that he was a critic, that his response to a work of art was always more likely to be analytic than aesthetic, and that such aesthetic responses as he did experience were usually to sounds, to words primarily and music there-after? Sophie had often told him that he lacked a visual imagination. He had not felt the lack till now.

There would be two more days of sight-seeing and five of meetings before James would be allowed to go home, two more lectures, visits to the opera and the ballet, to museums, exhibitions of ethnic ceramics, vintage cars and illustrations to books for children – what was he doing here? why had he come? Insulated by Jana and the spirit of Miss Hoost, he was no nearer understanding the reality of cultural deprivation in a communist country, and even without Jana he would have been cut off from contact by his utter ignorance of the language; he could not so much as order a meal on his own. Meanwhile he was depressed at the reception to his lecture, and extremely tired. "Look, I'm sorry about this," the Lecturer in English said. "Bit of a nonsense really. I'd ask you for a drink, but my wife's Bolivian. You're doing something at the British Cultural Section tomorrow, aren't you?"

"Thomas Hardy."

"Bound to get a decent turn-out. Always is there."

"Won't they be expecting something about trams?"

"Doesn't matter. Say what you like there. It's the English they go for – rolling periods and an educated accent, very keen on that."

There had been only one real moment of contact so far during the entire six days. Travelling back to his hotel alone by Metro, tired and sweaty with the central heating of a series of professorial offices, James had come accidentally between a small child and its parents as he entered a crowded train. The child's grasp had broken from its father's hand, and James had put out his own hand, and the child had taken it.

*

128

It was a full house at the British Cultural Section, forty people on folding chairs, their faces turned upwards to the platform, smiling because they were pleased to be there, pleased to understand what was said, pleased to recognise the titles of some of Thomas Hardy's better-known novels. If they had expected trams, they gave no indication of it. Fluorescent overhead lighting gleamed on the dentures of the older ladies, bounced off the beards and moustaches and glittered on the metal-rimmed spectacles of translators, which were like so many heliographs sending messages of comfort and welcome back to James, "We are glad to see you amongst us, Professor Elphinstone. We know who you are, and recognise you as an authority. Share your insights with us; we are ready and waiting."

Jana sat in the front row, laughing loudly at what she took to be the jokes, usually just before the end of a sentence so as to give the rest of the audience time to follow her lead. But they all laughed, all the audience laughed when encouraged, were attentively silent during passages of exegesis or extrapolation, applauded when James was introduced to them, applauded when he had finished his lecture, applauded after he had answered their questions. There was only one couple, who had arrived late and sat at the back of the room by the open door, who seemed a little worried, a little puzzled to be there, a little lost among the references forward (to Edward Thomas) and back (to Tennyson and Mrs Gaskell). These, James supposed, would be tram-people who had not been told. The man wore a leather coat; the woman's hair had been piled up in ringlets, and lacquered so that it gleamed like freshly-peeled conkers.

After the lecture there was white wine and the opportunity for members of the audience to meet the speaker socially. Some were introduced in an obscure order of precedence by the British Cultural Attaché; others bashfully introduced themselves. The man in the leather coat sat at a distance on a sofa, while the ringleted woman looked at an illustrated magazine, something to do with British

Aeronautical Achievement. Both refused wine. One of the translators was observing that Professor Elphinstone's work was not well-known in Czechoslovakia, meaning that it was not known at all. James had been advised to bring copies of his own books to cast like bread upon the waters, but it had smacked too much of self-advertisement, and he had not done so. He promised to send a book from England after his return, and was given a calling-card to add to his already numerous collection. The British Council had been surprised that James possessed no calling-cards of his own. Agronomists always carried calling-cards. The man in the leather coat was looking across the room at James, his face still wearing its puzzled expression. If he did not know where he was or what was happening, why did he and his companion not leave, since neither showed any interest in the free wine and the company?

Time passed. Five-forty-five became six-thirty, the wine was finished, and Czechs eat early; the translators drifted away. Would a seminar for dissidents have been rather like this, except perhaps for the presence of a secret policeman at the back taking notes? The British Cultural Attaché showed no disposition to suggest dinner; James had been taken to lunch on the day after his arrival, and there is a limit to what the British taxpayer's purse may be expected to bear. The two on the sofa were among the last to leave; the woman smiled at the Cultural Attaché from the door, and took the aeronautical magazine with her. "Always happening," he said. "Still, it spreads the word." James and Jana walked up Wenceslaus Square to the Museum Metro Station where James could catch a train direct to the station nearest his hotel. Jana herself lived in the other direction; her husband, a freelance photographer, would have fed the children, but Jana liked to see them before they were put to bed. James noticed the man in the leather coat and his companion in the concourse and again on the platform, where they took the same train as he.

He considered the matter of food. He had eaten nothing since breakfast but an apple, a bread roll and a raspberry milk shake. It was true that breakfast at the hotel was substantial if one wished to make it so, with a central table from which one might help oneself without stint to rissoles and sausages, hard-boiled eggs, pickled cucumbers and red cabbage, processed cheese, salami, corn-flakes, hard little apples, yoghurt, goulash, cold scrambled eggs with mushrooms, ketchup, rye bread and jam. The German tourists who occupied most of the rooms of the hotel would return to this table often, refilling their plates with delicacies for which they had not been able to create space the first time round, but James had not found himself able to do so. Consequently he was hungry. The hotel itself was situated in a wasteland of high-rise apartment-blocks, with no other places of entertainment or resort around it. It had its own restaurants, three of them, all over-priced, two with peripatetic violinists and in the third a waiter had asked if he wished to change dollars; James hated them all. Also, he discovered, he was suffering from a feeling of anti-climax. To deliver a lecture was no great matter; he had done so often before, and to larger, more diverse and more critical audiences. But in Prague he felt so isolated and so vulnerable, so much inclined to believe that he was wasting his time and should never have come that, particularly after the *Lear* fiasco, he had been anxious for this lecture to go well, and it had gone well, and yet here he was at just after seven in the evening on his way back to an hotel he detested with at least three hours to fill, either alone in his rooms or among Germans, before he could decently go to bed. A celebration of some sort, however mild, would have been in order. He could have asked Jana to dine with him, and she would have done so, leaving the children to be put to bed without her, but she had already given up so much of her time to him, and eating in a restaurant was always a problem for her, since the menus of Czech restaurants did not seem to mention vegetables to any great degree, and she would usually end up in an argument with the waiter over omelettes.

What a pother, what a silly business! He was too old to

indulge himself in such a gloom. James remembered that the Palace of Culture at Gottwaldova, where Jana had shown him the exhibition of vintage cars, had a Snack Bar; she had eaten cream cakes there with a pot of tea, and he an open sandwich. There had been an English menu, if one asked for it, and the prices had been reasonable, and the place crowded with what appeared to be genuine Czechs. Perhaps there would be some entertainment there, a concert or a multi-media show, which he could attend unchaperoned, but even if there were not, it would be more pleasant to eat his dinner outside the hotel than in. He would break his journey at Gottwaldova. The Palace of Culture, as he remembered, was next to the Metro station, and had a view over the city; he would look at the lights if there were nothing else to do.

James sat in the Snack Bar of the Palace of Culture, eating a hamburger with a fried egg on top and french fries on the side. That was not how it had been described, even in the English menu, but that was how it was, and there was no help for it. The Snack Bar was crowded. After a short while the man in the leather coat and his companion approached the table, and made signs to ask whether they might sit down. "Please . . . please . . . *prosim*," James said. The coat was not truly of leather, but of some plastic substance, and not black as it had seemed at a distance, but a mottled purple.

They sat, smiling nervously at James, who said, "I hope you enjoyed the lecture." The man, alarmed, looked sideways at his companion who replied after a little thought, "We enjoy." Conversation lapsed. A waiter came to the table, was, after consultation, given an order, and went away again. The woman moistened her lips with her tongue, and swallowed; clearly she was preparing to speak. James gave her the half-smile, half-nod of encouragement which hitherto he had reserved for his less talented pupils. The woman said something in Czech to the man, who produced a packet of filter-tipped cigarettes. She took one, and tapped it against the back of her hand. The

132

fried egg was congealing on top of the hamburger. James did not know which would be less polite, to continue watching the couple opposite or to look away. The man took a lighter from the pocket of his imitation-leather coat, just such a lighter as James had given to Pavel at Christmas, a heavy old-fashioned petrol-lighter with a cap. The woman inclined her head towards the man graciously, and the man flipped back the cap and turned the wheel, and the flame of the lighter leapt out towards her, catching one of her lacquered ringlets, which flared up, setting light to others. Miss Hoost, no doubt, would have reached across the table, and doused the flame with ketchup, but James found himself to be incapable of action of any sort.

The flame went out of its own accord, leaving most of the woman's coiffure intact, if a little lop-sided. She wiped away ash with a paper napkin, and said to James, "He is Pavel Borek. He has hear you are good friend to his son of brother. Please forgive my English no good, and speak slow."

What had been gained, what could the man possibly have gained from such a meeting? James had spoken slowly; he had used only simple words. He had told Borek what he knew of Pavel's father, of his coming to England, of his work as a farm-labourer, of his marriage and his wife's suicide, of his own death and its circumstances, attempting to mitigate the poverty and the loneliness of the man's life without telling lies. He had said what he knew to be true, that Pavel had loved his father dearly, and respected his memory. He had reported that Pavel himself, although unemployed as so many young people in Britain were these days, was in good health, physically A1 apart from his hand, which was . . . unavoidably and through no fault of his own . . . not exactly . . . not fully formed. *"Prosim?"* Disabled, in a sense; there was a physical disability. "Again, please!" Unfortunately Pavel, since birth had lacked a hand. "Hend?" James had restrained himself from

133

a cutting-off gesture which might suggest that Pavel's hand had been publicly amputated as a punishment for theft. "Hand," he said, "Pavel was born without a left hand, but is otherwise in excellent physical condition." Borek had lifted his own hand above the level of the table, and had examined it as if searching for some hereditary defect. "Perhaps the result of thalidomide," James had said, despairing of simple words, and the woman had said, "*Ano*, thalidomide!" and spoke rapidly in Czech to Borek, who nodded. "Really," James said, "he manages remarkably well. Your nephew is an extremely intelligent, likeable and capable young man," and Borek had smiled, and nodded again, and two tears had run down, one each side of his nose.

Information had been exchanged. Borek had two children of his own, a boy and a girl, whom he loved but no longer saw. His wife had divorced him at the time of his disgrace. The divorce had not been out of any animosity or as a reaction to sexual misconduct, but for the sake of the children who would otherwise, as the children of a disgraced person, not have been allowed to enter the conservatoire, far less the university. Borek himself had hopes of an improvement in his position; he had applied to be recategorised from hospital-cleaner to teacher again, not of course at a university but at a basic school, where he would teach spelling and the construction of simple sentences to the younger children. There was a new atmosphere these days, spreading from the Soviet Union; Borek had been told privately by a sympathetic party-member that his application was likely to be accepted.

Addresses had been exchanged. Borek hoped that Pavel would find time to write to him, preferably about uncontroversial matters. James had replied diplomatically that he was sure Pavel would wish to do so; the question of Pavel's ability to read and write had not come up, and James had not wished to bring it up. Borek had given James his card. Even Borek was equipped with cards, on which were printed his name and title, "Docent Pavel Borek", and

134

an address which had been crossed out and a new one written in by hand; the card had been yellow with age. As far as James had been able to make out, Borek now lived in an apartment-house, perhaps even a rooming-house; he seemed to occupy no more living-space than his nephew. The ringleted woman was a neighbour and good friend; if "good friend" were to be used in such a context, James wondered how his own position as good friend to Pavel had been construed.

They had travelled by coach, a journey of two and a half hours, from Brno to Prague, and must return. They had ordered only tea from the waiter, and it had been finished, and there seemed to be no more information to be exchanged, and they had stood, and shaken hands, and left James to the tepid remnants of the hamburger and the fried egg and to French fries which even Miss Hoost could not have revived. A two and a half hour journey each way! No doubt, the fare would be subsidised, but even so, the time and the expense! They would not have understood one word of his lecture on Hardy. What gain, what possible gain, what comfort could James have brought to such a man? And the woman had burned her hair.

James sat for a while before asking for his bill; it would be embarrassing to bump into Borek and his lady on the platform of the Metro. The waiter seemed perturbed by the amount of food left on the plate. "Sorry. Not as hungry as I thought. My fault. Delicious, however." On his way out, James noticed that there was a man waiting by the telephone box outside the WC who looked remarkably like the bearded translator to whom he had promised a copy of his Lawrence book. He paused on the steps outside the Palace of Culture; the lights of the city were bright across the valley. It would not do to ignore a man from whom he had parted cordially only ninety minutes before, and who at least spoke excellent English. James turned, and went back inside the foyer, but when he reached the telephone box again of course the man had gone.

"*Caj*" – they pronounced it "*chai*" – "tea". The word was

135

the same in Hindustani, which James found interesting. He had said as much to Jana, and she had replied, "No, it's Russian."

6

COTSWOLD SPRING

It seemed to James that spring had broken out at Little Easely during his absence. In Prague the weather had been a continuation of what he had left in Britain, but colder. Now he returned to find that all over the garden the heads of daffodils had lifted and opened into trumpets, that carpets of aconites had spread themselves under trees as if for a picnic, that *iris reticulata* and *scilla* had sprung up in all the borders, and by all the paths the petals of crocuses had been torn and scattered by capricious hedge-sparrows. Everywhere one looked there was the promise of tulips. These were Sophie's bulbs, of all sorts and sizes, bought on impulse from supermarkets, ordered from specialist nurseries; even wild garlic and bluebells had been transferred (illegally) from an abandoned quarry near Broadway. It had been an addiction, like gambling or alcohol, but in a smaller figure; she had been unable to resist them, planting some every autumn in beds and borders, in the lawn and orchard, in the crevices of a wall, forgetting within weeks where she had put them, to be delighted every spring by their unexpected appearance or to fret over bare patches where mice or eel-worms had devoured her pretties.

Last year she had missed them, all but a few early snowdrops, by dying in January, and James had taken little notice of the bulbs, but now he welcomed them as messages from Sophie, each one a letter in a bottle which would reach its destination long after the sender had moved on.

Such messages are not private; they can be shared. James

and Pavel had discarded the system of two lessons a week, and said goodbye to the Portakabin. Instead Pavel would hitch-hike from Oxford every morning from Monday to Friday. He would spend an hour and a half reading aloud, with assistance, from a book or newspaper, then there would be a break for coffee and a mutual discussion, then Pavel would make a written précis of what he had read, adding his own comments to it. Then there would be lunch of soup or salad, after which he insisted on doing odd jobs about the house as a way of paying for the lessons, and in the evening James would drive him back to Oxford. James had thought at first, since Pavel was so quick to learn, that the scope of the lessons should be enlarged to include most of the items of a secondary school curriculum, but Pavel was already numerate and could use a calculator, while James himself did not feel confident in either Algebra or Geometry, far less in the sciences, for which there was no equipment anyway to conduct experiments. History, some Geography, Sociology and Literature would be picked up to a degree from the books they chose to read aloud, Current Affairs from the newspaper. "It's amazing," James said to Pavel, "how little of one's formal education is actually useful in later life," and Pavel replied, "Nothing's much use in itself. You have to make use of it."

As for the odd jobs, once one begins to look at a building critically one discovers that it requires almost continuous repair like the Forth Bridge. Plaster had cracked in walls and ceilings. The paintwork was grubby indoors, needing to be washed down here and repainted there, and on the exterior of the house it had weathered, allowing the rain to rot the wood around the windows, which had to be patched with filler and liberally coated with preservative before being repainted. On fine afternoons Pavel would be up a ladder; on wet he would be repainting or plastering the interior walls, and had plans to revarnish the floor of James's study with polyurethane. He was only with difficulty restrained from a slate-by-slate examination of the roof. For most of these afternoons James would be left to his

138

own devices, but sometimes he would hold a ladder or, if minor carpentry were in progress, pass a nail, though Pavel assured him that both operations were unnecessary, since ladders firmly based will not fall unless one jiggles about, and Pavel had trained his mouth to perform most of the functions of a left hand. "I do it for the company," James said, and Pavel said, "I hate a liar." It was odd that they were so easy with each other, and yet Pavel had never been able to bring himself to call James by his first name.

Although James had promised the uncle that he would ask Pavel to write to him, he had not done so yet, or mentioned his meeting with Borek at all. It was certainly within Pavel's capabilities these days to write a simple letter, in English if not in Czech; it seemed to James that Czech must be a language which even some Czechs would have difficulty in writing. James examined the reasons for his reluctance. It was true that, when he had tried to introduce the uncle into their conversation during the early days, that attempt had caused a storm of weeping, but such a storm was unlikely to recur; Pavel had been weeping for his father, not his uncle. It was true that Pavel had not spoken of the uncle since, which might indicate either a lack of curiosity or a disinclination to know more. Nevertheless Borek had been to trouble to make a contact with James, and that must have been on Pavel's account, and Pavel should know it, and make up his own mind whether to correspond or no. But there had been a seediness about Borek, an accident-prone quality as instanced by the incident of the cigarette-lighter; James's instinct was to keep Pavel away from that seediness.

An instinct of this sort, James knew, was not always to be trusted; it might arise from the baser part of one's nature, beyond the reach of reason and good-will. Reluctantly he confronted this baser part. Was there still in him as a residue from early childhood a submerged colonialism by which all foreigners, and particularly those who spoke a language far from English, were in some way inferior? He hoped not. Was his distrust of Borek in fact a concealed

139

possessiveness, was it that James wanted to keep Pavel to himself? Reluctantly James decided that this was possible; a teacher may be possessive of his pupil, particularly if there is only one; teaching may in such a case be a form of creation. Nevertheless he had not invented the seediness; Borek was seedy. But seediness may be merely a consequence of poverty; probably most hospital-orderlies are seedy. Yet Pavel was poor, and not seedy. Seediness may come of middle age, of having known better circumstances, of being pushed below one's capacities; it may come of despair, which is, when one thinks of it, in real life more often seedy than tragic. Borek was blood kin to Pavel, his father's only brother; it was up to Pavel, legally an adult and no kin at all to James, to decide whether he wished to embrace or reject his seedy uncle. There really was no good reason against James's telling Pavel about the meeting with Borek yet James continued to delay doing so, and the longer the delay, the more difficult it became to explain. Meanwhile he made a search for the family camera, found it in a pine chest in which Sophie had kept objects which would one day go for jumble but not yet, and took photographs of Pavel which he despatched to Borek with a letter saying how much he had enjoyed their meeting in Prague.

It was odd, now James thought of it, what Pavel chose to ignore – not only the incident in the Portakabin when James had told him he had an uncle, but he had never questioned the man Baker's presence at the house on Christmas Day or referred to the greeting Baker had addressed to him in Czech.

James had read the book Baker had given him. It seemed to be a plodding sort of book, not good or bad enough to be worth much attention, inelegantly translated, published in Czechoslovakia in 1967, in Milwaukee in 1984, a collection of essays on the general topic of the contribution of individualism within the framework of a collective society. There were analogies with painting and with music, the suggestion that what may seem at first to be at odds with the social order may, by a shift in perspective, be seen to be

140

an integral part of it, that human beings may approach the same end by different means, that only by the study of various forms of imperfection can one reach a real under-standing of what is perfect, and so on, and so on. The philosopher Borek was like a man in a blindfold, venturing cautiously but with some courage along a path which dozens of other people trod every day; it was hard to see why Baker should admire his work so highly. James had given Baker an account of the meeting in the Snack Bar, and added that he himself had decided not to return to Czechoslovakia, particularly if Borek were to be involved, since James's opinion was that almost the last activity a person hoping to be reclassified upwards in the labour-market ought to undertake would be the organisation of an illegal seminar, and Baker had replied, "As you wish, as you wish!" in a very breezy way.

"One is bound to speculate how he knew, first of my visit, secondly of my concern with Pavel."

"One doesn't need to speculate very far. It's obvious that I told him, or at least made sure that he was informed."

"Without consulting me?"

"The decision to make contact with you was his. Why trouble you, when he might have decided against making the attempt? Or been prevented from doing so."

"His interest did not seem to be in me, nor in my giving any kind of seminar to himself and his friends."

"Exactly. No point in spoiling your visit with the anxiety that you might be accosted by a dissident. Just going through Customs is hairy enough without fretting about the secret police. Anyway the British Council doesn't approve – have to keep your nose clean; official guest; they must have told you. Borek, as I said, might never have turned up. The time to worry was when he was sitting there, across the table."

"His principal interest, indeed his only interest, seemed to be in his nephew."

"Exactly."

"Why exactly?"

"It's always useful for a Czech national to have a blood-relation living in the West."

"In what way useful?"

"When he's an old-age pensioner, he might be allowed to visit. Did you enjoy the book?"

"The other point of speculation, I suppose, is how you yourself knew of my visit, since I never spoke of it, and went off at short notice."

"Oh, my dear James, these things get about. Between All Souls and the Athenaeum, one lives in the smallest of worlds." James did not believe that the man Baker was an *habitué* of either All Souls or the Athenaeum; he had his own obnoxiousness, which was not the obnoxiousness of either. Nevertheless it was true that the academic world is not large, and that its secrets are ill-kept; there was no point in speculating further.

Since his return he had revisited Fawley Woods twice, both times alone. He had been unable to sleep one night, and the idea of going back to look at the badgers had come after hours of wakefulness unalleviated even by the bubble. He had driven to the place where the track widened, and had sat in the car with the lights off to clear his night-vision, and had then discovered first that he could not enter the woods without making enough noise to alarm the wildlife of four counties, and secondly that he could not remember where the sett was, although he would recognise it if he came across it, because of the fallen tree. He had told Pavel of his failure, and Pavel had drawn a map from memory. "You don't want to bother too much about noise; you always think you're making more than you are. It's when you get there you have to be quiet. You sit downwind of the sett, get comfortable, and then don't move. You start to itch after a bit. She'll have had her cubs by now – if they're still there, that is; the whole family might have moved on."

So, on his next sleepless night, having drunk a cup of tea while committing the map to memory, James had returned to the woods, and found his way in what seemed to be the right direction, until challenged.

"Halt! Who goes there?"

Yes, there was the fallen tree. The voice came from some distance away and from what James assumed would be the downwind direction. "Friend."

"Advance, friend, and be recognised."

"It's James Elphinstone. How do you do?"

"They told me you might be along one of these nights." "They" would be the Badger Protection Commando, informed by Pavel; there seemed to be no secrets in that world either. "Come to have a look at Missus and the young 'uns?"

"If I may."

"There's room over here with me."

The old lady's camouflage merged into the dark. Only her face showed as a lighter blurr under the red beret. James joined her at a tree-stump from which one still had a good sight of the entrance to the sett. "Seen any more of our friends?"

"The wall-eyed bugger was around about a fortnight ago, walking on his own; he must be a local. I let him see me, and he gibbered a bit, and sloped off." She patted the tree-stump, and James sat beside her. "Quiet now! Two little mice, eh, or we'll see nothing." Almost at once James began to itch.

After two hours it had become clear to James that he was not made for badger-watching. His figure was too stringy for sitting on tree-stumps; it had become accustomed to leather armchairs, which support the back and do not abrade the arse. He had not thought it necessary in late April to put on thermal underwear when he dressed, but came now to believe that long-johns would not only have warmed his legs, but have provided an extra layer of insulation against the points and bumps of a weathered stump over which ivy has grown. Also he was a critic; it was not natural for him to observe any phenomenon without comment, and he found the imposed silence irksome.

The sow had emerged first from the sett, snuffling the air and making a small circle of exploration before defecating in what James knew, from Dr Neal's book, to be a spoil-pit, and then returning to the entrance to call her two cubs, two triangular faces, each with its white blaze, appearing in the entrance-hole one after the other, and then the two small bodies running to her, falling over themselves and whickering. "Twelve weeks," the camouflaged old lady whispered. "Lovely!" The sow cleaned their fur by licking, butting them with her head and holding them with a paw to turn them over and keep them still; she paid particular attention to their hinder parts. There was no sign of the boar; James supposed that he might be denning somewhere else. When the sow was satisfied with her cubs' cleanliness, she began to drag bedding into the sett, scraping together bundles of bluebell-foliage, clasping the bundles to her chest with her front legs, and backing into the entrance, while the two cubs ran about, squealing and getting in the way, or attempting to imitate her.

So it had gone. The sow did not tire of her work or the cubs of their game. It was enchanting to watch them; it was a revelation and a privilege. James tired. It was uncomfortable; it was cold; it was inconvenient to be stuck on an old tree-stump for bloody hours, unable to move or speak when one wanted to go home. The eyes of the old lady glowed, but the glow did not keep James warm. He shifted on the tree-stump, not for the first time, and wondered whether, if he were to be racked by coughing, the badgers would be alarmed and go back underground. One could not help a cough, or be blamed for it. A paroxysm of coughing would be natural in a man nearly seventy, huddled in damp woods an hour before dawn. He gulped in a preparatory way, and his Adam's apple slid smoothly up and down his throat as if it had been greased as a preventative against coughing. The old lady by his side pitched suddenly forwards among the dead leaves, the bracken and the bluebells. There was a large animal, James saw, on top of her, a full-grown badger which had attacked her from behind. Once again, as in the Snack Bar when the woman's hair flared up, James was afflicted by paralysis.

144

All the grease on his Adam's apple had gone, leaving his throat dry, and all that came out when he shouted at the animal, was a croak, which had no effect on it whatever. The badger had rolled the old lady on her back, and was about to disembowel her. James stretched out his arms to push the badger off her, and felt fur under his palms. Let it turn and rend him; he was ready. The badger took no notice. The old lady seemed to be in hysterics, laughing and giggling and hitting at the badger with clenched fists. Its snout was already grubbing inside her camouflage-jacket. She rolled away from him, but already in the badger's mouth James could see – oh God! not a breast surely? no, it was an apple. The old lady struggled to her feet. The sow and her cubs had already bolted down the entrance to the sett, no doubt anticipating dinner. "Bloody George!" the old lady said. "Always does that. Can't wait. You haven't got a sandwich on you, I suppose?" She sat on the stump again, and George put his head on her knee, and whined, the apple already gone. She felt in a pocket, found another apple, and gave it to him, and George in return vented a strong-smelling liquid from his anus onto James trouser-legs. "Musked you," the old lady said. "Good sign. He likes you."

James said, "Yes, I've read about musking. Very flatter-ing." He wondered how easy the stuff would be to wash off.

"Look, you're not used to this; you must be knackered. Why don't you get off home while there's a break in the action?"

"Thank you. I will. It's been extraordinarily interesting."

"Coming again?"

"Not for a while, I think. But I've no doubt we'll meet."

"Hope so."

James drove home carefully, and went to bed. Since he neglected to set the alarm, he overslept, and was wakened by Pavel at ten o'clock with a pot of tea.

"No doubt you've already been informed where I was last night?"

"No. Haven't got the phone, remember." Pavel looked at James's trousers, lying over the back of a chair, and sniffed. "I can guess, though."

The boar, sow and cubs were taken in early May. The telephone rang at seven in the morning. "It's Amelia Walton-Brown. We met in Fawley Woods. Sorry to wake you. Emergency. Pavel not there yet, I suppose?"

"He doesn't usually get here until nine-thirty."

"I'd wait, but I've got to get to hospital. Wrist's swollen up. Bright red, puffy, and hurts like hell. Broken a bone, must have. Can't drive myself, stands to reason, so I've phoned for an ambulance. They were a bit reluctant, I can tell you, but there's no time to lose."

"I'm sorry. An accident?" She lived, James deduced, somewhere isolated, or was at odds with her neighbours. Did she expect him to drive her himself? No, for she had already arranged for an ambulance.

"Buggers knocked me over, kicked me about a bit, and hit me with the butt of the gun – trying to cover my face at the time. Lucky they didn't use the spade or I'd've lost a hand. Tried to stop them; couldn't. Rolled down the bank. They didn't bother with me after that. Lay there listening. Heard everything. Shit!" Her voice thickened. She had wept, James thought, and would weep again. "Useless old woman, that's the trouble. Taken the lot, all four. If I give you a couple of phone numbers, can we meet at your house? Wouldn't ask, but it's urgent; got to move quickly. Bloody fond of old George, you know, him and Martha, made friends, always a mistake. Want to save them if we can."

"Of course."

She gave him three telephone numbers, all of people living in villages south of Oxford. "Breaking security," she said. "Can't be helped, know you're sympathetic. Won't all be able to come, but we need an action group bloody pronto. Lucky young Pavel's unemployed. Christ, this wrist hurts! If I get stuck at the hospital or the ambulance is

146

late, start without me."

"Do you want me to phone the RSPCA as well? Don't they have inspectors to deal with this kind of thing?"

"Option to be discussed. Thank God! there's the bell. Could be the postman, but I don't get letters as a general rule. Don't forget to phone the comrades. Counting on you."

How could they start without her when only she knew the details of what had happened? He remembered Pavel's remark at the burning of the van, "I know those men." She had lain there in the dark, helpless, and heard the men and the dogs, the roaring of the boar as he tried to defend his family, the whimpering of the youngsters. Once discovered, since they were required alive, they would have been caught in nets, and dragged through the woods to the van. Perhaps the cubs had been clubbed to death or killed by the dogs to save trouble, since they were too young to make sport. The old lady would have heard all of that, lying among damp leaves. James dialled the first of the three numbers he had been given. *I know those men.* If Pavel knew who they were, he would know where they lived, and consequently where the badgers would have been taken. A young voice answered. James said, "Hullo! Is Felicia Bartlett at home?" and the young voice answered. "I'm Felicia. Who wants her?"

There was no reading aloud that morning, and no précis. The old lady arrived first. She had been in Casualty only long enough to have her wrist X-rayed and set in plaster, and had then, since she could not afford a taxi, persuaded the ambulance-driver to bring her straight to Little Easely. It was perhaps easier for the old lady to persuade such people to assist her than it would have been for most other ladies of her age, since she was a Lady as well as old; her poor old fellow, Sir Redvers Walton-Brown, had been knighted for services to public works in Africa, but after an economic crisis and two revolutions his ex-employers there had defaulted on his pension, which was why he had left her so ill-provided.

147

Then Pavel arrived, and very soon afterwards Greg and Felicia on the same moped; the third telephonee, Dave, worked in a garage part-time, and had not been able to get away. Felicia turned out to be older than she had sounded on the telephone, perhaps in her late twenties. She had the clear eyes, clear skin, the curly short hair and straight-forward boyish manner of an Ian Hay heroine, but the time of such heroines had gone by; to be a good sort was no longer enough, and Felicia had begun to know as much. She had worked in a second-hand bookshop, organised car boot sales of unwanted objects for Amnesty International, studied Physiotherapy and Bio-feedback at evening classes, and now travelled the villages of South Oxfordshire in a van, trying to sell macrobiotic wholegrains and pulses to villagers who preferred sliced white bread and reconstituted fish-fingers. So much energy, so much good-will, and most of it wasted! Felicia was like a bomb waiting to go off, but the priming mechanism had begun to rust.

As for Greg, he was clearly a creature of the nineteen-sixties; there are many like him still to be found in country districts where the people are not fashion's slaves. He had a full beard and moustache, both beginning to grey, and his hair was tied back with a bootlace into a pony-tail. Round his neck was a cheap brass chain from which depended a kabbalistic medal in iron, which had either been painted or was showing signs of rust. Greg's whole appearance was an affirmation, a living label which read, "I am faithful. I may age, but do not change." He and his wife kept a village sub-post-office and general shop, which is to say that she kept it, and he dragged in the heavier bags and boxes, and sometimes served behind the counter. Bustling about making cocoa and looking for biscuits to put on a plate, James said to himself, "Do not scorn this Greg – Does not James Elphinstone still wear for choice the corduroy trousers, crew-necked sweaters and open-necked shirts which were the fashion when he was a young don?" Greg and Felicia were two of the people slightingly described by the man

148

Baker as dotty but not dangerous, but they had come when called, and would put themselves at risk.

The five of them sat around the kitchen table, and discussed what to do. They had one advantage; they knew the enemy. Although the men had again worn balaclavas, in which even a wall-eye may pass unnoticed, there was no doubt that these were the men of Christmas Night. Three men with a lurcher and a Jack Russell, they had warned the old lady off, but she would not be warned. They had expected to find her at the sett, and had dealt with her. One of them had even told her as he kicked her that it served her right for not taking a warning. Both Pavel and Greg knew who the men were, or at least who their leader was; he used various helpers. He was Jimmy Tuttleby, said to be a gypsy from Yorkshire; he owned a scrap-yard and the caravan-site next to it, and traded in horses which he kept in a field at the back. He was known to the police and the RSPCA, the registration numbers of cars and vans seen in suspicious circumstances had been tracd to his yard, but there was no proof. The people who lived on the caravan-site must have seen enough to convict him, but dared not inform; Tuttleby was a dangerous man, held in fear by most of those who knew him.

"There's no deterrent, you see," Greg said to James. "You can't expect people to inform. Even if he was prosecuted and convicted, he'd only be fined, usually less than he could make by trapping another badger. He'd pay up, walk free, and beat the informer to pulp the day after. It's what nobody takes account of; you've got to go on living with such a man; it's not like a story you see on the television, with end credits and the adverts after. In Redditch where I used to live, I know people as have seen a badger dismembered in their neighbour's back garden. They had to keep the kids indoors, and close the curtains, but they still wouldn't go to the police."

The old lady would talk; she feared nothing. But she could not make a positive identification. She had tried to pull away the balaclava from the face of one of the men; that

149

she had failed probably accounted for her being still alive. Even if she were to lie, the only member of the gang she could describe from personal knowledge would be the wall-eyed man, who might not have been with them, and by producing an alibi would discredit her for ever with the police and RSPCA. In any case the wall-eyed man was only a hanger-on, a bully-boy; the badgers would not be at his premises. Only Tuttleby would do, and the old lady had never seen Tuttleby plain; it would be asking for trouble to describe him from notes supplied by Pavel and Greg. Yet, if the police were to obtain a warrant to search Tuttleby's premises, it would have to be on positive identification; mere supposition would not do.

"It's a non-starter, the police option," Greg said. "It always is, in my opinion." If the badgers were to be rescued, only the Commando could attempt it, and the attempt must be soon.

Tuttleby lived on a straight road, the Fairmile, between two villages south of Oxford. His house was at the half-mile point, the scrap-yard next to it; more scrap had overflowed onto what had once been a garden behind the house, at the end of which was a long wooden shed with two doors, therefore probably partitioned into two rooms. The shed had a concrete floor, Pavel thought, but the wooden walls could not confine a badger if it wished to leave. Therefore, if the badgers were in the shed, they must be in metal cages like those in the van which had been burned in the wood. The cages would not have burned, James supposed. Probably the men had returned by daylight and carried them away.

Rescuers would need a crowbar for the doors of the shed, a hammer and cold chisel for the padlocks of the cages. No problem! The absent Dave would be able to supply them from the garage where he worked. The problem would be to get the doors open and the padlocks broken without being discovered. Once again there was a police option. If one knew for certain that the badgers were in the shed, that would be grounds for a search-warrant; once the badgers

150

had been located, a watch could be kept until the police arrived. This was the common-sense option and almost legal, since it only involved breaking open the shed doors, which would easily be forgiven. It was not seriously considered by the action group, already in love with rescue.

None of the five was an expert with the cold chisel. How long would it actually take to break the padlocks? Felicia telephoned Dave at the garage, and he confirmed that he could supply the equipment and would come himself to deal with the padlocks. The whole operation might be completed in five minutes, even if both doors had to be broken open, provided that the badgers themselves were co-operative and had no objection to finding their own way home. Greg and Felicia would have to reconnoitre the ground that afternoon; the rescue would take place after dark. Should it be left until three in the morning, when the occupants of the house would be asleep? No, because the dogs would be out. Better to choose a time when the Tuttlebys would be watching television, and the dogs might be indoors. Between eight and eleven p.m. one might reasonably expect violence on at least one television channel with a decent quotient of shots, screams and the scrunch of broken bones to mask any noise from the shed, and if there were violence to watch, Tuttleby would be watching it. Greg consulted the newspaper. There was violence on both the major channels that night, and a comedy programme which would include much pre-recorded laughter and applause. Nevertheless they would require a diversion.

So it was that James parked the Volvo some fifty yards from Tuttleby's house that evening, walked to the front door, and rang the bell. He was in no danger; Pavel had insisted that he should not be, and he was not. James and Tuttleby had never met, and James did not live in the area; it was remotely possible that Tuttleby might remember the Volvo, but that was why it had been parked at a distance. It was Pavel and the others who were in danger, James who must avert it. He was a motorist whose car had broken down; he could not discover what was wrong; the engine had cut out, and would not start; he would be extremely grateful if he might use the phone to get help from the AA, and would gladly pay for the call. In this way, it was hoped, James would distract the attention of the Tuttleby family and their dogs. He was wearing the trousers which George had musked, and which had not been cleaned since, because Pavel had told him that he might wish to return to the sett one night, and it would be reassuring for George to know that James was already a friend. If it were possible for James, in the course of phoning or asking permission to phone, to bring those trousers into the proximity of the Jack Russell, they would interest the dog far more than the distant presence of strangers with a crow-bar at the back of the yard.

James heard with satisfaction from inside the house the sound of shots and a police siren. Both dogs set up a barking as the bell rang. The door was opened by a young man of about Pavel's age, but more sturdy and surly.

"I'm terribly sorry to disturb you. I'm afraid my car seems to have broken down."

"It's a scrap-yard, not a garage."

"I saw your light. I was wondering if you'd be kind enough to let me use your telephone."

"Phone-box in the village."

"How far is the village?"

" 'Bout half a mile."

It had not been contemplated that the Tuttlebys might refuse to allow their telephone to be used. Thus do liberal and well-intentioned persons deceive themselves by their assumption that others will have the same generous and reasonable reactions. If James were not allowed to use the telephone, the whole plan of rescue would go awry. Some-how he must contrive to spin out the process of refusal. He must argue, cajole, perhaps be taken suddenly ill. "I'm afraid I'm not supposed to walk long distances," he said. "Especially uphill."

"It's all on the flat."

152

From the front room, a shout. "What is it?"

"Somebody wants to use the phone."

"We're watching television." Both dogs were still barking, one from the front room with the family, the other by the sound of it on a chain outside the back door.

"Says he's not allowed to walk."

"It's a free country. Every bugger's allowed to walk." The door of the front room was opened, and the Jack Russell emerged like the Hound of the Baskervilles but considerably smaller, and attacked James's trousers. The young man pulled it away, and held it by the skin at the back of its neck, still snarling and struggling. A middle-aged man stood at the door of the front room. This would be the infamous Tuttleby. He wore a knitted cardigan over an open-necked shirt, and was running to fat, an ordinary man, home-loving, television-watching; it was hard for James to associate him with what had happened at the sett.

The Jack Russell was still attempting to reach James's trouser-leg, and there was the steady thump of the lurcher, at the full extent of its chain, against the back door. James said, "We have a bitch of our own. That would be the attraction. I'm afraid she's on heat," and heard himself adding totally unnecessary details, "A Sealyham. Her name is Mrs Fingers."

"Okay. The phone's in here. What's the number?"

"I'm afraid I'd have to find it." "I'm afraid" seemed to be the key words in James's dialogue for this scene. But he was not afraid, not for himself. "I'm afraid they don't put the phone number on the AA card any more. There's a twenty-four-hour service in Oxford."

"Book's under the phone." And the phone was on a small table just inside the door of the front room. The man sat in an armchair facing the television; a woman and a small girl were sharing the sofa. Nobody turned down the sound, or even offered to do so, which was, of course, all to the good. James picked up the telephone directory, and the Jack Russell broke free and went for his trousers again. James dropped the directory. "Find him the number, and

153

shut that bloody dog in the kitchen."

On the television a police car containing the crooked sheriff, who had for reasons not immediately apparent been handcuffed to its steering wheel, plunged into a canyon, bounced off several rocks, and burst into flames. The sheriff managed to get the gag out of his mouth just in time to let out several piercing screams before being incinerated. Everything was with the conspirators tonight.

James was told the number of the Automobile Association in Oxford, and managed to misdial one digit without the young man's noticing. The dog was taken to the kitchen as the telephone was answered.

"Hullo? Is that the AA?"

'What?''

"I am a member. My car has broken down. I'll give you my membership number." James hoped that no one in the room would notice that he was not giving his name. He had decided that a certain degree of efficiency would add variety, and so conviction, to his performance, and had the plastic card ready. "33FY 0057 6103 MFX. The card expires at the end of December, 1988."

"Who do you want to speak to?"

"I'm not quite sure; it's a minor road. Silly of me! I'll ask the people here." The young man had returned from the kitchen, whence the Jack Russell could be heard complaining in a highly satisfactory manner, and James asked him, "Where am I? They want to know."

"Tuttleby's Yard."

"Do you happen to know the number of the road? I came through a village some way back, but I'm afraid I didn't notice what it was called."

"Amford."

"Hamford?"

"Am. Ford. Next one along's Graceham. Grace. Ham. You're 'alf-way between."

"I don't know what he's talking about. I think he must have the wrong number." James could hear the faint voice of a man at the other end saying to the woman who had

154

answered. "Put the phone down, then," and the woman reply, "What if it's something to do with Auntie Bea? They won't phone again if we hang up."

James said, "They want to know which way I'm facing," and the man in the cardigan said, without shifting his gaze from the television screen, "What does it matter which way you're facing? There's no other bloody cars broken down on this bloody road."

"Of course. You're right." The woman at the other end said, "Is it something to do with Mrs Beatrice Whetstone?" James said, "I think I may be facing towards Graceham, but in any case there aren't any other cars on the road. A silver Volvo." Had he said too much? Had he seen the back of the man's neck stiffen in the armchair? A foolish anxiety! Oxfordshire was full of Volvos, and Bedfordshire also, most of them silver. "I'll wait in the car, then, shall I?"

"You've got the wrong number."

Both telephones were put down simultaneously. James could not have managed it better if he had written the scene himself. He said, "Thank you very much. Please let me pay you for the call."

"You can give the lad a quid."

It was a mark-up of a thousand per cent, and James paid it gladly. "Please don't see me out. I can find my own way." The surly young man accompanied him to the door. "You've been so kind. I can't tell you how grateful I am." Both dogs were still barking as the door was shut in his face. James felt the glow of pleasure only to be obtained by a job well done, which lasted until he was joined back at the car by Pavel and the old lady, and informed that no badgers had been found in the shed.

Dave had returned to his village. He was a member of the Voluntary Fire Service, and there was a practice that evening. Greg and Felicia were waiting in Felicia's van, emptied of macrobiotic wholegrains so as to be available for badgers if any of them needed transporting, and parked further down the road in the opposite direction.

"What do we do? Go home?" The feeling of anti-climax

155

which follows a performance played at full stretch had combined with the disappointment to make James feel sick, literally so; he hoped he would not vomit.

"Pavel doesn't want to."

"They've got to be here somewhere."

"In the house, you think?"

"The dogs wouldn't stand for it."

The scrap-yard was full of abandoned automobiles, broken and rusting; they would not be secure to keep an animal. And the caravan-site was hardly . . . "I suppose," James said, "that all those caravans are occupied?"

"Oh, yes," the old lady said. "Of course. Yes."

"Dave's took the crow-bar."

"Taken!" The old lady was looking at him, surprised. Pavel's head was turned away. He had never spoken sharply to the boy before. "I'm sorry," he said. "Nerves. Please forgive me. There's probably a spanner or wrench or something in the tool-kit of the car. Who lives in the caravans?"

"Nobody special. People who haven't got anywhere else to live. It's not holiday homes."

"I was wondering whether any of Mr Tuttleby's own people lived there. Greg said there was a gypsy connection."

"Dunno."

"Well, we should proceed cautiously in any case?" Had James assumed command? Had Pavel, in the presence of outsiders and after having been publicly reproved, relinquished command to his teacher? There seemed to be a vacuum, and James had filled it. They took a spanner and a large screw-driver from the tool-kit of the car and a rubber torch from the back seat, and went to join Greg and Felicia. Two Senior Citizens (one with a broken wrist), an Ian Hay heroine, a faded Flower Child and a boy with only one hand, they were not a force to deter gypsies.

The caravan-site was separated from the house by the full width of the scrap-yard; they would not be likely to arouse the dogs, though some of the caravan-dwellers might have

156

dogs. A string of coloured lights had been hung above the entrance to the site, either as identification or invitation, but most of the bulbs had burned out and had not been replaced. "I don't think we should use the torch until we have to," James said, so Pavel and the old lady, who had the keenest night-vision, led the way, and Greg, who had discovered that he was almost blind in the dark, came last holding onto Felicia's hand. It did not occur to Greg or to any of the *force de frappe* that he might have been better left in the road; they had entered upon this adventure together, and would stay together until it was concluded.

The caravans had been set up in staggered rows of six and five. Some had small gardens, and most had dustbins, and all, of course, had steps at the side, which had to be avoided. One could tell which were occupied by their lighted windows. The badgers would not be confined in any of those, or in any of those unlighted which were near the entrance. The rescue-party went through the first row, then right and left and through the second, left and right, and found a clothes-line strung between two caravans, which caught Pavel across the throat and brought a gasp from the old lady. They went through two more rows, and came to a patch of slippery concrete. "Stand-pipe!" the old lady said. Greg was helped to negotiate the concrete, as he had been helped under the clothes-line, stubbed the toe of a trainer on the rim, and moaned softly; Greg's image of Greg had taken a beating this evening. They went through another row of caravans, all dark, and blundered into a post-and-wire fence which had eluded even Pavel's night-vision. Something snorted in the darkness, waved a monstrous head, and ran from them. Felicia put her arm round Greg's shoulders to calm him.

"What? What?"

"Horse."

They were at the end of the site. The row of five dark caravans was between them and the stand-pipe, beyond which was a row of six, four of them lighted. If the badgers had been hidden in a caravan, it would be in one of these

157

five. Which? The oldest and most dilapidated probably, but in the darkness one could not tell which that would be; even the lighted caravans had not seemed new. Pavel mounted the steps of the nearest van, and tried the door. It was locked, but all the doors would be locked against transient squatters. Could they break open five doors without being discovered? The nearest of the lighted caravans was not fifteen yards away. As if to underline the danger, the door of that caravan now opened, and a man could be seen standing in the doorway, the light behind him, pissing on the steps. He would have no night-vision at all; he would not be able to see the rescue-party, provided that it kept quiet and did not move, nevertheless . . . The man spat, and went back inside. Pavel said, "I'd better try. I'll be as quiet as I can. Have you got the screw-driver?"

"Wait." The old lady raised her head, loosened the muscles of her neck with both hands, gulped air, and began to scream. Greg said, "She's gone mad," and again Felicia held him to calm him. The sound was horrible, not human. James had heard it before, though only at a distance. Lying in bed at night, he had heard that screaming from beyond the orchard, and had thought it to be the cry of some animal caught in a trap. Greg began to moan again, "Jesus! Jesus!" Already in his mind's eye he saw the gypsies grasping staves and shot-guns, and when his friends ran from them, as they would have to do, Greg would be left, blind and stumbling among the concrete and the clothes-lines, to be kicked and clubbed. The old lady stopped screaming. "Listen!"

Nothing. Then a sound at some distance, not an answering scream, nothing one could put a name to, only a sound. The old lady moved swiftly towards it, as one possessed. The sound came again; it was from the caravan furthest from them, at the other edge of the site. The old lady made a series of four harsh croaking sounds, then repeated them. Again the sound from within the caravan was not similar; it was more like a human being sobbing. The old lady began to whimper; James had heard George make that sound

158

when asking for a second apple. "Here!" the old lady said.

It would be the oldest of the caravans on the site, the one no longer habitable even by the poorest and most desperate of Mr Tuttleby's tenants. The steps were broken and slippery; the door gave easily to the screw-driver. "I'll go in," the old lady said. "They know me." She touched James on the shoulder. "You come with me. He musked you." James had half-expected the four badgers to rush out when the door was opened, but of course they would be caged. The old lady said to Pavel, "Close the door behind us; we'll have to use the torch. Wait out here with Greg and Felicia. Try to keep Greg quiet. We'll call if we need you. They mustn't be frightened."

Then James was inside with the old lady, and the door closed behind them. There was a strong stench in the caravan, a badger stench and something else. The sound had ceased when the door was opened, but something was moving at the far end. The old lady shone the torch towards the movement, and they saw the blaze, white on black, and the grey body. The old lady began to make a purring sound, but desisted almost at once, as George backed away as far as the cage would allow, whimpering. "He's frightened. Don't be frightened of me, old chap. Where are the others?"

The others were not frightened; they were not encaged. The others lay on the floor, higgledy-piggledy in their own blood, the sow and her two cubs; their throats had been slit, preparatory to skinning them. James was glad that they had not yet been skinned. George's throat had not been slit, because he was the most valuable of the four. Much money would be won and lost on the length of time it took the dogs to kill George slowly in a pit. But all four badgers had been taken, because there was a value even to the cubs; their pelts were valuable.

"What a piece of work is a man! How noble in reason! How infinite in faculty! In action, how like an angel! In apprehension how like a god!" "Can you break the padlock?" the old lady said.

159

"I'll have to get Pavel."

A screw-driver and a spanner were not as effective as a hammer and cold chisel would have been, but they managed because they had to manage; the old lady would not have left George; she would have faced Tuttleby and all his crew, and died so. She remained by the cage as they worked, crooning, "Poor old fellow! Poor old fellow!" to the frightened badger until the padlock was broken. Then she said, "Keep away. We can't know what he'll do," and, when she had been obeyed, gently opened the door, whimpering and purring, to let George out.

Perhaps he would not come; perhaps he was too frightened. He could smell the blood; he had seen what happened; he would be in shock. They waited, and he began to move forward. The old lady had switched off the torch so as to reassure him. "Open the door, and stay outside. We need the light," she said to Pavel. She and James stepped aside to give George a clear path to the door, but as their night-vision adjusted, assisted by the light from the open door, they could see that George could move only with difficulty, because the men had broken a back leg. He would need help to get away, provided he would accept it.

The old lady said to James, "Let him smell your trousers. He has to know we're all friends." Very cautiously, James put a trouser-leg forwards, and George butted it aside, but not, as far as one could tell, with any hostility. The old lady sat on the floor among the blood and the mess, and George moved with difficulty towards her. She scratched the back of his head. "Poor old fellow! Get as far as the door, and we'll take you the rest of the way. You're not so old really, are you? You're not heavy yet, not twenty kilos yet; you've still got some fattening up to do after the winter." She began to move backwards on her rump towards the door. Twenty kilos seemed heavy to James, far too heavy for either himself or the old lady to carry, even if her wrist were not in plaster, and it seemed unlikely that George would allow anyone else to carry him. George was following the old lady, dragging himself through the dirt and blood.

160

"Walk with him. Come on, old fellow; do your best. I wish we'd brought some apples."

In this way they proceeded very slowly to the door of the caravan, James moving beside George, not knowing whether he was doing any good or no. The old lady crooned, whimpered, kept up a gentle encouragement of noise, and somehow George moved himself towards her. When she had reached the open door, she moved down a step, so as to bring her body below the level of the floor, and opened the front of her camouflage jacket, still purring. "Hold me," she said. "Don't let me fall down the steps." Pavel and Felicia held her, and George, all eighteen kilos of him, crawled inside the camouflage jacket, and the old lady fastened it over him. "Now," she said, "I'm afraid you'll have to carry me. Go as slowly as you like, but try not to fall over."

They carried the old lady horizontally, face upwards, on their shoulders. James and Pavel, who were much of a height and had the better night-vision, walked in front supporting her rump and her lower back; her legs dangled down before them, the feet bouncing off James's raglan overcoat and Pavel's donkey-jacket. Felicia and Greg put their own shoulders below hers, and linked arms to support her head, while the old lady used her own arms to keep George from sliding off her chest. She could not be put down before they reached the van, because there would be no way of getting her up again. They wished that, before lifting her, they had thought of bringing the van to the entrance of the site, but they had not done so, and must endure the longer portage. They remembered the locations of the stand-pipe and the clothes-line, and took a route to avoid them. Once Greg stumbled, and his breathing became laboured; too much home-brewed beer, too many hand-rolled cigarettes had affected his puff, and he and Felicia were shorter and were carrying the heavier end. Yet he endured.

They reached the van, and managed to open the back doors without spilling their burden. Lowering the old lady

161

to the level of the floor was a problem in logistics, but their fatigue allowed them no time to solve it, and in the end it solved itself by a process of general collapse in which luckily she ended on top. "I'll stay in the back with George," she said. "We'd better take him to my place. He won't be fit for the woods yet."

James heard himself saying, "I have a cellar if he prefers to live underground."

"And a camp-bed?"

"Will he need a camp-bed?"

"I'll need a camp-bed."

"I have a camp-bed."

"Right. Good show. He will need *some* bedding, of course." James glanced at his wrist-watch. It seemed a little late to go out and collect the foliage of bluebells. "Sacking or straw will do. And we'll want something to make a splint."

"Are you sure you'll be all right in there? Wouldn't you be more comfortable in my car?" She had been through more than any of them, and must now travel over twenty miles with her wrist in plaster, lying on the floor of the van in the dark with a wounded animal. "It's a bumpy journey. You may have trouble with your wrist. Pavel could stay with George if you're worried."

"Doesn't know him. Poor old fellow doesn't know what's happening. Needs reassurance. Don't worry about me. Elated. Famous victory." She began to giggle. "Home, James, and don't spare the horse-power. I hope you're not a teetotaller. I'll need something more than cocoa when we get home." It was not quite a victory, of course, not with the sow and the two cubs murdered. That would hit her later.

James said to Felicia, "I'll go on in front. You follow." As he and Pavel walked back to the Volvo they saw by the light of the few remaining coloured bulbs that there were two children standing at the entrance to the caravan-site watching them, a boy of about twelve years old, a girl a little younger identically dressed in jeans and padded wind-cheaters, both dark-haired and of a swarthy complexion. James and Pavel approached until they were almost level

162

with the children, and then stopped. The two sides looked at each other in silence, like opposing armies before a battle. How much had the children seen? Could their silence be bought? Probably not; they would take the money, then tell, but one had better try, since the Volvo would have to pass them, and they would be able to read the registration number. James took a step towards the children, and they turned and ran back into the darkness of the site.

James found in the freezer a carton of spaghetti-sauce Sophie had made two years earlier, and it was heated and eaten with fettucine which must also have been two years old, and all the apples in the house were eaten, and all the cheese, and three bottles of Rioja drunk. George was given warm milk with soluble aspirin dissolved in it, and the old lady made a splint for his broken leg from a piece of firewood and a cotton vest torn into strips, and he was bedded down on sacks in the cellar with James's trousers to make it seem more like home, and a camp-bed was made up for the old lady to sleep by him, since she resolutely refused the comforts of the spare room. James told of his adventures at the Tuttleby residence, and somehow they became hilarious in the telling. "And then I dropped," he said, "I dropped . . . the directory . . ." and could not continue for laughing, and they all laughed, spluttering the crumbs of wholemeal bread and cheese; the old lady wept with laughter. Later there were tears of another sort as Greg, being far gone in wine, mourned the passing of the Age of Aquarius, when his mind and that of his wife Jinny had first been blown at a pop festival in Windsor Great Park, and everything had seemed possible. Now it had all drained away, all the ease and comradeship of that lovely Age, leaving Greg and Jinny beached like whales in a sub-post-office in Oxfordshire. James wanted to say that this was not peculiar to the Age of Aquarius, but a characteristic of all Ages, and was itself called age, but with a discretion unusual to him kept this insight to himself, and allowed

163

Greg to enjoy his grieving and to be hugged by Felicia, and then by the old lady, and to have his upper arm gripped by Pavel, after which James gripped Greg's other arm, and the Age of Aquarius was momentarily recreated in the kitchen of the Manor at Little Easely. Neither James nor Pavel mentioned the two children at the entrance to the caravan-site.

Lying in bed he thought how Sophie would have enjoyed the evening, not the slaughter in the caravan, of course, but the good-fellowship afterwards. He wondered whether, during their last years together, he had deprived her of company she might have relished, selfishly assuming that she found his own society sufficient, as he found hers. He had retreated from what was, in his own terms, failure, and had taken her into the fortress with him, and never considered that she might have found it confining. Lying in bed he wished that she could have been with him at the Tuttleby residence, and praised him afterwards.

Next day the vet was summoned and came, cocked his head on one side, raised one eyebrow, lowered one corner of his mouth, cleaned the wound, renewed the splint and bandage, and prescribed a course of antibiotics against infection, one a day to be given in food. James said to the old lady, "What do badgers eat?" and she replied, "What have you got in your dustbin? He's particularly fond of potato-peelings."

In fact the dustbin of an elderly gentleman living alone is not rich in food for badgers, even for a badger off his grub, as George was at first. The antibiotic spansules were pushed singly into grapes, and he made no difficulty about taking them, but hardly touched the dish of worms which James had spent two hours in digging from the garden. The old lady continued to spend her nights and much of the days in the cellar, talking to George or simply sitting by him with one hand resting on the top of his head. "I don't like doing it," she said. "He's got to learn to distrust humans. But it's the only way for a while." Tucked away in the cellar,

164

she did not interrupt the lessons, but would join James and Pavel for lunch, and then, encouraged, would speak of her observations in Fawley Woods since the death of her poor old fellow, and of the old days in Africa when, being childless, she would accompany him on the survey and actual making of roads. "Never out of each other's pockets. Married bliss in a tent, bloody embarrassing; of course the native boys used to listen. Never experienced an orgasm until I was thirty-five, and then broke the mosquito net. Pardon my French. Surprise to us both."

On the third day George recovered his appetite. More potatoes were peeled than James and the old lady could consume. She re-stocked the freezer with shepherd's pies, and Pavel went home in the evenings with foil dishes of hot-pot he had no way of heating up. Slugs and snails were gathered from the garden, the cheapest of sausages brought from the village shop, and rotting fruit cadged from the greengrocer in Chipping Norton. George throve, and grew restless. The vet returned, and removed the splint. On the evening of the tenth day, watched from front gardens by village children and from behind curtains by their parents, George was enticed into the back seat of the Volvo, and driven to Fawley Woods. They followed the track to its end at an abandoned farm, made sure that there was nobody about, and put him out.

They stood by the car, three humans and a badger. George lifted his snout, and moved it in the air, then lowered his head and trotted a few paces up the track. The humans remained very still, watching him. He stopped, and looked back at them. "Go on, you fool," the old lady said.

"Go on, George."

Pavel said, "I feel a bit choked."

"I suppose we'll miss him."

The old lady's voice hardened. "Get on! Move! Go!" She mimed throwing a stone. "Hate humans, you hear me? Hate them!" George trotted on up the track, then went sideways into the woods. "If he's got any sense, he'll get

165

out of here altogether. I'll stay out of the way for a while anyhow."

"Can we give you a lift home?"

"Rather walk. Better on my own for a bit. Liable to blub, not a pretty sight." She shook James's hand, kissed Pavel on the cheek, and walked away past the ruins of the farm. Unlike George, she did not look back.

"We still have things of hers at the house."

"She'll let you know when she wants them. Is it all right if I stop over?"

Consequently Pavel was actually in the house that evening when the telephone rang, and Father Doubrava from the Czech Catholic Hostel in Notting Hill Gate informed James that a Mr Pavel Borek had arrived in London and had given James's name as a sponsor.

7

WORMALD

James said, "I'm afraid I have to go to London tomorrow, so we shan't be able to work. Shall I drop you off at Oxford on my way, or would you rather stay here all day?"

"Is anything wrong? You look a bit funny. Is it about your son?"

"No. Nothing about Richard. I have to see somebody. It's rather unexpected." It did not seem to James either necessary or wise to tell Pavel yet about Borek's arrival. First James must find out what all this was about, then decide what to do about it, then, if his decision were to consult, he would consult. *"The trouble with you, Jimmy, is that you won't enter any situation you can't control."* Well, at the age of sixty-eight, though he had achieved some degree of self-awareness, he was unlikely to respond to it by any essential change. Nor did it seem to James that he had any choice about entering this particular situation, inasmuch as he had already entered it, for in fact Sophie was wrong to this extent, that the most important and demanding situations in one's life cannot properly be likened to the mere breaking of plates in a Greek taverna, since the moment of entry is seldom clear except by hindsight, and the entry itself will change the situation and the nature and extent of its demands upon oneself.

Pavel was watching him, and with some concern. James supposed that he had been making faces again. James's face did move to match his thoughts; this was not a failing of old age, but had always been so. During his first year at

Oxford, in the Trinity term of 1939, he had cycled with friends to the theatre in Stratford-upon-Avon to Shakespeare's *King John*, and cycled back by moonlight. *Be thou as lightning in the eyes of France!* His face had been working so under the gibbous moon that a motor-cyclist, coming the other way, had run into the ditch. "Gibbous", an archaic word. James said, "I'll be back by the evening. You could try reading to yourself, if you like. Not aloud: in your head. See whether you can keep the sense of it, or whether you just go to sleep."

Next morning he drove to London, found a parking-place with considerable difficulty in the Holland Park area, and walked about a mile to the Hostel, which was smaller than he had expected, a narrow building of three floors and a basement, with the windows at the front all bricked up.

There was a blank double-door with brass knobs and a brass letter-box, all recently polished. To the right of the door was a single bell which, when pressed, brought no response. Was it out of order? Had it sounded within the house? James pressed it again, and listened, but could not tell. To the left of the door there was a panel of twelve bells, set one above the other like the bells of a rooming-house. Well, the place was a hostel, but surely its occupants must be transient people, unlikely to be allotted separate bells? The top bell was labelled, "Fr Doubrava", the one below it, "Rev X. Smolik", then there were three English names, and then seven labels with no names at all, only dirt and thumbprints. He rang Father Doubrava's bell. Since it was at the top, presumably the good father would have three floors to come. Nobody came. There was a spy-hole in the right-hand section of the black door, and behind it, he began to believe, an eye watching him. He said very loudly, "I am Professor Elphinstone. You're expecting me," and an old lady across the street turned in surprise to look behind her. The door was opened by an elderly man in cassock and cardigan. Behind him in the hall James could see the philosopher, Borek, still wearing his coat of purple plastic.

168

"Come in, come in! You know this gentleman."

There was a strong smell of cooking in the hall, meat of some sort, probably with paprika, prepared and consumed the night before, since they would hardly have it for breakfast. James said, "Yes, we've met. Once. In Prague. How do you do?" and shook Borek's hand. The hand was damp, and even in the gloom of the windowless hall James could see that Borek's face glistened with sweat. Borek cleared his throat, and managed a couple of sentences in Czech which may have been an apology. "Come! In here!" the priest said, dancing away without a handshake. James said, "I'm afraid I don't speak Czech, as Mr Borek knows. Beyond 'prosim' and 'dobry den', I'm a complete –" and balked at the word "illiterate", which would in any case have been the wrong word to use "– completely ignorant of the language." He was (he could feel it) himself sweating a little, more than a little; the situation had already become confused.

"Yes. In here! Please!"

"In here" was a room just off the hall, at the foot of the stairs and facing the front door. It was not a reception room or office, but seemed to be a combination of common room and dining hall, with a bar and a sink at one end, a table covered with oilcloth and a stack of plastic chairs at the other, and two elderly armchairs and a coffee-table between. The smell of cooking emanated from this room, and was stronger; there was braised cabbage in it as well as paprika. Perhaps these people did eat goulash for breakfast; James remembered the rissoles and sauerkraut of the hotel in Prague. The priest was pointing to one of the armchairs, "Please sit. Be comfortable," and, when James sat, took the other himself, while Borek stood by the bar, shifting from foot to foot, until the priest indicated that he should bring one of the plastic chairs to sit between them.

"You said Mr Borek gave my name as a sponsor? To whom? To Immigration? Or, for that matter, Emigration in his own country?"

"To me?"

169

"Has he a visa?"

"Oh, yes."

"I find that surprising."

"He has a Visitor's Visa for three weeks. Of course, he must put up money to be sure he return. Fifty dollars a day at the special rate. Maybe twenty-three thousand crowns."

"A hospital orderly? He could lay his hands on so much?"

"A good friend help him to find it. A lady who live in the same building." James thought he knew the lady, and wondered how she had been able to lay hands on twenty-three thousand crowns either. He himself had received ten crowns to the pound, but Czech nationals travelling the other way, he had heard, must pay forty. "When he goes back," the priest said, "he can reclaim this money."

James felt a lifting of the heart. "He intends, then, to return?"

There was a silence, during which the lifted heart sank again. Borek asked a question to which the priest replied with some impatience. The priest said, "They come to us. They imagine freedom they will live in, but there are practical difficulties. Possibilities are not as easy as you think."

"His intention is not to return?"

"The British Home Office, they don't open their arms, you know; it's not easy to defect. Maybe they allow three months. You appeal; you keep appealing. After a year, you hope maybe they will let you stay; they can't send you back to prison, but you don't know. It's a very unpleasant battle. One has to be good nerves for it."

"What will happen to the lady's twenty-three thousand crowns?"

"Maybe she lose it; maybe she knew that. Of course, if he is a Chartist, maybe it will be easier with your Home Office."

"I had the impression in Prague that he might be about to reconsider his attachment to the Charter. Even so, it's surprising that he should have been given a visa."

170

Again there was a silence, but this time Borek did not break it. It seemed to James – but perhaps he was reading too much into the silence – that the priest himself was not comfortable on the question of the visa. Was there a visa at all? Had Borek been smuggled over the border? But no; he would be in Austria in some camp for defectors; he could certainly not have escaped, in his purple plastic coat, by aeroplane to London, and even if he had, lacking a visa, he would have been held at Heathrow. Had he used James's own name in some devious way to deceive the authorities, an English professor from Oxford who would stand sponsor for him? – but a retired professor and only of Literature, and what was that to the Czechs or even to the bulldogs of Heathrow? The priest said, "He have a nephew. UK citizen."

"I know that. He knows that. But how could he prove that?" The man Baker's hand was in this somewhere. James could smell the civet.

"There was invitation from this nephew. A written invitation, you understand? It must be produced in such a case."

"Yes," James said, and turned his gaze fully upon the philosopher, Borek, who sweated under it even more profusely than before. "Yet when he arrived here, he asked for me, not for his nephew. I understand your concern." Pavel might just, these days and probably with help from his teacher, be able to compose an invitation in English, if he knew where to send it, but not in Czech. Did this priest expect James to take Borek away with him like the puppy suggested by that Samaritan woman? "I am, of course, well acquainted with Mr Borek's nephew; he is my pupil. I'll consult with him, and one of us will let you know within the week what he proposes. Meanwhile, I take it that Mr Borek will be able to remain here with you?"

"We have so little space. We have one defector already staying here a year; your Home Office make difficulties. Of course there is a small fund to help with money at the beginning, but even so . . ."

171

James rose with some difficulty from the elderly armchair, and Borek stood at once, like a naughty child
reproved for sitting down in the presence of his betters. A
puppy! Borek's facial expression, half-timid, half-ingratiat-
ing, might be observed any day from behind the bars of the
cages of the Lost Dogs' Home. ''I'm afraid I can't take Mr
Borek with me, but if money and space are the immediate
problems . . .'' He felt for his wallet. Was there enough in
it? A mistake to make generous gestures unless one were
sure that one had the money to back them up! Yes, there
must be eighty pounds. ''Perhaps you'd be kind enough to
accept this as a contribution; it should pay for a boarding-
house, if you have no space here. I'll consult, as I say, and
come back to you.'' He offered Borek his hand again, and
feared for a moment that the man would not release it.
''Please tell Mr Borek not to worry. I'm sure something can
be arranged.''

Pavel, of course, had not written the invitation. Equally, of
course, the man Baker had done so. Taxed with his offence,
he was totally unapologetic. ''It was a virtuous act, James,
by any definition.''
    ''Forgery?''
    ''To no one's harm, and someone's service.''
    ''And the twenty-three thousand crowns?''
    ''Will be taken care of. Have been.''
    ''And if I inform the Home Office?''
    ''Why should they care? Civil servants are only inter-
ested in facts – inconvenient facts to suppress them, convenient to use them. The fact is that Borek's nephew, his
only brother's only son, is a citizen of the United Kingdom
both by *jus solis* and *jus sanguinis*, his mother being English.
Borek is a known dissident who has blood kin in this
country; there's no reason for the Home Office to refuse
asylum. Provided that nobody tries to hassle them, or
complain when they lose the correspondence, they'll
almost certainly accept him. In any case, James, you know
perfectly well you wouldn't grass on the man; it's not in you

172

to do so."

"And, until the Home Office accepts him, you expect me to look after him?"

"Not at all. No obligation. You collect him, and hand him over to us. We'll see he's looked after."

"Who exactly are 'we' in this case?"

"Me. Us. Caring people among the Czech community. My dear James, we should be honoured by the presence amongst us of a distinguished philosopher."

"That's a bloody awful book, and you know it," James said, and hung up.

When James asked Pavel whether his uncle should be invited to stay at the Manor, Pavel blushed, hung his head, and seemed unable to reply. James said, "I really don't mind. It could be managed, at least for a while. It's entirely up to you." Pavel's blush deepened and he shook his head, which might have meant that it could not be managed, or that it was not up to him, or that he did not wish to meet his uncle, or merely that he felt unable to offer an opinion. "Don't you want to see him? You're certainly not obliged to."

"Don't know."

"I agree; the moral position is extremely confused. On the one hand, he appears to believe that you invited him to Britain. On the other, he may know perfectly well that you did not." Pavel's eyes filled with tears. In any situation involving badgers, Pavel was capable of decision and action, but family relationships brought him grief. No, be fair to the boy! He believed that he was in some way responsible for Borek's arrival, since if he had been born without an uncle it would not have happened. Since childhood Pavel had tried to protect older persons from trouble and anxiety; his sense of failure in this instance was acute. "Look!" James said. "Let's have him here until his visa expires; that'll be in just under three weeks. At the end of that time, he must decide whether we pass him on to Baker's people or he goes back to Brno. Right?" Pavel nodded. Tears still glistened in his eyes, but had ceased to form there. James said, "I think, if you don't mind, you'd better move in here during his stay, if only as an interpreter. You might be able to teach him a little English."

This time Pavel nodded. A decision had been made, and he had work to do. Pavel was sometimes very easy to please.

They would collect Borek on the week-end, when it would be easier to park. They would go down to London together, and bring him back by car. James supposed that he would have to cook for the three of them. Since Sophie's death he had been cooking as solitary people cook, not the solitary people who live in cities, buy prepared dishes frozen from the supermarket, and heat them up to eat in front of the television, but as Sophie would have expected him to cook. Sophie would have been distressed by Slimline Haddock Crumble with chemical additives in a foil dish; therefore James had been cooking nourishing stews and roasts one evening in three, and finished them up over the next two . . . Stews and stock, Sophie had said, like grievances must be brought to the boil and simmered every day. James seldom made stock, but continued, even though she had been dead over a year, to feel guilty whenever he threw out the carcass of a chicken.

Well, he would cook stews and roasts for the two Pavel Boreks, but they would not last three evenings, and if he were to serve one or the other every evening, they would become monotonous; he would have to enlarge his repertoire. Pavel would help; only small potatoes, Pavel had said, defeated him. They would prepare large potatoes or rice or pasta; cooking pasta is only a matter of dropping it into enough boiling water; anyone could do that. What a complicated business it was, having people to stay, and how fortunate that the house had three WCs!

They would have to share the bathroom, however. He looked at the clutter on the tiled window-sill above the wash-basin. How could any one person possess so many objects for the care of the teeth? There was a water-pick,

174

unused since water-picks went out of fashion, which must be over ten years ago. He touched the button, and there was still life in the battery. Perhaps Borek would use it; the Czechs must be at least ten years behind in dental hygiene. There were toothbrushes, inter-dental brushes, bottle-brushes in two sizes, Corsodyl Dental Gel and Blackmore's Herbal and Mineral Toothpaste. There were six disposable razors at various stages on the road to disposal and a canister of shaving foam (which destroyed the ozone layer, but James had been unable to reaccustom himself to lather). There were spare tablets of transparent soap from Sainsbury's, bottles of shampoo, most of them Sophie's; no guest must use those; he would remove them. Elastoplast, aspirin, antiseptic powder for cuts, anti-fungal powder for rotting feet, suppositories for piles – these must also be several years old, and perhaps should be thrown out. Boots' Cucumber Moisturising Cream.

The Moisturising Cream was James's own, not Sophie's. He had been troubled three years earlier by an itching which persisted and, since it had begun in winter, was unlikely to have been caused by the bites of midges. "A touch of senile eczema," the doctor had said. "There's not much else wrong with you."

James had instantly imagined patches of scrofula breaking out all over his body. He would be covered. "Can its progress be halted?"

"Very easily. Moisturise your skin, especially the legs."

"I do."

"Nonsense." The doctor scratched at a patch of scaling skin on James's right shin. "Dry!"

"I take a bath every morning."

"Do you? That's it, then. Water doesn't moisturise the skin. Water dries the skin." Not for the first time, James had marvelled at the infinite flexibility of the English language. "You won't thank me if I ask you to stop bathing, I suppose? Never mind. Get some cream at the chemist. You'll come up smelling of roses."

That had been the junior doctor of the local practice, a

woman, distrusted by many of the country people. Both James and Sophie had made a point of asking for her, since their own distrust was of the senior partner. The older villagers died off from cancer at an alarming rate because Dr Throwmore was reluctant to make the diagnosis, at least at an early stage when something might have been done to halt its progress. "You're old," he would say to a villager complaining of persistent pain, "you must expect aches and pains at your age," and when old Mrs Hardy had gone to him with falling hair and a wen on the side of her nose he had teased her affectionately, saying, "Vanity, my dear! vanity! all is vanity saith the preacher, eh?" and she had died within the twelvemonth in hospital at Oxford, rotten with tumours.

James had bought moisturising cream, and used it daily, always a little furtively in case someone came to call while he was still only half-moisturised. He would have to take the pot of cream into the bedroom, and moisturise there during Borek's visit.

The telephone rang, and it was his father. "It is another mark of the solitary person," James thought, "that his incoming phone-calls are either wrong numbers or unwelcome news." His father was using the pay-phone in the main building of Madras House. Calling from Maidstone at peak-time he would have to insert money almost at the end of every sentence; their conversation would be all pips. "James? Is that you? Wormald's been here asking questions," his father said.

"You're using a pay-phone, aren't you? Tell me the number, and I'll phone you back. Either that or put the phone down, dial the operator, and reverse the charge."

The pips went. "Shit!" James's father said, and James could hear a succession of tenpenny pieces being fed into the machine.

"If your money runs out, father, just reverse –"

"Did you hear what I said?"

"You said Wormald had been. Did he come to see you specially or is he thinking of joining the community?"

176

Could Wormald still be alive? If so, he must be James's father's age. It seemed unlikely that the Madras House would accept someone already over ninety.

"Don't be a bloody fool! He was talking to Matron."

"Yes?"

"Try to understand. I came downstairs from the bog, turned the corner, and there he was, wearing a raincoat and a brown suit, talking to Matron outside the shop."

"Were you able to have a chat about old times?"

"Kept out of the way. Hid." The pips again. "Shit!" More coins inserted. How many tenpenny pieces had been collected for this call, and why was it so important for James's father, who never communicated with his son for months at a stretch, to telephone at peak-time about the visit of an old friend? "Gone now. Did you hear that? Pissed off. Bugger talked to Matron, and then he left."

"When was this?"

"When do you think? Half an hour ago – had to get tenpences from the shop without Matron seeing – got no bloody money of my own. Why'd he come, eh? Talking about me, stands to reason, asking Matron questions, slimy bugger, always was! Bloody Funny Farm! You stop it."

"But Wormald must be your age, father."

"No, just as he was; that bugger never changed, used to dye his moustache. Couldn't lose him, infatuated with your mother, used to say we were the three musketeers, but I knew his purposes. Even came with us on our honeymoon, slept in the *dak* bungalow, and joined us for *chota hazri*. He never liked you."

"He never knew me."

"Said you broke things up. You better get rid of him."

"Father, are you telling me you've had some kind of hallucination, that you saw Wormald as you used to know him, talking to Matron outside the –"

"Saw the bugger. He was there."

"A ghost? Some sort of supernatural – ?"

"Never wore a brown suit before."

"There's no need to worry about the Funny Farm or

177

anything like that. These manifestations are quite common, I believe, as one gets older." James had no idea whether they were common or not, but the old man was clearly over-excited and must be reassured. Everything would be noticed at Madras House, noticed and discussed by the residents, noticed and noted by the staff, the tenpences collected in bulk from the shop, the agitated telephone call from the public box. James would have to talk to Matron, he supposed, except that Matron seemed to be part of the delusion, and it would only feed the old man's paranoia if he were to conspire with her. "There are more things in heaven and earth, father; the paranormal is more common than we think. Don't worry." The pips again. "Shit!" James said. "I'll call you back." Please God, let it not be the beginning of something serious. He would not be able to go down to Maidstone, at least until the Borek business was concluded.

He heard his father insert a single coin. "Last one," his father said. "Should've known better. Sorry. Panicked. Had to talk to someone. Should've known you'd never understand. It's all out of bloody books with you, son; it's all bloody theory. Wormald at the end of the corridor, hatching bloody plots with Matron, and all you can do is talk about bloody manifestations. Waste of money! Never mind. Handle it myself, always have done. You just keep your trap shut, not much to ask. I don't want Matron knowing I'm on to her – lose the element of surprise."

"Father –"

"Waste of bloody money. Should've known. There's the pips. Don't phone back." His father broke the connection. Probably, James thought, keeping his trap shut might be the wisest course for the time being. To talk to Matron would be to betray the old man's confidence and might actually bring the Funny Farm closer. James had enough on his plate at the moment. He must not be expected to worry about two problems at once.

By the third day of the visit it had begun to seem to James

178

that both Pavel Boreks were suffering from culture-shock, though of different kinds, and it expressed itself in different ways.

In Borek the condition was easy to identify; he had become almost entirely passive. Active enough in his own country, he had obtained a visa, booked a passage, boarded the aircraft, negotiated (perhaps with the assistance of other passengers) Customs and Immigration, found his way to the hostel in Notting Hill, and had thereafter abnegated any direction of events. He was like a pet, but not as responsive as a pet, more like a doll, or like a pet which does not know it is a pet, but only that it has been removed from its natural habitat and placed in another most unfamiliar; the philosopher, Borek, was like some bewildered non-venomous snake in his purple plastic skin.

It had been intended that Pavel should teach him English, at least the beginnings of spoken English, simple requests and pieces of information. If the reason for Borek's passivity was that he could not understand anything said to or about him or make himself understood, a condition the psychologist R.D. Laing has likened to schizophrenia, then the sooner he learned a little English the better. Unfortunately, Pavel had no experience of teaching, and Borek seemed to have forgotten how to learn, or else had no wish to do so, so the lessons did not progress; James did not listen at the door, but what he could not sometimes avoid hearing seemed to be mostly silence. He remembered that Pavel's own father had given up the attempt to learn English, and had settled for Radio Three, and, later, the services of his son as an interpreter. It had been a retreat from failure; any reasonably acute person could divine so much. The father's expatriate compatriots, people of no greater stature than he at home, had become publishers, broadcasters, the manufacturers of shoes or glass, research chemists, and he himself had only with difficulty obtained employment as an agricultural labourer; it must all be ascribed to his inability with the language, and that inability must be preserved if self-respect were to be

179

preserved. How had they managed, he and that village girl, on their wedding night? No wonder she had become depressed, had left home for long periods, and walked, at last, into the river with no kindly pastor to assist her towards immersion. *"She had all sorts, anyone who wanted, do it for a cigarette up against a wall."* Did Pavel now begin to understand something of the desperation of that despised and unhappy woman? "Whore"! – rather an old-fashioned word, I'm afraid, although not yet archaic.

These were early days, early days. Culture-shock of the kind Borek was suffering had a way of passing. If Pavel were unable to master it, James himself would teach Borek a little English by the Berlitz Method in which no Czech need be spoken. It would, of course, be better for all three of them if Pavel were able to master the teaching. It would bring Pavel closer to his uncle, whom at present Pavel appeared to dislike. This dislike was not overtly expressed; Pavel was never less than polite; yet James could sense it, and feared that Borek could also. Meanwhile Borek had developed a devotion to television. He took no interest in healthy walks, or being shown around historic buildings or demonstrations of interesting features of English life such as Morris Dancing and country crafts, but, like any child, would spend all day in front of the television set if he were allowed. By a happy chance Channel Four was showing (for the third time) *Closely Observed Trains*, a Czech film, so that they were able to watch it together. Pavel, James observed, was much moved by the film, but when James asked about Borek's reaction, Pavel replied that Borek had not enjoyed the film because it was not in colour.

Pavel was the worrying one, no doubt of that. The mainspring which drove him had lost its tension, and become as limp as boiled spaghetti. He could not understand why this should be; the spring was still there inside him; why did it no longer work? He had been kept going since childhood by his knowledge of the difference between himself and those amongst whom he lived. This difference had not lain in the lack of a hand; that was a disability to be overcome. What made Pavel unique and in important ways better than other people, better than his mother's family, better than the village schoolchildren and those in Care at the John Radclyffe Home, better than the clients of the Disability Centre and the unemployed lodgers in the rooming-house who fell so easily into despair, what enabled him to transcend disability and distress was the knowledge that he was Pavel Borek, son of Vaclav Borek, intellectual, freedom-fighter, who had stood tall among peers in a distant country, a Czech from Czechoslovakia.

This knowledge had been private; probably he had never even shared it with his father. *"I was the only person he could really talk to . . . He hated the English, but he didn't have any money to go anywhere else."* Pavel had not hated the English; he had made a point of not hating anyone, not even his mother's kin; he had risen above them. But secretly he had cherished his idea of Czechoslovakia and of his difference in being part of it; he had never allowed them to call him Paul. The idea had worked for him, driven him, and supported him, and it had not occurred to him that the idea was incomplete. All he had ever known of Czechoslovakia was his father, and he had loved his father; that had been enough. Now here was his father's only brother, also Czech, also an intellectual, and if he had not fought for freedom yet he had suffered for it, and this man was (as it seemed to Pavel) a slug, entirely without self-reliance, altogether dependent on others and apparently content to be so. This man was everything Pavel had all his life refused to be.

The shock was grave. In four days, Pavel seemed to have grown thinner; he had developed an occasional tic at the right side of his mouth; he blinked and seemed often to be on the verge of tears; it was clear to James that he was not sleeping. He found it difficult to speak to Borek, far less teach him; he took no joy in peeling large potatoes for him, but went out whenever he could into the garden, there to work as if in punishment, digging with one hand on the spade and the other arm held across it. James lay awake at

181

night, knowing that Borek, across the corridor, was lying awake, and that Pavel was awake in Helen's room. It could not go on. Something would have to be done.

Into this already worrying situation a man in a brown suit came walking.

Pavel was in the garden, Borek watching television in the living-room. The man in the brown suit came to the back door, entered uninvited, and found James chopping onions in the kitchen. Sophie's old cookery books, still on the kitchen shelf, had encouraged James into what were still only minor flights of ambition, but he had at least discovered how many variants there are upon the basic stew, had bought venison at the fish-shop, and was preparing a marinade.

"Professor Elphinstone?"

"Yes. Who are you?"

"I don't think we need to go into that, sir. You may take it that I'm officially accredited."

"To do what?"

"Enter these premises. Ask a few questions."

"Are you, indeed?" James wiped one oniony hand in his hair as Sophie had used to do. The man was from the police, he supposed, Special Branch or some such. James had been told by the British Council that he should report to the police in Prague the day after his arrival there, but when he had mentioned this to Jana she had only giggled, and said, "No necessity. They know you are here," and certainly the police had never required his presence, so perhaps the British Council had been basing their briefing on British practice, and it was the British police who required Czechs to report. "May I see your accreditation?"

"Never shown."

"Why not?"

"Official secret."

"I see. And you yourself are?"

"That, sir, is also for me to know and you not to find out." The man was smirking. He had made a joke which

182

was also a threat.

James looked at the man in the brown suit, and the man looked back at him. There was an air of the second-rate about the man; he was a hanger-on. If his gaze was direct, it was because he had been told as a boy that masturbators cannot look people in the eye; it was the way one identified them, like the green socks of homosexuals. Therefore the man, finding himself unable to give up masturbation, had trained himself to meet eyes instead. The brown suit had been bought off the peg at some multiple outfitters', and the grubby mackintosh worn over it almost certainly let in the rain. Gravy had dried on the man's moustache. "Wormald!" James said.

The mouth of the man in the brown suit opened and remained open; his direct gaze had become a stare. Then he said, "Crossed line here somewhere," and left the kitchen.

James followed the man out into the road, interested to know what he would do next. Wormald was sitting in his car, speaking agitatedly into a radio-telephone. He saw that James was watching, and shook the fist of his unoccupied hand. James shrugged, and went back into the kitchen.

After a short while Wormald returned. "I am informed, sir, that there is no acceptable way in which you can know who I am. I must ask you, therefore, how you come to be in possession of classified information."

"There's no secret. My parents knew your father in India. He was rather a joke, I'm afraid."

"You'll have to do better than that, sir. My father is still alive, and practising as a turf accountant in Lewes."

"A bookie? How extraordinary! It would have been your grandfather, I suppose. Old men forget. I'm a grandfather myself, but I married late, and my daughter's children are still infants."

"My father inherited the business from his father. However," Wormald took a small notebook from the inside pocket of his brown jacket, and wrote in it, "I've made a note of your allegation."

"I'm sure you'll find it's true. The gravy was the clincher.

183

Do you want to talk to my guest, Mr Borek? He doesn't speak English, you'll find, not even in the most basic way, and I don't speak Czech, but no doubt you do. How really very extraordinary! Your grandfather accompanied my parents on their honeymoon, you know. They often spoke of him. But of course you've met my father."

"No."

James remembered. They had not met. His father had hidden from Wormald. Stupid to have mentioned it. Change the subject. The note-book was still open. "Shall I take you to Mr Borek?" No need to mention, unless pressed, that there was someone in the garden who could interpret.

"If you don't speak Czech, sir, would you mind explaining your connection with Borek?"

"I've been teaching his nephew to read and write. And I have been to Czechoslovakia this year, as no doubt you know, but only for a fortnight on a Specialist Tour for the British Council."

"And your speciality is?"

"Literature. I am – was, until I retired – a professor of English Literature."

"Litt-ra-ture." Wormald wrote it in his book. There was a heavy patience in his voice. James felt an irritability rising within him, which clearly he must control. These tactics seemed so heavy-handed. Obviously many people would lie to Wormald, but these were facts which could be – must already have been – checked.

"And this nephew? Is he also Czech?"

"English. His father was Czech. But the nephew was born to an English mother, and has been brought up entirely in England. He has never, as far as I know, been out of this country."

A grunt. "You've no direct connection, then, with this man, Borek."

"Dr Borek?" James remembered the "docent" on Borek's card; that must mean doctor; he should have thought of it earlier. The man had been so diminished by Wormald's

184

tone that he could do with a little elevation. "I met him casually in Prague after a lecture. We spoke of that and other matters, mainly his nephew, and I gave him my address. It's quite common in Europe for professional colleagues to exchange cards."

"He's a doctor, then?"

"Of Philosophy."

"Ah! I thought maybe, working in a hospital, he might be medical. But he wouldn't need to be a doctor, I suppose, just to polish the floors."

"You seem to know something about him already."

"We always know more than we let on at the beginning. First rule of the department." Note-book closed with a snap. James had told the man nothing which was not already known. "You do realise, sir, being an intelligent man, how very thin all this sounds? Reduce it to the basic facts, and it's very thin. We reduce everything to the basic facts, and build from that; it's the only way to make a case. How long's he staying?"

"His visa is for three weeks."

"That wasn't the question."

"I have no plans for Dr Borek to stay here after his visa expires."

"*You* have no plans. No. Right." The note-book opened again, a further note made, the note-book shut.

"Don't you want to see Dr Borek? Or my pupil, his nephew? I imagine that you already know he's staying here."

"I don't speak Czech."

The note-book was opened and closed seven more times during the next hour before Wormald left. During this time, Pavel actually came to the kitchen window and went away again, but Wormald showed no disposition to interview him or Borek. Instead he and James discussed James's own short-lived attachment during the late nineteen-fifties to the cause of unilateral nuclear disarmament. They discussed an advertisement published in *The Times* in 1973 protesting at the restrictions placed on academic freedom in

Chile, which James had signed, along with many other British academics and literary persons. James had put his signature to the advertisement, and contributed a small sum towards the cost of it, at the request of a colleague, which is what one does in such a circumstance if one does not actually disapprove of the cause advertised. It is what one does, but was clearly not what Wormald would have done. They discussed the single occasion when Richard, long after leaving home, had been busted for the possession of an illegal substance; he had become a little less streetwise as he had entered his twenties. The busting was news to James, to whom Richard had not mentioned it; nevertheless he and Wormald discussed it. As the discussion proceeded James found his political views moving leftwards. Finally Wormald departed, promising to keep in touch.

When Wormald had gone, James telephoned his father at the Madras House. "I owe you an apology. You did see Wormald, or at least his grandson. He wouldn't have been plotting against you, though. It's me he's after."

"Told you. Never liked you."

"He seems now to like me even less. Tell me, how did your Wormald happen to end up as a bookie in Lewes?"

"Bit of a story there. Bloody man took early retirement. Had to. Fiddled the imprest. Pretended it was a peptic ulcer, but everyone knew. Great relief to your mother and me. Bought a bungalow in Sussex, took to eating lentils, married a bookie's widow, and went in for lay-preaching. Messy business!"

"You're all right, father, aren't you?"

"Lord, yes, I'm all right. What day is it?"

Such a visit could not be fudged over. James held a council of war over the venison, which was a little tough; it should have marinated for longer. Did Wellington hold such a council with his allies before Waterloo? Probably not; the Prussians arrived late. When everything has to be translated, a council of war is a cumbersome mechanism by

186

which to reach a decision, particularly since, as usual, Borek offered little in the way of information, nothing in the way of advice.

"What does he actually want to do? Does he want to go back when his visa expires or try to extend it?" Pavel's mouth twitched at the prospect of extension. "Does he want to apply for asylum, and if so did he do anything about that at the hostel?"

Borek had pushed all the vegetables to the side of his plate, and was applying himself to the thorough mastication of two pieces of venison at once. His reply was indistinct.

"He hasn't made up his mind. I don't think he's done anything about it."

"We mustn't rush him; it's an important decision." James meant that, as long as Borek had not yet decided definitely against returning, he must not be pushed towards a decision to defect. "Please tell him I do understand his uncertainty."

"I'll tell him he's got you into trouble with the police."

"Please don't do that. Tell him that since the police – Special Branch, MI5 or whatever, we don't know who they are – but since his arrival here has aroused their interest, it might be as well to declare himself one way or the other. Otherwise he gives cause for suspicion, do you see? They're very suspicious, these people; it's a habit of mind with them."

"I can't say all that; I don't know enough words." Jana had never said she didn't know enough words, but had used her powers of improvisation freely. "I'll tell him the police want him to go back."

"Tell him the police want to know what he intends to do."

Borek nodded. His attitude to dauphinoise potatoes had become clear, as it had on previous evenings to potatoes baked in their jackets, to fettucine and to rice. His attitude to carrots, cauliflower, leeks and green peppers had been similar. Even cabbage, which is eaten everywhere in

187

Central Europe, had received a very muted welcome. James remembered that the Czechs like potato dumplings, but did not feel he could rise to them. Well, Borek had taken it in that the police would want to know his intentions, but was not giving out anything in return. They would watch television, all three for a while after dinner, and in the morning James would telephone the hostel.

Father Doubrava was of no great comfort, however. No, Borek had made no application for asylum as far as the fathers knew, but he would have to do so.

"Why have to?"

"If the authorities allow such a man to leave, they expect him to defect. They will not be pleased to get him back; they will have to return the money. Also they wonder why he does not stay. Why do the British send him back? There will be a question."

"He'd never seen his nephew, never knew he had one. Then he received an invitation. He applied for a visa quite openly, met the boy and stayed with him for the allotted period of time, and then returned home. What's wrong with that?"

"If he is an old-age pensioner, nothing; he can come and go, and maybe in time he is remaining in England, and he will save the Czechoslovak government a pension. But, if a known dissident is given a visa, they do not expect he will return, and if he do return, it is a surprise for them, which they don't like. He should know this already without explanation."

"He seems to be a man of very little personal initiative."

"He is a strange man; we thought so here. He has no expectations. You should get rid of him to his nephew, and they work something out together."

That was out of the question, but it would be as well to begin the process of getting rid of Borek to the man, Baker. But, when James followed his call to Notting Hill with one to Nuffield College, he was told that Dr Baker had gone away for a while, and left no date for his return.

Puzzled and worried, James proceeded to Borek's first

English lesson under the new arrangement; it was to be given in the study, well away from the television set, and James and Pavel would conduct it together. They would use a cheap tape-recorder, a Czech/English dictionary, and a copy of *Teach Yourself Czech*, all purchased the day before from Oxford. They had barely begun, however, when they were interrupted by the arrival of the old lady. Objectively so little time had passed since the freeing of George in Fawley Woods, only ten days – three weeks since their adventure at the caravan-site – but it seemed months. Her wrist was out of plaster, but she wore an elastic bandage, and Felicia had brought her in the van. James supposed that she had come for her things.

"Sorry to butt in. We should have phoned first, but it's urgent. Council of war."

"We've just had one."

"Eh?"

"Sorry. Pavel and I and his – someone who's staying here, a Czech philosopher – we had a council of war last night; they seem to be in the air. I hope nothing's happened to George."

"Worse. Felicia brought this." The old lady was carrying a copy of the *Oxford Mail*. "We'd better sit down round a table."

They left Borek to study the dictionary and to listen to the tape-recording of conversational phrases supplied with *Teach Yourself Czech*; it would be the wrong way round for him, but he might learn something from it. They sat round the kitchen table as they had done with Greg three weeks earlier to plan the rescue, but this time the danger was not to badgers but to themselves and, although it might be less immediate, it was nevertheless a matter to be discussed with urgency.

A news item in the *Oxford Mail* had been circled by a felt-tipped pen. The Field Commander of the Badger Protection Unit, Cotswold Area, had done this before giving the paper, now a day old, to Felicia, who did not take the *Oxford Mail*, as the old lady did not, and James did not. The news

189

item recorded the conviction of Walter Hookham, thirty-five, unemployed, a married man, resident of the Fairmile Caravan Welcorama, Graceham, South Oxfordshire, for trapping a badger, which had been found caged in his caravan. He had pleaded guilty and asked for six other offences to be taken into consideration.

"Six other offences!" James said. "Yes, I agree. That's extremely worrying."

Pavel said, "I don't get it."

"One has to consider what is known and what is not known. Tuttleby knew that more than one person had been concerned in our raid, had seen the dead sow and the cubs in the caravan, and had released George and carried him away, because no one person could have done it alone – breaking into the caravan, breaking the lock on the cage, carrying away an adult male badger with a broken leg. There would be, therefore, not just a single witness, but witnesses, three or four of them, who could give evidence against him if the case should ever come to court, and whom it might be difficult to frighten into withdrawal. Because these people themselves had acted illegally, they were unlikely to bring a case, and the days passed, and they did not do so, but if he himself were to pursue them with any form of vengeance, then they would certainly inform against him. A stalemate. Better to write off the whole affair."

"He couldn't know who we were. At least . . . " Pavel remembered the two children at the entrance to the caravan site.

"Up to a point. He would not think that Amelia could have been one of the raiders because of her age and because his people had left her injured, but he would believe that she had informed and incited those who did make the rescue. His people knew Amelia and where to find her, in Fawley Woods almost every night. Unless . . . "

The old lady shook her head. "Have to be there. But I know places to hide."

"They know where you live, however; you shouldn't be

190

alone." It seemed to James that the whole world would soon be moving into Little Easely Manor, but the old lady would be a welcome visitor, as Pavel was. He hoped that she would not wish to sleep in the cellar again. "You'd better move in here at least for a while, but even this house will not be entirely safe, though of course it's not isolated. Tuttleby doesn't know me, but he's bound to wonder just why an elderly gentleman should have decided to telephone the AA from his house at such a convenient time."

"Those two kids saw us."

"Yes. They ran away into the caravan-site, but they may have come out again once we were in the car. A silver Volvo. They may have taken a note of the registration number. Consequently Tuttleby may already have made enquiries; most people of his sort, I believe, have contacts with the police; he could hardly operate if he did not. He may have paid for access to the police computer. We don't know how much Mr Tuttleby knows or may have guessed, but as long as we had seen the badgers in that caravan there wasn't much he could do about it. But now, of course," James finger tapped the paper, "if those badgers have been taken into consideration on someone else's confession, someone who actually lived on the caravan-site, Tuttleby is free to act."

"Tuttleby paid him to confess?" the old lady said.

"Paid him. Frightened him; the man has a wife, and perhaps children. Probably a bit of both."

Felicia said, "The Field Commander told me you'd think of something. He said you'd analyse the situation, and come up with a preliminary course of action."

"He seems to have a higher opinion of me than is justified by my record; I don't know why he should."

"Greg and I had to make a report. We wrote you up."

Pavel said, "I think we ought to keep the Professor out of it. I don't want him worried. He's got enough worries at the moment, mostly because of me."

"I don't think I can be kept out of it. Amelia and I are

191

already in it, like it or not."

"That's the trouble with worries," the old lady said. "General rule is, the more you've got, the more you get. They settle in, and put out a little sign, 'Worries welcome here'."

8

THE BATTLE OF
FAWLEY WOODS

He would analyse the situation logically, and come up with a preliminary plan. Who were at risk? Himself and the old lady, the others only insofar as James and the old lady might lead to them. Was the risk real? Yes, because Tuttleby had made, in effect, a public declaration in the law courts of his freedom to proceed, and would not have troubled to obtain the freedom if he had not first formed the intention. Caveat: one could not know whether any other people were dangerous to Tuttleby, who might just as well be protecting himself against an impending prosecution by the RSPCA; the "six other offences" had not been specified in the newspaper's report, and might not include the trapping of the Fawley badgers at all. This induced confession of Walter Hookham, unemployed, could not be taken as positive proof of Tuttleby's intention to avenge himself on those who had burned his van and stolen a badger worth a thousand pounds, but it would be prudent to behave as if it were.

Question: James and his friends knew that the two episodes were connected, but were they right to assume that Tuttleby knew? Answer: he would be a fool if he did not make the assumption. Preparations had to be made, but against what? It was unlikely that Tuttleby's people would attack the house directly. Even in his own locality, he would not go so far, and Little Easely was over twenty miles from the scrap-yard. The wall-eyed man might be local, or at least local to Fawley, but could be so easily identified by his wall-eye that Tuttleby would be unlikely to use him for any major mayhem. Would Tuttleby burn the Volvo as his own van had been burned? Well, if that were all, let him; the vehicle was insured, and would be a small quittance if he would be content with that. Probably he would not be content; in any case, one could not make the offer. Nothing must be made easy for Tuttleby; these people feed on weakness. The Volvo must no longer be parked outside at night, but locked in the garage. To burn a van on a hillside among conifers at night while its owner is engaged in criminal activities at some distance is one thing; to break into a locked garage in a small village and set fire to a Volvo GL Saloon, the property of a retired Regius Professor, is quite another. The police would have to investigate arson seriously, and such creatures as the wall-eyed man might crack under interrogation. Nevertheless James resolved to instal burglar alarms.

The old lady was the vulnerable one, and so, of course, were the badgers. Defensively considered, the old lady and the badgers constituted the same problem, since she would not allow any restraint on her movements which would leave them unprotected. George was still denning at Fawley Woods, though at a different sett. He had taken up with his daughter of the previous year, one of the three cubs who had been so reluctant to move out at Christmas. The old lady had agreed to leave her cottage, at least for a while, since it was just outside her own village and comparatively unprotected, and had taken over Helen's rooms from Pavel, for whom one of the attic rooms had been re-opened, but she would not give up her nightly visits to the woods. She knew hiding-places, she had said, and it was true she did, but would she remain in them if the badgers were endangered? The old lady's method of protecting them up to now had been to make her presence known; she could not be trusted to lie low for long.

What could Tuttleby actually do? One must try to put oneself inside the mind of the man. *"He'd pay up, walk free, and beat the informer to pulp the day after. It's what nobody takes*

194

account of; you've got to go on living with such a person." If Tuttleby's people were to beat the old lady to pulp they would kill her; they might easily have done as much when George was taken. They had broken her wrist then, and she had rolled away from them downhill into darkness. If she had been unable to get up again, and had died of exposure, that would have been murder, though not intended as such. *From the fury of the Northmen, good Lord deliver us.* Tuttleby, Greg had said, was from the north, a gypsy from Yorkshire. If the old lady were to leave her hide, confront his people, receive a beating, and die of it, murder in the woods by a person or persons unknown would be hard to bring home, however strongly a certain person might be suspected. Very well! the old lady must be made to understand that she must not leave her hide, and James must find some way to keep in communication with her. A walkie-talkie radio perhaps might do it; he would make enquiries; if she were able to summon assistance by such a means, there would be no need for her to confront intruders. As for Tuttleby, he would be a fool to proceed to murder; it would be, quite literally, over-kill.

James found that he was sweating. Sophie would have told him to close his eyes, breathe deeply, shake out from the wrists the tension in his fingers which were in danger of breaking the pencil. He did so, and returned to the assessment of Tuttleby's intentions, of which murder would not be one. Tuttleby would wish to do damage and have that damage known, to inspire fear, to demoralise the old lady's friends. He might achieve that much by an attack on the old lady's cottage, now vacant; it might be vandalised, even burned, all her precious things, all the mementoes of her life in Africa with her poor old fellow destroyed. Even this was likely to cause an investigation which might involve him; again the link would be the wall-eyed man who had shot at her in the woods. The old lady was, after all, a Lady, a person of some note, well liked and well regarded in the locality, her eccentricity prized as a talking-point; she was not the cowering occupant of a semi in Kettering. Yet it

195

would be so easy to vandalise that isolated cottage at dead of night, so hard for the police to make a case, however strong their suspicions. Tuttleby need not even have his own people do the work; local yobboes could be hired through a third party. Luckily the old lady had no great attachment to possessions, but the cottage itself was valuable to her, inasmuch as she had nowhere else to live.

James's pencil wrote, and drew a line under what it had written – *"ACTION. TEMPORARY TENANT."* For a while someone else must occupy the old lady's cottage, someone who would appear to be renting it, who, if asked, would deny any knowledge of her present whereabouts, but would give a full account to James of any such enquiries. This someone would probably have to be a member of the Badger Protection Commando, persuaded by the Field Commander to move house for a while, but first James would try the calling-in of what seemed to him to be a debt. He telephoned again to Nuffield College, and this time was told by the porter that Dr Baker had returned.

"Didn't you get my message? I phoned two days ago. They said you were away."

"I was."

"Why? The whole question of Borek is still unsettled. He appears to be unable to make up his mind. I've had people at the house enquiring."

"What people?"

"A person. Someone from MI5, I think. He wouldn't say, of course. I imagine that's usual."

"Really? Did he talk to Borek? They're not usually very good at foreign languages. MI6 ought to be better, though I'm bound to say they're often not."

Was there no subject on which the man Baker was not odiously well-informed, or was it perhaps that he invented his information? James said, "He did not wish to talk to Borek. He wished to talk to me, and did so."

"Yes, that's their way. Bullied you a bit, did he?"

"I think you'd better talk to Borek yourself. He doesn't appear to have much in common with his nephew, or any

196

particular desire to enjoy what democratic freedoms we are able to offer him, beyond colour television. However, although the matter is clearly of some urgency, that is not my primary reason for telephoning; I think we may agree to put Borek on the back-burner for a while. There is something else I should like you to do for me. It's time the obligations began to go the other way."

And amazingly Baker agreed to rent the old lady's cottage for a month. James, much cheered, went into Oxford the same afternoon to enquire about a walkie-talkie.

He had looked under "Radio Communications" in the Yellow Pages, and found himself amongst house-plants in the blue perspex shopping precinct which these days linked the Cornmarket and Paradise Square, talking to a young man in whose voice the accents of Oxfordshire, Bromley and what may have been the West Coast of the United States carried on a shifting battle for dominance. This young man used some words unfamiliar to James (module, cellnet, alphanumeric), others which seemed to have suffered a change in meaning (mode, systems configuration), and put them together into sentences which made no sense whatever. In James's experience only educationists spoke in such a way. Nevertheless, just as with the educationists, meaning could be teased out if one persisted.

The young man was of the opinion that, if one wished to maintain communication across hilly country with a partner seven miles away and moving about amongst woods, a two-way radio would not do the job; it would be better to make use of a hand-portable cellular telephone with long-life batteries rechargeable by the cigar lighter of one's car. This opinion of the young man may have been influenced by the fact that his shop was furnished all over with portable telephones, and contained no two-way radios at all that James could recognise, but it did suggest another possibility. A two-way radio would allow the old lady to communicate only with the Manor; a cellular telephone would give her access to the RSPCA. also, to

197

the police, the Field Commander; she would have many sources of support, provided that she could remember the telephone numbers and press the right buttons in the dark. The cellular telephone, the young man said, had a memory of ninety-nine numbers, with speed-dialling and illuminated ten-digit display. James's brain had already begun to fog; he was of the generation which had difficulty with all but the simplest functions of a pocket-calculator; a memory in it brought on amnesia in him. There was a status indicator, the young man said, and a last-number recall, and a mute mode, which appeared to mean that the old lady would be able to speak to Tuttleby's people without James hearing what she was saying, when surely the opposite of that would be more useful? There was call restriction and an electronic lock, which would prevent the badgers or any passing fox from making unauthorised use of the instrument. The old lady could adjust the ring-tone level, and keep one call on hold while answering another. Including the leather case, with spare battery and cigar-lighter adaptor, the telephone would cost one thousand, one hundred and eighty-five pounds.

"One can't rent them?"

"Oh, yes. There is a rental provision, subject to credit-worthiness. Three-yearly or five-yearly?"

"Are those the options?" A three-yearly lease would cost £43.50 a month, a five-yearly £30.05. That would be . . . that would be altogether . . . James looked about for paper and pencil, and the young man pushed buttons on a plastic wafer. To rent a hand-portable cellular telephone for the shortest period of time allowed would cost over fifteen hundred pounds; it would be cheaper to buy outright. James had seen these things advertised on television among the detergents and chocolate bars. In the television commercials, people fishing in the middle of a lake, shooting amongst heather, even tennis-players had them. Three million unemployed, and tennis-players were paying fifteen hundred pounds for a portable telephone to keep this young man in potted plants! Yet the old lady's life might depend on it. *I will do such things.* He had savings as well as his pension; he could re-mortgage the house if he were short of money. What need had a dead man for savings?

The young man was looking at him curiously. "You're really serious, then?" Bromley and the West Coast had dropped out of the battle for his accent, and were taking a break at the commissary. Oxfordshire alone was easy to understand.

"What made you think I might not be?"

"People come in here to talk mainly, make themselves feel good; it's all pretence. It's a show-case, this shop; we really only sell to businesses."

"But you can tell I'm serious?"

"It was the pain in your face. Not understanding a word I was on about; you still don't understand it. But screwing yourself up to spend the money. Hilly country . . . moving about in woods . . . I'm not lying to you; the phone would work in those conditions. But mostly people buy them to fit in their cars, and they only use them to impress their passengers. I mean, if you really have to call Head Office, you can stop at a phone-box."

"I really am serious."

"You'd better hire it for a week, then, to see if it suits you. I'll need a deposit, mind, and something for insurance. And try to keep it out of the rain."

While James was in Oxford, Pavel went down to the stream, and chose fifteen pebbles, smooth and flat and oval and each weighing between seventy and a hundred grammes. He washed them and dried them and made a satchel out of old curtain-material and twine to hold them. Then he walked into Chipping Norton. Pavel was still required to pay rent for his room in Oxford, but he had spent nothing on food during his time as a guest at the Manor, so he had a little money of his own. He bought a piece of soft leather from Kirsty, who made mocassins in the back room of the Craft Shop, and leather thongs from Henry Pacey, Boot and Shoe Repairs, and took these back to the Manor, where he already knew that there was a bradawl in the cardboard box in the bottom drawer of the kitchen dresser. When James returned, Pavel was at the kitchen table, constructing a sling. A catapult would have required two hands but, by fixing a hook to his belt from which the sling would depend, he could load it from the satchel with one hand, then pick it off the hook to use it, then return it to the belt to load again.

After tea Pavel drew a target with chalk on the wall of the garden shed, and spent the next two hours and much of the next day practising until he could hit the centre of the target from different angles and at distances of up to fifty yards, and reload in seven seconds. And at night he went out again to see how great a range he could manage with his night-vision in the dark. By then several targets had been chalked on the wall of the shed because, as Pavel became more and more accurate, his pebbles broke through the wood.

James himself, observing this methodical pursuit of excellence, hearing the regular smack of pebble against wooden wall, went to the cupboard where the shot-gun was kept, unlocked it, took out the gun and balanced it between his hands. But it would not come to that; it could not come to that. He put the shot-gun back in the cupboard, and secured the door again with lock and chain as required by police regulations.

The old lady slept through it all by day, and spent the night with her darlings in the woods after a hearty dinner of stew. As for the philosopher, Borek, he continued to pass his days watching colour television. Borek was on the back-burner, though one could not be sure he knew it.

"You distrust me," Wormald said. "I have to live with that."

"Most people distrust the Security Services these days, don't they? There's been so much publicity about your mistakes."

"I never said I was from the Security Services. I might be

200

a private detective, pursuing enquiries."

"You might. It seems unlikely. Are you?"

Wormald shook his head. "You know better than to ask. And, if I was to answer, who's to say I'd be telling the truth? You talk about mistakes. It's a point of view, but are you seeing the full picture? What looks like a mistake could be deliberate disinformation. Everything you read, everything you hear, could be disinformation. You're a thinking man. Reflect on that."

"Are you suggesting that the Government would spend millions of pounds of taxpayers' money, attempting in courts all over the Commonwealth to stop the publication of books, prosecuting people under the Official Secrets Act, hounding newspapers from injunction to appeal, decision after decision –"

"Exactly!" Wormald stretched his feet out in front of him, and helped himself to another Chocolate Chip Cookie. "End result! – the public is sick and tired of bloody security and the newspapers are as jumpy as kittens. Well worth the money! Look at it another way. Compare the entire cost of every branch of the Security Services added together to the cost of Trident; it's a gnat to a dinosaur. Consider the billions spent every year by every civilised country on weapons which are never intended to be used, which is just as well because most of them don't work anyway. It's all a matter of how you look at it; the Security Services are only a little bit of marzipan on top of a very indigestible cake."

"What I don't understand is why you never talk to anyone else in this house, why you should spend your time entirely with me."

"You are the nub."

"I don't understand you."

"Find the nub, and keep your finger there; that's the way I was trained, and the way I continue to train myself; I don't change. 'Finger-on-the-Nub Wormald', they call me. In this situation, Professor, you are the nub."

"What situation?"

Wormald took out his note-book, turned it back to front,

201

lifted the back flap, and prepared to read from it instead of writing. "Look at it my way. Consider the points I'm making. Begin with this nephew. He's a cripple, isn't he? – what they call 'disabled'. Nice enough lad, I dare say; I've noticed him around, doing odd jobs. But he can't read or write, and nobody's ever heard him speak a foreign language."

"He can read and he can write."

"Your doing, I suppose?"

"And, as it happens, speak Czech."

"How do you know that?"

"He speaks to his uncle."

"Does he?" The note-book reversed. A note made. Then the note-book was returned to what the young man in Oxford might have called its reading mode. "Right! I'll continue. This nephew takes up with you – no harm in that; you're his teacher, one to one, volunteered for the job and have since extended the scope of your duties beyond the confines of the Adult Education Centre at . . ." Wormald held the book a little further away from him, and squinnied at it; James was fairly sure that the squint was put on . . . "at Littlemore – yes. You have abandoned the classrooms and periods arranged for you, in order to continue working at your own home and his. More convenient for you, I dare say. More private."

"Yes."

"Now, just to establish the time-sequence, your first meeting with this nephew is in October, 1987. Six months later, never having visited Eastern Europe before, on your own initiative and request you undertake a Specialist Tour to Prague, your speciality being in . . . English . . . Litt-ra-ture. In the course of your specialist duties, this man Borek, who actually lives two and a half hours' journey from Prague, at a place called Brno where he is employed as a hospital orderly, just happens to bump into you, whereupon you exchange addresses. Now, this hospital orderly, Borek, has no means of knowing he has a nephew in Britain, and the nephew has no means of knowing where

202

his uncle lives, yet within a month of your visit the uncle receives an invitation, written in perfect Czech, from the nephew to visit him, and although the man is a known dissident, the authorities let him go."

"There's an error in your *résumé*. Dr Borek did know he had a nephew. I told you the other day, we discussed his nephew when we met."

"How? How did he know?"

"I'm afraid I can't offer you any more biscuits. You've finished the packet." James supposed that he would have to tell this man about Baker's interest at some time, but he ought in fairness to speak to Baker first.

"You must agree, sir, errors and omissions excepted, it's a very fishy story. And, being as you're the nub of it, I intend to keep my finger on you. My own experience has always been that, provided I keep it there long enough, something is bound to break. There's no Marmite, I suppose, in this house? We get so little time for food in my business, we have to catch the flying moment on the wing."

Did James remember, could he recall the details, had there not been a woman in Shropshire, Hilda Murrell, an old lady like his own old lady, who grew roses and campaigned against the erection of nuclear power-stations, and who had been accidentally murdered in her own home by the Security Services? That was the horror of it; there was no protection against these people.

After the planning, after the decisive action, came the attrition and the fatigue. By the end of three days it began to seem to James that the most damaging action Tuttleby could take was to do nothing. Not half a week gone, and James was already exhausted, partly because he was sleeping badly, and partly because the tenor of his life had become one damned thing after another.

He had been driving the old lady to the woods after dinner, and picking her up again at dawn, then, at her suggestion, taking Pavel over in the afternoon to check that

203

there were no indications of day-time investigations of the setts. The old lady had made no demand that James should drive her; she had been used to walking over fields from her own cottage, and now wished to drive herself; her own car had been brought to the Manor by Felicia. But one had to be sensible; old bones mend slowly; the frequent changing of gears in a ten-year-old Renault on country roads would play hob with the old lady's wrist. The alternative was that Pavel should drive her in the Volvo with its power-steering and automatic gear-shift, and indeed he had passed his test at the Disability Centre, and had a licence to drive, but only, it was discovered on examination, cars which had been specially adapted for the disabled. Felicia herself had offered to move in as driver and spare cook, but if Tuttleby's people were keeping the Manor under any kind of observation her presence might identify her as a member of the Commando. Also Wormald would want to know who she was, and might enter her name in his note-book as a person of possibly subversive views, whence it would find its way into the memory of some computer, and give her grief in the years to come.

So James drove to and from Fawley Woods twice a day, only twenty-eight miles altogether; there was no reason why it should tire him so.

The house was filling up. Elsie had grown used to Pavel, and seemed to like him, but had not known what to make of Borek on her previous visit, and now there was the old lady, of whom even less could be made since she was asleep. Elsie, in face and body-language, expressed the grievance naturally felt by one who is being asked to clean up after more people than one has bargained for. Also the gardener was displeased by the holes in the wall of the shed. Nor could Borek be entirely neglected by a conscientious sponsor. James tried to find an hour a day to work with him on a basic English vocabulary.

Pavel said, "You can't go on like this. You'll wear yourself out."

"Am I looking that much under the weather?"

204

Pavel said, "Yes."

A fine evening in May. They sat together on the wooden bench beneath the yew tree which shaded the lawn. On the branch above them a blackbird chattered. The same blackbird, or his father, had resented James's and Sophie's sitting there two years before; there had been a line of grossly possessive blackbirds living in that tree.

Pavel said, "It's the worry, isn't it? You do a lot of worrying. You ought to share it."

"Yes, I'm sorry. I've never been very good at that, as I discover. I used to think I shared most things with my wife, but sometimes I wonder whether I really did. It seemed to me that you and I shared, to an extent, on the night we set fire to the van, but in that case you were the one who did the sharing."

"We used to do reading."

"We shall again. I've never known anyone with more aptitude for learning."

"It's easy when you do it every day. And if you enjoy it. You can learn anything if you enjoy it. I've brought you trouble in every way. With the badgers. And . . ." Pavel jerked his head in the direction of the living-room where the television set was kept.

"That's hardly your fault. Someone wanted him out, and made use of us both. It'll pass, all that, whether he goes back or stays."

"Who's that man keeps coming round and eating biscuits?"

"The grandson of someone who knew my parents in India. He's in the Security Services, I think."

"I could go with Amelia at night, and learn the hiding-places. Then I could teach the others, and we'd do one night each a week."

"Might help." He should have consulted Pavel earlier. It was comforting to share; one swiftly lost the habit, living alone. And always having to be in control, of course, inhibited it. "What we really need," James said, "is to find some way of bringing all this to a head."

205

Baker was coming towards them across the lawn. Whenever one achieved a moment of peace, James supposed, Baker would find some way to break into it. How jauntily the man stepped! He was like a magnetic field, never content unless everyone was aligned in his direction. He was carrying some instrument in a leather case.

"I've brought you this, James," the man Baker said. "It's only borrowed, I'm afraid, so I'll need it back, but I thought you might find it useful. It's an infra-red camera. Might give you the chance to get those chaps off your back for a while."

The old lady had spoken of her need for an infra-red camera, which would allow her to photograph the trappers without their knowledge, and of the impossibility of ever getting one because it was so expensive. Pavel's mouth had opened. James knew that the boy longed to handle the thing, so he took it from Baker and gave it immediately to Pavel, who sat there, running his hands over the outside; Pavel would consider it impolite to do more in Baker's presence. James said, "That is extraordinarily kind of you. I was thinking just now that we ought to try to find some way to bring matters to a head, and this may afford the opportunity. I really am grateful. I find it difficult to express the depth of my gratitude."

"My dear James, you have, after all, done a great deal for us." One must be careful not to resent the fact that yet again Baker gave no indication of who "us" were.

"Would you like to have a word with Dr Borek while you're here? I'm sure he'd be glad of it; he gets very little opportunity to converse in Czech."

"I've done that, put a bit of spunk into him; he was rather deliquescent, I thought, not suitable in a house-guest. I told him he'd be coming to us in a week; we'll handle his application for asylum. He'll probably go on to the States – hundreds of television channels there, all in colour, twenty-four hours a day. We'll find him something undemanding to do, teaching Freshman Philosophy in a liberal arts college, something like that. It's been good of

206

you to cope so far, but one mustn't take advantage." Again, infuriatingly, just as at Christmas, Baker spoke to Pavel in Czech, and again Pavel coloured, and replied in English, "Thank you." Baker said, "I think you'll find our philosopher much perkier when you go in. I've told him he's got to take part in the life of the household, go out a bit, help with the shopping."

"The life of the household is at the moment, as you know, under some strain."

"Exactly! Let him take a bit of it. No reason why he shouldn't go badgering from time to time, if you can find a use for him. They have conservation in Czechoslovakia too, you know, just so long as it doesn't get in the way of industrial production."

Later, when James, Pavel and the old lady examined the camera, and marvelled at it, they discovered that, stamped indelibly into both camera and case, were the words, "Property of the Ministry of Defence."

James negotiated a further month's hire of the hand-portable telephone, and Owen, the Technical Officer of the Badger Protection Commando, came over from Marston to instruct the Little Easely Detachment in its use. Owen was seventeen years old. His parents had bought him an Apple Macintosh home-computer for his thirteenth birthday, and he had gone on from that. By the use of computer-graphics, Owen was able to produce maps of every badger-inhabited area of the county for which the Commando had records, with each sett marked, and notes of the age and sex of every badger denning in each, and which other setts each badger had previously occupied. It was as well that Tuttleby had no access to these maps, unless he had a mole at the office of the Nature Conservancy Trust to which copies were sent updated on a monthly basis.

A hand-portable radio-telephone was nothing to Owen. Hitherto the machine had been used below its capacities. When James had brought it back from Oxford they had decided to make an immediate trial of it, and the old lady

207

had taken it out that night with instructions to telephone the Manor at eleven, but she had forgotten that it had to be switched on before it could be used, so that when James, after a sleepless and anxious night had collected her at dawn, he had found her tearful and apologetic. George had tried to search the machine for apples, she said; if he had broken it, she would pay off the cost, but it would have to be on a weekly basis from her old-age pension. The next night a proper test had been made by James himself from the track where he parked the car, telephoning to Pavel at the Manor, so that the old lady was taken through the sequence she must follow, first to switch the telephone on, then to press the Call Button to make sure that a frequency was available (which at that time of night it always would be), then to press the buttons of the telephone number required, which would be shown in figures on a lighted panel to confirm that she had not pushed the wrong ones. This Call Button and lighted panel were new to James, since the cordless telephone at the house did not have such features, nevertheless he and the old lady had mastered the use of them, but the further functions of the machine were beyond him.

Owen clicked his tongue over the telephone, which did not seem powerful enough to him. He agreed with the young man in the shopping precinct that it would work better than a two-way radio, because a two-way radio in such country and over such a distance would be unlikely to work at all, but Owen would have preferred a larger model with a battery roughly the size of a hat-box. That the old lady, pushing seventy and with one wrist still knitting, would not have been able to lift it, let alone carry it about woodland at night, was of little importance to Owen, whose interest was in the perfect, not the possible. This machine, he said, with its inadequate power-source, would allow the old lady to telephone New York or Frankfurt, because the call would be routed by satellite, but she might have difficulty in reaching South Oxfordshire. Nevertheless he loaded its memory with the telephone numbers of the

208

Manor, the police-station at Chipping Norton, the Field Commander, Felicia, Dave, Greg and the home number of Jim Heritage, the RSPCA Inspector, and he spent an hour instructing Pavel in its use, explaining to James and the old lady that they were not of an age to understand much of what he said; the micro-chip gap was too wide; they would be better off with Pavel as middle-man.

As for the infra-red camera, offered with such pride, it threw Owen into his scornful mode. "Infra-red", he said, had declined by misuse into a generic word like "hoover" and "filofax". Probably the camera functioned either thermographically, producing images created by heat and not by light, or by light-emission-intensification, more probably the second, which was the method used by the Natural History Unit of the BBC. True infra-red film was only manufactured in the United States, and could only be bought in batches worth £50,000 each, which was why nobody ever used it. James forbore to point out that the Ministry of Defence was well able, and usually eager, to buy things in £50,000 batches, particularly from the United States, since he recognised in Owen's scornful attitude to the common misuse of specialised words something curiously close to his own, so he only asked what one would actually see when one looked through the view-finder of the camera in Fawley Woods at night. Owen replied that, if the instrument were thermographic, wherever there were living objects, one would see shapes which appeared to be made up of tiny glowing overlapping fish-scales, while, if its function were by light-emission-intensification, one would see woodland animals moving about in a greenish monochromatic murk. It seemed important to James to know which since he doubted whether glowing fish-scales would be accepted as evidence of identification in a court of law, and Owen himself looked through the view-finder, and reassured James that it would be greenish murk, in which Tuttleby's people and the surroundings in which they were committing their criminal acts should be recognisable, provided that James were

209

careful to hold the camera still. James thanked Owen, and offered tea, which was accepted, and a lift home, which was refused. Owen's metabolism seemed to function at the same advanced rate as his brain. He managed to get through half a pot of Sophie's Plum and Almond Conserve on buttered toast before setting off to hitch-hike back to Marston in good time for supper at his own home.

James looked at the technical equipment laid out on the desk in his study. Even without the additional batteries desired by Owen, it all seemed rather a lot for the old lady to carry, but both these objects had their cases with leather shoulder-straps, and she did not complain, but walked about in a dream of pleasure at having an infra-red camera in her possession at last. As James drove her to the woods that night, she held it in her lap, stroking it and making little crooning noises as if it were a favourite animal. "I suppose you think I'm bonkers," she said to James, "but I like to get on terms with things."

James had taken the opportunity of Baker's visit to speak to him about Wormald, but, as was usual with that elusive man, had little joy of the conversation.

"He doesn't believe Pavel wrote the letter of invitation. He's right, of course; it's beyond belief."

"Have you told him who did?"

"Since he has only asked the question by implication, I've been able to avoid giving an answer; it seemed fairer to speak to you first, since it's your own confidence I should be breaking. Consequently Wormald may believe that I wrote the letter myself, or caused it to be written. From his point of view, the whole sequence of events becomes extraordinarily suspicious."

"To a man like that suspicion is a habit of mind. My dear James, when it comes to the men in brown suits, as others have discovered before you, there's no objective reality. Whatever you tell him will be twisted until it fits a conspiracy to subvert. He hasn't asked Pavel himself about the letter?"

"He hasn't spoken to Pavel. He hasn't spoken to Borek.

210

He speaks exclusively to me. He calls it keeping his finger on the nub. He even went down to Maidstone, and made enquiries about my father. He was seen in the corridor, talking to Matron."

"What a silly fellow, and how vexatious for you! I do see that, and I sympathise, James; you're clearly taking all the weight. These chaps have no idea how to behave; they're mostly misfits, you know. Just the same, I would prefer it if you could keep quiet about our people's involvement for a little longer. Once we take Borek over, and he puts in his application, there'll be no problem, because he'll be a known dissident seeking asylum, and it won't matter who wrote the letter, which becomes merely a device to get him out, do you see? Meanwhile let Wormald do the talking; they love to talk; they have so little social life."

"When are you planning to take Borek?"

"I told you, within the week."

"And if Wormald continues to harass me? If he – what do they call it? – 'pulls me in' for interrogation? I can't afford to go. I have people here who need my protection."

"He won't. If he does, I may be able to get him called off. Our people have their own lines to the Security Services."

What people? What people? Baker's friends were not Amnesty or International PEN. They were not, could not be, the *ad hoc* groups of distinguished academics, National Theatre playwrights and Booker-prize-winners who would from time to time launch an appeal to secure the release of some distinguished dissident from confinement. Who were these people of Baker's with their lines to the Security Services, and how was he able to borrow an infra-red camera from the Ministry of Defence? James said, "You've no idea. They actually have a file on me. Aldermaston! Chile! A pupil of mine at York went on to join some anarchist group, and apparently I'm responsible. Even my own son!"

"Can't do anything about that, I'm afraid; they have files on half the country, the Security Services and the police; they swap them, you know, like cigarette cards. They've a

211

file on me, I imagine, since I'm an economist; if I were a sociologist, it would be twice as thick. Console yourself, James: there's safety in numbers. Meanwhile I must be getting back to Amelia's cottage to heat up my TV dinner. I never thought I should miss dining in hall. There have been no enquiries about her apart from the neighbours, by the way. Your Mr Tuttleby is obviously biding his time."

James remembered that Mowgli in Kipling's *The Jungle Book* had been pestered by a vengeful tiger, Shere Khan, and had rid himself of the persecutor in some resourceful way. How had that been done? *The Jungle Book* was in an edition of his childhood, clearly printed on India paper which was still unyellowed; he had passed it on to Richard, who had passed it back. Yes, here was the story. Mowgli had instructed two wolves, Akela and Grey Brother, to watch Shere Khan, had chosen a time when, heavy with food and drink, the tiger had gone to sleep in a ravine, and had then driven a herd of buffalo over him. Not much help in that.

He put to the old lady Pavel's suggestion that various members of the Commando, most of whom had their own transport, should take turns in watching the sett at night, but the old lady resisted it. She would allow Pavel into her space, but Felicia, Greg with his faulty night-vision, even Dave were not naturalists. They would not be able to avoid causing noise and nuisance, alarming the woodland fauna, particularly the badgers who might move to somewhere more difficult to guard. The old lady was sorry to be negative in her approach (how easily one picked up this jargon from the television; it was the American influence, of course), but implored James to think again.

On the afternoon of Tuesday, May 24th, two days after Pentecost, eighteen after Borek's arrival in London, Pavel returned quickly from the woods to where James waited in the car. "Something to show you." James went with him to the sett. Two of its entrances had been blocked, and a steel tube about five feet long had been left in a third. Pavel said, "That's been done deliberate. Today. They

212

want us to know."

"What's the steel tube for?"

"Listening. They put it down and listen to find out if the sett's occupied."

"Done today? This morning?"

"Has to be. Wasn't here yesterday, and Amelia's been on watch all night."

"They want us to know?"

"Signpost. Telling us. Daring us."

"We could inform the police."

"They know we won't."

Both Pavel and the old lady had explained to James the disadvantages of telling the police when one believed that a sett was to be raided; if these disadvantages had not existed, the Commando would not have been formed. Naturalists have learned that, in the calendar of crimes, the taking of badgers comes very low down. There are areas of Coventry and Birmingham where the police will not go except in pairs, but a station sergeant thinks nothing of sending a single constable into woodland at night to apprehend eight men with spades and shot-guns. No wonder that the constable makes a lot of noise, and loses his way, allowing the men with spades to disperse and return the next night. "Can't blame the bugger," the old lady had said. "Most people are scared of woods, particularly in the dark. Startle a pigeon, and you think you've walked into an ambush. Put up a pheasant, and it's Alamein." The only useful way to involve the police was to immobilise the trappers' vehicle while they were digging at the sett, and then to phone the police to catch them in possession. That would not work tonight. Tuttleby would be unlikely to leave his van unguarded again, and in any case where George was concerned the old lady would not allow the trappers to get as far as possession; she would be at them first.

Tuttleby hoped for confrontation. What would be the worst he could do, short of murder? James decided that probably the worst would be to kill the two badgers slowly with dogs and spades *in situ*, while forcing the old lady to watch. "What they don't know," he said, "is that we have the infra-red camera. If we can photograph them digging, it doesn't have to come to possession." Under the 1973 Act, it is an offence to dig at a badger-sett; the prosecution is not required to prove possession. James had bought a copy of the 1973 Act from Her Majesty's Stationery Office, and Pavel, as an exercise, had read the Act aloud and made a *précis* of its provisions. The problem was that, if Tuttleby's people did not know they were being photographed, they would continue to dig and would send in the dogs, George and his new mate would be under threat, and it would be impossible to prevent the old lady trying to defend them. Tuttleby would have the confrontation he desired, and which James wished to avert. In spite of the infra-red camera and hand-portable telephone, they would be back to the same unfortunate odds, two old-age pensioners and a cripple against at least four men with dogs and probably a gun.

But the cripple had his own ideas. Pavel never went into the woods these days without his bag of pebbles and his sling. "Don't forget it's dark, and we've got night-vision," he said. "You get the photographs, and then I'll stop them digging." There was a sweetness in the air. Honeysuckle had grown over the dead oak, and was in flower. Wild honeysuckle was a memory from James's Devon childhood, but by the eighties had become a garden plant; one did not expect to find it in a wood in Oxfordshire. The scent of honeysuckle, and Pavel's eyes sparkling as they had not done for all the length of his uncle's visit, and somewhere above and beyond the wood a skylark singing; the whole countryside and season conspired to create a pathetic fallacy. "We'll manage," Pavel said. "Don't you worry. We'll manage together."

Yet it would require planning. They had been challenged, but must seem to have declined the challenge. Tuttleby's people must be tricked into believing that the Little Easely party had chickened out of a confrontation,

214

leaving the badgers defenceless. James, Pavel and the old lady would arrive early and be in position, concealed, before dark. This would allow their night-vision to adjust as the light faded, and give Pavel time to cut away any scrub and branches which might impede his field of fire. The Volvo must be hidden. It must certainly not be left on the track, nor could it be parked among other vehicles outside the cottages on the top road as it had been on Christmas night, because Tuttleby's people would be looking out for it. At the bottom of the track, where George had been released, there was the derelict farmhouse, its windows broken, holes in the roof, its yard a tangle of nettles, convolvulus, briars and woody nightshade, which had grown over the empty bottles and cans, sherds and blue plastic sacks left there by the last tenants. This farm had out-buildings, barns even more ruined than itself, surrounding three sides of a trampled space to which sheep were still brought for dipping. They could open the gate to this enclosure, the old lady said, and then a barn-door, drive the Volvo into the barn, and close all behind them. Even local people would not expect a car to be hidden there, and Tuttleby's people, always excepting the wall-eyed man, were not local.

This was the division of responsibilities: the old lady to choose their vantage-point, and provide hiding-places thereafter, James to take the photographs, Pavel to break up the dig, and cover their retreat. He was not to aim at faces, except in the most grave emergency, but he had trained himself to hit the two-inch centre of a target chalked on the garden shed in the dark at a range of fifty yards, and a man's knee-cap is larger than that; a terrier is larger than that. Each of the three usefully employed, each content and confident in the task. Then, during a high-tea of boiled eggs and wholemeal toast consumed before setting off, Borek announced that he wished to be one of the party.

The conversation which followed was largely given over to confusion and controlled hysteria; Pavel's inadequacy as an interpreter contributed equally to both. Borek's face

wore a fixed smile like that of a Boy Scout in Bob-a-Job
Week, through which he continued to eat slice after slice of
buttery toast. Sweat ran from Borek's brow down the side
of his nose, splashed over the smile, and mingled with the
butter, but he ate on. James's voice became so heavy with
patience that he could hardly haul it up as far as his
epiglottis. Inwardly he cursed the man Baker who had put
it into Borek's head, even to this point of obstinacy, that he
should contribute positively to the activities of the household. As for Pavel, he seemed about to burst into tears.
How sanguine the boy was in the presence of physical
danger, yet how emotionally unstable in any situation
involving his own family! Pavel's attitude, James knew,
would be ambivalent. A small part of him would rejoice
that his father's brother and fellow-countryman was at last
beginning to behave in a manly way, but the larger
common-sensical part knew well enough that to take
Borek, a person totally unversed in woodcraft, into their
company was likely to bring the whole enterprise to ruin.
The situation was saved by the old lady, who pointed out
that there was a job Dr Borek could very well do for them,
an important job which would otherwise have to remain
undone, and that was to guard the car. Since Dr Borek had
not so far been seen even in the village, except on the day of
his arrival, he would be an unknown quantity; the
appearance of a stranger, unable to speak English, sitting in
a vehicle which had already been parked in a deserted barn,
would be bound to confuse anyone who might happen
across it, and furthermore, now she thought of it, with
someone remaining in the car, the barn-doors could be
barred on the inside, and opened for them by Dr Borek on
their return from the woods.

So it had gone. The Little Easely detachment was in
position. Pavel had selected three sites from which he could
cover the sett, and had worked out ways of moving silently
from one to the other. A separate vantage point had been
found for James as photographer; even if he were to decide
that a different angle would produce a better picture, he

was under instructions not to move, and had promised to obey. He and Pavel had suggested to the old lady that her part of the business had been successfully completed, and she should wait in hiding, ready to make a diversion if that should become necessary, but of course she would not. She would wait with James, and watch; she could make a diversion well enough from where she was.

They heard the clock of the village church chime eight across the valley, then nine; the wood had grown dark. They heard the sharp alarm call of a tawny owl, hunting in the field beyond, but the daytime birds had fallen silent. Even the woodpigeons, who are great complainers and shifters about, had gone to roost; they would complain again when Tuttleby's people disturbed them. Perhaps Tuttleby's people would not come. Perhaps it was all for nothing, to be endured again night after night, the preparation and the waiting and the weary return to the Manor at dawn, until one night it would become too much trouble, and the badgers would be taken. James did not understand why the trappers should do their business at night, when the badgers might be expected to be out foraging, instead of by day when they would be sure to be at home, and the old lady explained that dirty deeds were usually done in the dark for fear of interruption, but it was true that May, when the nights were short and forage abundant, was not the most convenient month, and that the reason why some entrances to the sett had been blocked and gear left about was not only as a challenge to themselves, but in order to perturb George and his mate, and keep them underground.

Ten o'clock. They should have brought a thermos and sandwiches. Was that the sound of a van? No, only a charter aircraft on its way to Birmingham airport from Majorca. Ten-thirty. Eleven. Eleven-thirty. Every limb was already stiff, and five hours to go before dawn; he would never be able to hold the camera steady. The church clock chimed the three-quarters. James no longer noticed the chiming of the Little Easely church clock. Perhaps it had

217

ceased to chime. There had been an appeal for the church tower – Coffee Mornings, Jumble Sales and specially printed tea-towels on sale at the butcher's; the woman at the corner had opened her garden to the public but nobody came. There was a flurry of woodpigeons moving from tree to tree. A dog yapped; twigs snapped; someone on the bridle-path above was laughing. These people exercised no caution at all.

The trappers left the bridle-path, and began their progress downwards, slipping on leaf-mould, bumping against tree trunks, ripping themselves free from the trailing brambles; they sounded like the Gadarene swine walking over Rice Krispies, and must be, James thought, to some degree in drink. He could see the lights of their torches between the trees, and must remember not to look directly at those lights. "Here they come, the buggers!" the old lady whispered; she was regretting not having joined Pavel in practice with a sling. The dogs had already arrived at the sett, two Jack Russells this time and the lurcher, and following them were – yes, five men, three wearing balaclavas and two in flat caps, one of them Tuttleby, so confident was he in his mastery, Tuttleby in a jacket of no doubt genuine leather, no purple plastic for him, Tuttleby in a cap of light blue corduroy and trousers of cavalry twill. James's imagination had become fevered. He could not know the material of the trousers or of the cap, nor its colour, but had invented them out of the purest hate.

Three men with spades. No gun that James could see; if they were challenged, the spades would do their work. Three dogs. Tuttleby in a flat cap, leather jacket and light trousers. And with Tuttleby another man in a cap; James had seen that man before somewhere also, not at Tuttleby's house or at the caravan-site, somewhere else; he was sure of it. He raised the camera to his face, and looked through the view-finder. The world turned green, but even in the murk it was easier to distinguish details. The terriers seemed to be wearing collars of an odd design, as if each had a battery attached to it and Tuttleby was holding some

218

kind of panel; James had seen something like it before at the University of York, where it had been used to control model boats on the lake. One of the men with spades began to dig. The terriers, over-excited, were being held back by another. James sensed the old lady stiffening at his side, if she tried to move forward, he would have to hold her and the camera too. Click! The first photograph. No one would notice the noise of the shutter when the dogs were making such a din, or the whirr of the camera winding on the film for another exposure. Click! The fifth man had his back to the camera. James willed him to turn, and he did turn. Click! The man was Wormald. There was no possibility of error; his green face, like the belly of a fish, stood out from the darker green of its surroundings.

Suddenly the portable telephone began to ring. It was not a ring exactly, more of a buzz or brrr, but unmistakeably the sound of a mechanical instrument of communication.

The men at the sett froze. The old lady fumbled and panicked, trying to turn the telephone off; she had never before received a call during all the nights she had taken it to the wood. The freeze would not last for ever. Tuttleby's people would move in concert towards the source of that sound, and Pavel would not be able to stop them. James took the telephone from the old lady, and moved the switch from "Standby" to "Talk"; so much it had in common with the machine at the Manor. The buzz ceased. "Thank you," James said in his most carrying voice, "yes, we're in position," and then with a hazy memory of films put out by the Ministry of Information during the 1939–45 war, "Wilco and out."

Tuttleby said to Wormald, "You've set us up, you bugger!"

Wormald said, "Not to worry. It's a misunderstanding. I can fix it."

Click!

Tuttleby said, "You'll fix fuck-all, mate. You've fixed enough. Now it's me fixing you," and he nodded to the men with spades, who, James supposed, although

219

unequipped with light-emission-intensifiers, were close enough to see or sense the nod.

Wormald produced a gun, an automatic of some sort, squat and stubby, not round-bellied like a pistol, from inside his jacket. "All right," he said. "That'll do. You'd better go home. I'll handle this." Then the two Jack Russells bit him in the ankles, and brought him down, and one of the men in balaclavas sliced into his wrist with a spade so that his grasp was loosened, and the gun fell out of his hand. "Don't," Wormald said. "Get those dogs off. Don't! Oh, Christ!" Tuttleby's people wore heavy boots with steel toe-caps. They kicked Wormald in the groin, and in the ribs, and in the head. At first Wormald shouted, and then he screamed, and then he groaned, and then he whimpered, and then he was silent, and Tuttleby took the gun, and left with his people and with their dogs, stumbling up the slope to the bridle-path, and then away. During all this time James continued to take photographs, while the old lady, rigid beside him, did deep-breathing-exercises to keep herself under control.

When Tuttleby and his people had gone, James said, "I'll take the camera back to the car. Will you see if anything can be done for Wormald? Pavel will help you. I'll come back. There may be a first-aid kit in the boot of the car. I imagine he won't want us to phone the police, or even for an ambulance."

James left the woods by the track, and walked swiftly towards the barn. The moon had risen. One had not noticed it among the trees; it was still a week from the full, but gave enough light to see by. There was a car parked outside the farmhouse, an expensive car, a BMW; it was the man Baker's car. The man Baker himself had left his car, and could be seen in the trampled ground outside the barn, the doors of which had been opened, presumably by Borek. The man Baker was holding a single-barrelled shot-gun, and Borek was with him.

James said, "What on earth are you doing?"

"Just going up to the woods."

"Don't bother. It's all over, bar the wounded."

"Who's wounded?"

"Wormald."

"How horrid for him! Nevertheless I think we'll go."

Borek said something incomprehensible in Czech, to which Baker replied sharply and monosyllabically. It seemed to James that Borek was in some fear.

"Where are you going with Dr Borek?"

"Taking him with me. I told you we'd collect him."

"I'd leave him here if I were you. You can collect him tomorrow."

"Oh no, I don't think so."

James walked forwards through the open gate, and Borek came towards him like a child to a protecting parent. Baker spoke sharply again in Czech, and half-raised the shot-gun. Instead of halting, as he had clearly been instructed to do, Borek increased his speed, and placed himself first next to and then behind James, so that the shot-gun, by then in a position to fire, was pointing at his protector.

Baker said, "Just step aside, James, would you please?"

"Why?"

"I told you. Dr Borek and I are going for a walk."

"With what object and to what destination?"

"That's nothing to do with you."

"I'm his sponsor. He gave my name to Immigration." For some reason the man Baker intended to kill Borek, although James did not see why; presumably all the talk about asylum and teaching Freshman Philosophy had been lies, and instead Baker had induced Pavel's uncle to leave Brno in order to murder him in Oxfordshire. It would have to be prevented; James was, in a sense, responsible. Baker took a step forward, bringing the shot-gun uncomfortably close; even if he took no aim at all, he could hardly miss from such a distance. Borek, from behind James's back said something which sounded as if it were an entreaty, but to no effect. James could see that two ducks had been etched as decoration into the stock of the gun. It was his own gun, stolen from the locked cupboard in the study.

221

Baker said, "You are not his sponsor. This man is not Pavel Borek."

"Who, then?"

"Just someone paid to do a job."

"Paid to get himself murdered?"

"I don't suppose that part of the assignment was fully explained to him."

"He's a spy or what? Czech agent? Something like that?"

"No, no, no; he's a person of no importance whatsoever in himself. His sole importance is as raw material."

"I don't follow you." James shifted from one foot to the other, and the raw material at his back, believing him to be about to move away, clung on with both hands like the Old Man of the Sea.

"Have you really learned nothing from poor Wormald?" the man Baker said. "All that interminable conversation at the kitchen table, and you still haven't grasped the nature and purposes of the Security Services? Try to understand now. This country has no secrets of any value. The sole function of the Security Services is to maintain a climate in which they themselves can continue to operate. That is true of Wormald's division, and of my own, and of all divisions. At a time when this climate is under threat by a general lowering of barriers politically between East and West, we need an incident, and to create such an incident a dead Czech agent would come in handy. Now, I've no doubt that there are Czech agents around, but why go to the trouble of catching one, who would be disowned anyway, when it's so much easier to create one? The purpose of the man at your back is to supply a Czech corpse who may or may not be Pavel Borek. That will allow us the creative freedom either to present him as a Czech agent, intercepted on his way to the American air-base at Upper Heyford, or as a genuine dissident seeking asylum, who has been shot to discourage the others."

There was no control over these people; they could do as they wished, being outside the law. James saw that it must be the same all over the world, the Security Services of

222

every country devoted only to their own perpetuation, their ultimate loyalty given, not to the governments which at least in theory controlled them, but to each other.

Baker said, "If you insist on my shooting you as well, there will be two corpses, which is really one more than necessary, but probably one could make something interesting of them."

"If you don't shoot me, I could make a fuss. Tell the truth. Expose you."

"This country is crammed with people trying to tell the truth about the Security Services, but nobody takes any notice; it's all old hat. Anyway, how can you be certain I'm telling you the truth myself? Now please step out of the way, James. I detest waste, but if you give me no alternative, I'll shoot you both."

James said, "You may not be able to. It's a single-barrelled shot-gun. While you're re-loading, he'll run away."

"He may not have the nous. Or I may catch him. Or if he does escape, we'll say he shot you. James, James, you stand there like a metaphor for the death of liberal England, intent on sacrificing your own life to protect someone you really rather dislike. Please do step out of the way." And Baker pressed the button which released the safety-catch.

James said, "The lives of most of us are metaphors, though we rarely know for what. This was sometime a paradox, but now the time gives it proof." He moved forward sharply two paces, taking Baker off guard, and the gun went off. James could see the surprise and shock in the man's face, but whether because he had pressed the trigger without meaning to do so, or because at that same moment a smooth pebble weighing about a hundred grammes came out of the darkness and struck him in the temple, James could not be sure. The pebble had on the man Baker's temple the same sort of crunching effect as on the wall of the garden shed, seeming to make a hole in it from which blood spurted, and he fell sideways, as once the giant Goliath must have fallen and, as James supposed, as dead.

James himself remained upright, held by the grasp of the man at his back. Then his own knees buckled, as he was released, and he fell forwards on the trampled earth to lie beside Baker, while the man who may have been the philosopher Borek ran whimpering into the dark wood.

James lay where he had fallen. What he had read long ago was correct: the immediate shock of the explosion acted as an anaesthetic, and he felt no pain, or at least none of any consequence. There was a pain in his chest, but it was not much of a pain, and either it would go away, or it would get worse. He did feel a little cold, but, lying in the open between cow-sheds at midnight, even in May that was to be expected. The plexiglass hemisphere of the bubble, set at its smallest diameter, fitted snugly over him. Sophie was with him in the bubble, he knew; it had always been able to accommodate them both, though truth to tell he had sometimes excluded her. Outside the bubble he could see Pavel in the moonlight. The boy had dropped to his knees, and was bending over James, his face distorted as in one of those photographs taken with a wide-angled lens which one sees in the Sunday colour-supplements. James would have liked Pavel to join himself and Sophie in the bubble, but of course there was no room for him, and this was a pity because, James discovered, he had loved them both.

Then Pavel moved, not his good arm but his stump to meet James's hand. The tiny pink buds met the iridescent surface of the bubble, and it burst; it ceased to provide a protection which was no longer needed. The stump passed through where the bubble had been, and met James's hand, and James felt a spasm of what could have been either pain or the most intense joy, and quite simply, like the bubble, ceased to be.